CLANDESTINE LOVERS

FRIENDSHIP CHRONICLES 3

SHELLEY MUNRO

MUNRO PRESS

Clandestine Lovers

Print ISBN: 978-1-99-106332-8
Digital ISBN: 978-0-9941483-8-4

Editor: Evil Eye Editing

Cover: Kim Killion, The Killion Group, Inc.

This book is a work of fiction. The names, characters, places, and incidents are products of the writer's imagination or have been used fictitiously and are not to be construed as real. Any resemblance to persons, living or dead, actual events, locales, or organizations is entirely coincidental.

Munro Press, New Zealand.

First Munro Press electronic publication August 2017

First Munro Press print publication June 2023

DEDICATION

For Paul, my partner in crime and fellow adventurer.

"If we were meant to stay in one place, we'd have roots instead of feet."

—— Rachel Wolchin

INTRODUCTION

THINK FINDING THE PERFECT lover is difficult? Ask Susan Webb—she *knows* it is. Lonely, tired of dull routine and dud men who only think with their lower brains, she takes a calculated risk to shake up her lackluster life.

Now she's set to take part in a reality dating show. Her objective: to find a good, honest man who's up for enjoying lots of sexy fun on the road to love. Failure is not an option.

One look at his older brother's *Farmer Seeks a Wife* candidate, and Tyler Penrith is intrigued. Prim and proper on the surface, she has a secret smile in her eyes and an exotic dancer sway to her step. And calamity follows her around like a tame dragon.

Susan might be in his brother's age group, but Tyler's not about to let Nolan waltz off with the first woman to snare his attention in ages.

As the show's ratings go through the roof, Susan finds herself falling for the wrong man—and her simple plan for happiness on the brink of falling apart.

Warning: Contains sibling rivalry, lots of sneaking around, sexy times in the great outdoors, a bright blue vibrator, and a reality show that's giving everyone something to talk about.

CHAPTER ONE

Do not screw up this speed date. This is your chance to find love. A husband. Everything you want for the future.

"No pressure," Susan Webb whispered as she navigated the gravel path alongside the grapevines and went *off-piste* onto the freshly mown grass. Immediately, the heels of her black-and-red sandals sank halfway to China.

The cameraman following her snickered and kept filming while her arms windmilled wildly to maintain her balance. Thank goodness she'd donned a pair of sexy black briefs this morning. The thought raced through her mind as she teetered on the brink of flashing her bottom to the viewers of *Farmer Seeks a Wife* reality show.

"Here, let me help," a husky voice said.

A muscular forearm curved around her waist, the man's strength holding her upright. A hit of citrus and leather engulfed her while heat massed in her cheeks.

Slowly, Susan turned her head to study her savior. She recognized his chiseled features immediately. Her chosen farmer—Nolan Penrith—and he was even hotter in the flesh. His light brown sun-streaked hair was neatly trimmed but still flirted with the collar of his cream shirt. He wore jeans and a brown leather jacket. Her gaze skirted down past his hips, lingered on the bulge at his groin and moved lower until her stare hit his brown boots. A soft chuckle dragged her attention northward to meet a crooked smile and brown eyes full of amusement.

"Ah, sorry," she said, fervently wishing she could have a do-over. She'd ogled his junk, for goodness sake, right after almost flashing the reality show viewers. Time to fix this situation. She *had* to create the right impression. Her future depended on her actions today. "I'm not usually this clumsy."

"No problem," he said. "Let's get you safely to the meeting spot so we can have a chat."

Susan nodded, embarrassment quashing her ability to format further sentences. Luckily, her mind was still in working order. She grasped one of his arms and attempted to jerk her right foot free, preferably with her sandal still in place so she didn't wobble like an undignified stork.

"That's not the way," he said, a laugh in his voice, and he tugged her back then scooped her up into his arms, striding away and leaving her sandals embedded in the lawn.

Susan became aware of the breeze at her butt and started to struggle. *No, no, no!* This was not happening.

"Don't worry, I won't drop you. A little thing like you doesn't weigh more than a bale of hay."

"That's not what I meant," Susan said, the chill on her backside confirming her fears.

A bark of laughter escaped the cameraman. Susan froze. She was gonna commit murder—if she didn't die of mortification first. She glared over Nolan's shoulder at the man, but all she could see was the blink of light on the side of the camera that indicated everything—including her butt—was being faithfully recorded. *Gah!*

Nolan set her on her feet, and she instantly flicked the back of her red dress down over her panties.

"*Oops*. Sorry about that, darlin'," Nolan said. "Would you like something to drink?" He gestured to a jug of water and another of juice.

Heck, yeah! A margarita would be good about now. "W-water will be f-fine." At least it would be something to do with her hands. Nolan had apologized, so she couldn't hit him. The cameraman, however, was riding a shaky line.

Aware of the camera, she resisted the urge to snap out an insult or roll the cool glass across her cheeks to dispel her embarrassment. Instead, she took a quick sip and fought to regain her equilibrium.

She needed to flirt, needed to speak intelligently, needed to show herself to best advantage.

She needed to excel.

Nolan helped himself to a glass of juice and gestured to the tartan blanket, spread on the ground not far from the table holding the refreshments.

Susan crouched and placed her glass within easy reach, then she gingerly knelt and curled her legs to the side, taking great care not to flash her panties. Again.

Nolan dropped to the blanket with casual ease. "So you're looking for a husband?"

Straight away, her hackles rose and an indignant retort sped to her lips. In her peripheral vision, she noted the cameraman shift positions to get another angle for his shot. She bit back her grumpiness and strove for a witty comeback, something to wow.

"A-are you l-looking for a wife?" *Better, but what was with the stuttering?* She didn't usually stammer. She managed to shape her lips into something resembling a smile. Her friends would see the jagged edges, but it was her best effort when all she could think of was her bottom broadcast on national television.

"It appears so."

The weird inflection in his tone tugged at her curiosity, and she opened her mouth to ask a question.

Before she could speak, he said, "I'm Nolan, which I'm sure you already know, and you, according to my list, are Susan. Tell me a little about yourself. I believe you work in an office? What do you do in your spare time?"

Oh, heck. Minefield alert.

She hesitated, frantically wondering how to break the news of her career change. "I'm r-really excited to be here, N-Nolan, and it's great to meet you. Um…I…ah…like to dance. I go out with my f-friends to clubs and r-r-rugby matches. Sometimes we go shopping or to m-movies." Her heart hammered like the beat in a fast dance, and she caught her bottom lip between her teeth before releasing it to force her features into a happy, confident mask.

"Not many shops out in the country."

"No, I don't suppose there are." Her fixed smile wobbled and tried to slink away to hide. Was he trying to sabotage her? Had he taken an instant dislike to her?

Too bad.

If they were destined to be together, he needed to know she possessed a steel rod of determination in her spine. She added a touch of sweetness to her smile and hoped she didn't look like a caricature. "The internet works well for shopping. You can buy just about anything online these days from farm equipment to dresses." *Yay! No stuttering this time*.

His brown eyes glazed over and he sipped his orange juice.

Heck, she was losing him.

"Do you enjoy your job?" he asked. "If we hit it off with each other, would you miss not working?"

"I don't work in an office anymore," Susan blurted.

"Oh?" His dark brows rose to emphasize his surprise. "You gave up your job? You must be very certain of your future."

"No, I have a new job. One of my friends owns a club, and I work for her now."

"What sort of club?"

Susan's heart skipped several beats, leaving her breathless, definitely anxious. "What qualities do you want in a wife?"

"One who answers questions. What sort of club?"

"A burlesque club," she said in a low voice, mortified heat blooming fiery-hot again in her cheeks. She shot a glance at the camera, saw the man zoom in on her face, recording every bit of the unfolding drama.

"You like to dance." It sounded like an accusation.

He was judging her, reading between the lines and making mistakes with his version of the facts.

Susan gave a clipped nod, unhappily aware of the camera. She refused to lie. That was no way to start a relationship. So she was going to crash at the first interview. Didn't matter. She'd done her best, and if she was bowing out of the reality show straight away, she might as well give *Maxwell's* a shout out and gain some exposure.

"I work at *Maxwell's*, a burlesque club on K' Road in Auckland," Susan said. "I take care of the accounts and wages and dance on stage several nights a week."

"You're a stripper," Nolan said, eyes narrowing into

disparaging slits.

"You need to educate yourself about burlesque." Susan kept an even tone, refusing to stoop to his level. "Burlesque is not the same as stripping."

"But you do perform on stage."

"Yes, and I'm rather good at it. *Maxwell's* is a very busy place." Nothing less than the truth, and even she heard her shimmering pride.

Nolan stared, and his intense gaze ricocheted through her body, frisking every pleasure point during the journey. A pity he'd set himself up as judge of her morals when he held so much sex appeal.

"I wonder if you'd find the countryside a little quiet," he said. "We don't have shops or movie theatres or clubs."

"I'm open to trying new things," Susan countered. "I've never lived in the country, but I'm sure I'll keep myself amused."

"I see."

"What do you envision your wife doing?" Susan made a concerted effort to control the combative note in her voice. "Will she help you on the farm or stay home and bake cookies?"

Nolan flashed a wide grin, and her breath caught at the flash of dimples. A smile took him from handsome to plain stunning. He kept grinning instead of answering her questions, making for a long camera silence.

Susan rolled her eyes, feeling immeasurably older, even

though he was two years her senior. "Well?"

"The other girls have flirted with me and fluttered their eyelashes. A couple of the women gave me good views of their best assets." His gaze dropped to her chest. Tiny wrinkles fanned from the corners of his eyes in another display of humor.

"I flashed my butt at the viewing audience." Susan shot a glare at the cameraman. "I think I've shown more than my fair share of assets."

"I didn't see," he pointed out.

"Not my fault."

"You have two more minutes," the cameraman said.

"What do you expect from a wife?" Susan asked again.

"I want a woman who attracts me sexually, someone who enjoys sex. I'd expect my wife to work alongside me, taking an active part in running the farm and socializing within the community. I want someone to share my life. In return, I'll do my best to make my wife happy too."

His words were unexpected and warmed her heart. A partner. He wanted someone to stand alongside him. *Be still my heart.* That was exactly what she wanted from a man—someone to share good times and bad.

"I want a man who is attractive and attentive, one who will treat me as an equal and share life in all its different facets. Our needs are similar."

He scratched his chin, the faint abrasion of fingertip and the beginnings of stubble a rasp in the expectant pause.

"Maybe."

"Time," the cameraman said.

Nolan unfolded his long limbs and stood before extending his hand. "I'll carry you to the gravel."

"No, it's fine," she said hastily. "I'll go barefoot." She slid her hand free and offered him a dazzling smile. "Thank you for chatting with me. It was nice to meet you."

"Don't I get a goodbye kiss?"

"Sure. Why not?" At least she could tell her friends she'd scored a kiss from a sexy farmer. She lifted her head, expecting a quick, polite peck on the mouth.

Instead, he framed her face with his hands, holding her firmly. He grinned as he lowered his lips. Her heartbeat stalled on seeing his intent. Then he was kissing her, slowly. Thoroughly. Not exactly the kiss for a first meeting, but she guessed the circumstances warranted different. His scent wrapped through her senses, and her knees went weak, only his strength holding her upright.

"Ahem."

The loud interruption came from behind Susan.

Nolan pulled back and grinned over her shoulder. "Yeah, I know. Time for the next prospective wife." He glanced down at her, his expression softening and brushed his fingers over her cheek. "Beneath the quick mind and sass, you're very sensual. I like it."

He released her hand and stepped back, leaving her reeling. Only the chuckle of the cameraman—his face once again concealed by his camera—jerked back her composure.

"Goodbye, Susan," Nolan said.

"Goodbye." Susan paused to yank the spike heels from the ground and padded to the edge of the gravel before slipping them on her feet. She replayed their conversation and came up with the conclusion.

She'd blown her speed date.

Nolan watched Susan retreat, intrigue warring with his need for retribution. His mother had to accept he was capable of choosing a wife. A thirty-year-old man wasn't a kid, damn it. Aware of his loosening grip on his temper, he sucked in a breath, let it ease out and scanned his list of dates.

The next woman was one of his choosing and satisfaction brought a grim smile. Judging by her photo, she was an attractive blonde and her hobbies shadowed his interests. And the bonus—she'd grown up on a farm, so she'd know the ins and outs better than most of the girls his mother had chosen for this debacle.

His grandfather had suggested he refuse to participate in the reality show, but his grandmother, in her wise way, searched for the profits. If he played things right, businesses in their community might benefit. The film crew and the people involved in the project would bring spending power and maybe a few nosy visitors. This promotion was good for the town of Clare, and his grandmother had pointed out, he might have fun and make new friends along the way.

He thought fleetingly of Yvonne and her two kids. He already knew how to have fun...

Yeah, mind on the job.

Whittling the group of twenty women down to eight wasn't gonna be easy. Blast his mother for putting him in this position, entering him without seeking his permission.

"I know my son," she'd said, her shoulders square and chin raised in the face of his fury. "You'll make a good husband, but you won't meet anyone if you insist on spending your time at the farm. You need to get out, meet suitable women."

What she'd meant was she hadn't approved of him spending time with a divorced woman, or another man's children.

His mother had reached for the kettle and filled it with water to make a pot of tea while he'd stormed out and ended up at his grandparents' house in nearby Napier. He and his grandparents had drunk cups of tea, eaten pieces of shortbread and discussed his objections.

They'd changed his mind, and while he didn't agree with his mother's skullduggery, he had to admit it was fun stepping out of routine. The visit to the big smoke to meet the show's producer and the other farmers had sealed the deal. He wasn't the only farmer here under duress.

"You ready to see the next woman?" the cameraman asked.

"Yeah."

The cameraman contacted the producer and soon his next date walked toward him. She was stunning, and even better in person. Her clothes were smart but casual, and he noted she didn't have trouble with her shoes. Her smile was wide and bright and she gave him a swift hug. Oh yeah. He liked this one.

Two hours later, the speed dates were done, and his head whirled with faces and impressions. Jennifer Williams, the producer, had suggested the men take brief notes, and he was glad he'd taken her advice.

"You ready?" the cameraman asked. "I'll show you to the meeting room. They've organized drinks and something to eat while you farmers decide which chicks you're going to pick for the next round."

Nolan blew out a burst of air. "Easier said than done."

"I'm glad it's not me," the cameraman said. "I bet some of those chicks will cry buckets."

Hell. Nolan hadn't thought of that. He'd worried more about trying to pick the right mix of eight women. Now he had to worry about women and tears? *Bloody hell.* As he followed the cameraman, he wondered if their drinks ran to alcohol.

SUSAN SPOTTED CHRISTINA AND sank onto the chair her friend had saved for her. "How did it go?"

Christina wrinkled her nose. Her bracelets jingled as she shunted a glass of wine toward Susan. "If your date went as badly as mine, you'll need a drink."

"I was craving a margarita before we even started talking."

"That bad, huh?"

Susan's tummy hollowed at the memories. "You go first. What was your farmer like?"

"He said—bluntly, I might add—that I was more bohemian than I appeared in my photo."

Susan stared at her friend. "Bohemian?"

"Yeah. Evidently jewelry that clacks will scare his animals."

Susan glanced down at Christina's three golden bracelets and started laughing.

Christina's lips twitched. "Your date can't have been that bad."

Susan laughed harder and nodded at the same time. Once she'd gathered herself, she said, "You were right to warn me about wearing my spike sandals. I wish I'd listened. I sank into the grass the second I stepped off the path and my farmer came to my rescue. He literally swept me off my feet and carried me to our meeting point—a picnic blanket."

"That sounds romantic."

"It was nice until I realized my skirt was tucked up and the cameraman was busy filming my butt."

"At least you listened about the sexy lingerie."

Susan snorted—a half laugh and half whimper. "If that's meant to make me feel better it's not working." She flicked a lock of her straight hair out of her face. "And it got worse." Words tumbled from her as she related details of her speed date.

"Oh well." Christina lifted her glass of wine in salute. "At least we've had a nice outing to a vineyard. The wine is good. The food looks delicious."

"And we can laugh about it together."

"Exactly." Christina clicked her glass against Susan's. "To friends."

"To friends," Susan said and grinned as she thought of two of her other friends. "Maggie and Julia will get a good laugh."

Two hours passed before the producer called the women to assemble. The tension in the meeting room was thick enough to slice with a knife. So many women who wanted the same things as she—a steady man to love and share their lives.

A secure future.

There was something wrong with society if this many

personable single women couldn't find a mate. Or maybe featuring on a television show attracted their participation. Susan didn't know. There had to be a better way to meet a man.

Besides, the idea of leaving her job at Maxwell's... She loved her new job, the dancing giving her a physical outlet and pleasure she hadn't known she'd craved.

Nolan's questions about living in the country had given her things to mull over. Leaving her friends and her job in exchange for a quiet life in the country would be a huge step. Maybe fluffing her speed date was a good thing. Two of her best friends had found husbands already. Maggie had married their mutual friend, Connor, while Julia had married Ryan. Both women were shiny examples of love, and Connor and Ryan were awesome.

No, she wouldn't panic or settle for second best.

Almost twenty-nine wasn't exactly ancient. The right man would come along, and if he didn't, then she'd deal. She had a great group of friends, both male and female. Love and friendship. Yeah, she had that already.

"I want you to split into your groups again," Jennifer Williams, the producer shouted above the din made by a room full of anxious women. She was a tall and very thin woman, dressed in tight black jeans and a body-fitting green T-shirt. A no-nonsense kind of woman, she wielded her power by sheer force of presence.

The women quieted, and Jennifer repeated her request.

"Line up behind the signs for your farmers, please, then I'll call groups one-by-one."

"Good luck," Susan said to Christina.

"What I'd need is a miracle," Christina said. "It doesn't matter. It's been a fun day."

"True. Tonight we can commiserate over margaritas. Julia and Maggie will want the deets."

"Done deal." Susan gave her friend a swift hug and headed for her group. Who wanted a judgmental man in their lives anyway?

Not her. She'd worked hard to scrub the trait from her personality. Seeing it from the other side, she understood how her friends felt when she'd passed sentence on their actions. If she'd learned anything in the past five years, it was that nothing was black and white. Shades of gray swirled everywhere, and there was nothing wrong with the color.

She took a seat. None of the other girls wanted to chat, so she sat quietly and pondered her next step. If she asked, Connor would probably set up a blind date for her with one of his rugby mates. The guys in Ryan's band were cute. It wasn't as if she lacked opportunities to meet men.

Perhaps she was setting her standards too high?

She considered that for about two seconds. No, she wanted a husband like Connor or Ryan and refused to settle for less.

Jennifer strode into the room, the heels of her boots

making a snappy beat on the wooden floor. "Ladies, Nolan is ready to share his choices."

"It makes us sound like items on a dinner menu," Susan murmured.

A blonde woman beside her frowned. "That's a perfect description. I wonder who gets to be dish of the day."

Susan let out a chuckle, but none of the other women appreciated the humor. Their swift glances held panic and censure. Susan was still grinning when she entered the private room.

"Ladies, please stand behind the chalk line and smile at the camera," Jennifer instructed in a firm voice.

The women shuffled into position, and the tension ramped up a couple of notches. Susan's heart thumped extra loudly, then the drumming evened out as she realized she didn't want to win a man in a competition.

No, she'd return to work and tonight, while they were at the pub and comfortably ensconced with margaritas, she'd ask for suggestions of ways to meet men.

"We'll start filming in a few minutes. Hailee Raymond, our hostess will have a quick chat with Nolan, and then Nolan will announce his eight chosen women. Afterward, Hailee will interview each of the successful dates. Are there any questions?"

"Do you have some tissues handy?" one of the women asked.

"I have my assistant standing by," Jennifer said in a brisk

voice.

Susan didn't care enough to cry when she received her rejection. That thought alone cheered her. She wasn't invested and didn't care about Nolan's opinion of her personality.

"Anything else?" When no one replied, Jennifer said, "Quiet on the set."

The silence grew deafening, and Susan had an awful urge to giggle. Determined not to create another spectacle, she bit her bottom lip.

The assistant darted forward. He lifted his board and clapped it down. "Action."

Hailee, the gorgeous blonde hostess, took her cue with the smoothness of a professional. "Nolan, you've speed dated your ladies and spoken with them. Was it difficult to narrow down your choice to just eight?"

"Very difficult, Hailee," Nolan said, appearing comfortable in front of the camera. "Each woman is beautiful, and any man would be lucky to have them at their side."

Hailee grinned, her teeth a flash of bright white. "Quite the smooth talker, aren't you? So how did you pick your group of eight?"

"I took into account common interests, how I thought our personalities would mesh and my gut instincts. They never steer me wrong."

Hailee nodded, then leaned toward Nolan in a

confidential manner. "What about physical attraction? Does that come into your equation?"

"Of course," Nolan said. "The woman I choose to take for my wife will be one who pushes my buttons. Physical attraction always plays a part in a relationship."

"Well, I think it's time to let these lovely ladies know your decision," Hailee said. "Tell us who you have chosen."

Nolan ran his gaze down the line of women, his expression suitably somber. "The ladies I've chosen for the next stage are Maxine, Elle, Tamara, Lucy, Anna, Cherry, Jasmine and Susan."

"Ladies," Hailee said in a bright tone. "Step forward."

Shock made Susan slow to react. He'd called her name. While there was physical attraction, on her side at least, they were poles apart in the interest department.

Susan joined the other squealing women, her focus on Nolan's handsome face. For an instant, their gazes connected, and she propelled a silent message his way. *What on earth are you playing at?*

CHAPTER TWO

THE AFTERMATH OF NOLAN'S announcement was surreal, or at least it felt that way to Susan. A strawberry blonde woman burst into tears, a few seconds after Nolan finished his list of names. Her wailing acted like a prod on the rest of the group, and Jennifer's assistant dispensed tissues.

Susan waited to speak with Hailee while groping to understand Nolan's choices, and in specific, her.

"Are you excited to make it to the next stage of the competition?" Hailee asked.

"I'm more surprised than anything," Susan said. "I didn't think our speed date went very well."

"Oh?"

"We didn't exactly hit it off. Nolan suggested that since my experience with country life is nil I wouldn't enjoy the isolation and lack of facilities." No way was she going to mention the reveal of her high-cut lacy panties. Maybe the cameraman would take mercy and leave that part on the cutting room floor. But then again, recalling his snigger of appreciation, perhaps not. She'd have to wait and see.

"Maybe he took one look at you and decided you're worth taking a chance on," Hailee cooed.

That was spreading the bullshit a bit thick. Susan wasn't pretty in the conventional sense. Dressed right, she could stretch her appearance to striking. No, most people who checked her out probably thought prissy, although since taking up dancing, she'd slid out of that slot.

"I think he took pity on me," Susan said. "I almost took a nose dive while I was walking to meet Nolan. The embarrassment at being such a klutz put me off-balance from the start of our date."

"Oh? Tell us more."

"I don't think so," Susan said with a smile to mute her bluntness. "I believe the cameraman recorded everything on film. That's all I'm saying at this stage."

Hailee laughed, a tinkling sound that would've been right at home in a feel-good cartoon. "That sounds very mysterious. We'll look forward to seeing you on camera. Good luck with the next stage, Susan."

"Thanks, Hailee." Susan forced her lips to remain in their curve while her mind struggled with the people of New Zealand seeing her arse on film.

"And cut," the assistant said. "Well done, everyone."

Susan dropped into a booth at *Maxwell's* and watched a dancer go through her paces. "She's good," she commented as Julia Maxwell—an attractive blonde and her boss—slid in beside her. Christina and their other friend, Maggie—a full-figured brown-haired woman with an impish smile—joined them. A minute later, a waitress arrived bearing a tray of glasses and a bottle.

"Champagne?" Susan asked.

"Ryan and Caleb sprang for the bottle when they heard you'd made the next round."

"But they're in China doing a show."

Julia grinned. "I rang them. Ryan said they were cheering for you both, and they wanted to hear the results straightaway."

Susan ran a finger over the condensation on the neck of the bottle. "The champagne is chilled."

"Ordered before Ryan left. He and Caleb figured we'd celebrate or commiserate. Either way, champagne would work."

Christina chuckled, her eyes gleaming behind the lenses of her glasses. "Julia, I love your husband. He has style."

Julia nodded. "Yes, he does. Caleb too. You could always hook up with Caleb."

"I'm not upset about today, about not making the next

round," Christina said. "We had a lovely day and lots of fun. I don't need to snatch a man just because I struck out in the show. I like Caleb, but he's like a brother rather than a prospective lover, you know?"

Maggie fiddled with one of her brown curls. "What about your farmer, Susan?"

Susan scowled at her glass. "I don't understand why he picked me. He made it clear he thought I wouldn't enjoy country life. He didn't think I'd last the distance, and when he learned I danced burlesque that was the full stop on his decision."

"He's cute," Christina said.

"True. The physical attraction is there—at least on my side—but I hated his disapproving manner." Susan sipped her champagne, savoring the tickly bubbles bursting against her tongue. "Jennifer wants us to chat about our experiences online. Her assistant has set up blogs for us on the station website. Oh, and I gave *Maxwell's* a plug. Hopefully, they won't cut it from the final show."

"When is the first episode showing?" Maggie asked.

"Thursday night," Christina said. "Instead of taping the entire show then airing it, they want to keep everything current and show the episodes as they're filmed."

"Let's tape it and have a private viewing once things quiet down at the club," Julia said.

"I'm nervous and I know the results," Susan said. "From this point on, we're not supposed to tell anyone what happens during filming. They made us sign contracts before we left. We're meant to have our blog posts ready to go live once the first show has aired." A sudden thought occurred and she laughed.

"What?" Christina asked.

"For my first post, I might talk about burlesque and educate people," Susan said.

"Why don't you post photos of you in costume and maybe some from our training sessions? Do some little slices of your daily routine. You could take some shots in the office too," Christina said.

"Connor has a camera," Maggie said. "He's got a good eye for photos too. I'll ask him if he'll snap some shots."

"That's a great idea," Susan said, her mind full of possibilities. "I mentioned going to rugby matches, and I can do a few pics of Auckland too. Photos will help personalize my blog, and I won't need to write as much."

"A toast," Julia said, lifting her glass. "To Susan and her farmer."

"To Susan and her farmer," Maggie and Christina chorused.

"I can't drink to myself," Susan protested. "To my farmer and to absent friends for providing this delicious champagne."

"To Ryan and Caleb," Julia said, a soft smile sliding across her face.

Tyler Penrith accepted a cup of tea from Josie Murdoch

with a nod of thanks. His mother-in-law—a chubby woman with dark brown hair—reached up to pat his arm in a casual gesture of affection.

"How many stories did Katey wrangle out of you before she settled?" Eric Murdoch asked. In contrast to his wife, Eric was tall and slender—almost too thin—and his short hair was white even though he was a mere year older than Josie.

"Only two tonight," Tyler said. "The birthday party tuckered her out."

"Takes after her mother, that one." Eric reached for the biscuit tin, snagged a chocolate chip cookie and settled his backside on his favorite chair.

Lord, he hoped not, Tyler thought. He'd go gray before his time if his four-year-old daughter rivaled her mother for mischief.

"Eric, don't eat another cookie." Josie poked a finger into his belly. "They're for Katey's kindergarten class." She settled beside Tyler on the couch and focused on the television. "When does the show start? Has anyone seen my glasses?"

"A few minutes," Tyler said. "I was surprised when I heard Nolan was going on *Farmer Seeks a Wife*. I ran into Dad at the cattle sale. I thought he was pulling my leg until he informed me Mum had entered Nolan. She wants Nolan settled with a suitable wife."

Eric sent a longing glance at the cookie tin then turned

back to the television with a sigh. "Your glasses are on the kitchen counter. I thought Nolan was seeing the solo mum with the kids."

"Yvonne," Tyler said. "I thought so too, but obviously the gossips got it wrong."

"Quiet, the show's starting," Josie said, after her quick trip to retrieve her glasses. "This has to be the biggest thing that's happened in Clare since the Shakespeare sextuplets were born. I don't want to miss a word."

Obediently, Tyler turned his attention to the TV and the bubbly blonde hostess introducing the farmers. Nolan did a good job. He appeared confident and conversed easily with Hailee. He'd cut his hair and wore what looked like new clothes.

"Do you think you'll find the perfect woman here?" Hailee asked.

"I'm hoping so," Nolan said. "I'm certainly looking forward to meeting the lovely ladies in my group."

"I'm sure they'll enjoy meeting you too," Hailee said and beamed into the camera. "Come back after the break and meet the ladies who hope to steal Farmer Nolan's heart."

"Nolan came across as interesting and sincere," Josie said.

He had. His older brother bore a wide streak of charm when he chose to exert himself.

The ad break ran, and Tyler settled in to watch the rest of the show. The segment moved to Nolan meeting some of the women in his group. His brother remained charming, but he was blunt and abrupt with the women, grilling them about living in the country.

"Look at that woman's face," Josie said, her kindness showing in a sympathetic grimace. "Her eyes are welling with tears."

"Did he pick the candidates himself?" Eric asked.

"According to Dad, the women had to pick one of the farmers, complete a form, write an essay and send their applications to the station. Nolan received five hundred and twenty-three replies to whittle down to twenty."

"I imagine that must have been difficult—oh, my! That poor girl," Josie said.

Tyler watched the screen, spellbound as a woman with long, straight brown hair and a fire-engine red dress struggled to free her shoes from the turf. His brother strolled over, a smile twitching his lips as his gaze did a brief scan of her trim body.

"I'm not usually this clumsy," the woman said, the color in her cheeks matching her clothing.

"No problem," Nolan said. "Let's get you safely to the meeting spot so we can have a chat." He whisked the woman into his arms, and Tyler experienced a surge of envy. His lips twisted wryly. Maybe he needed to take advantage of his in-laws when they volunteered to babysit and get out more.

"Oh my," Josie repeated.

Eric let out a slow whistle while Tyler didn't bother wasting breath. He stared at the curve of the woman's bottom and the tiny pair of lacy black panties she wore beneath her red dress. Her flustered expression when Nolan set her on the tartan blanket cried out for a hug. Tyler grinned at the careful way the woman positioned herself on the ground. She didn't intend to flash again.

Once Nolan offered her a drink, he started his questions. "I believe you work in an office? What do you do in your spare time?"

The woman—Susan—hesitated. "I'm r-really excited to be here, N-Nolan, and it's great to meet you. Um...I...ah...like to dance. I go out with my f-friends to clubs and r-r-rugby matches. Sometimes we go shopping or to m-movies." She caught her bottom lip between her teeth before releasing it to offer a strained smile.

"The poor girl is nervous," Josie said with a sympathetic tut.

"Not many shops out in the country," Nolan persisted.

Tyler focused on the woman's face. She had a quiet beauty, the type that would creep up on a man and steal into his heart. Damn, was Nolan trying to kick her off-balance?

"No, I don't suppose there are." Her smile wobbled. "The internet works for shopping. You can buy just about anything online these days from farm equipment to dresses."

Josie gave a laugh of delight. "I like this one. She's handled the situation well and isn't letting Nolan bulldoze her in the same way he has with the other girls."

Onscreen, Nolan nodded at Susan's reply, and Tyler could tell he was enjoying his moment of fame.

"Do you enjoy your job?" Nolan asked. "If we hit it off with each other, would you miss not working in an office?"

"I don't work in an office anymore," Susan blurted.

Something in her tone had Tyler leaning forward, eager to hear what she'd say next.

Nolan's eyes narrowed as the camera panned across his features. "You gave up your job? You must be very certain of your future."

The woman gritted her teeth, and Tyler caught a flash of irritation in her pretty blue eyes. "No, I have a new job. One of my friends owns a club, and I work for her now."

"What sort of club?"

Susan ignored his demand for an answer. "What qualities do you want in a wife?"

"Interesting," Tyler said.

"I wonder what sort of club she works at," Eric mused.

Josie cocked her head, her eyes alert behind the lenses of the tortoise shell-rimmed glasses. "A strip club? A dance club? A casino?"

"I'd like a wife who answers questions. What sort of club?" Nolan insisted in a stern, don't-mess-with-me voice.

"A burlesque club," she said, her face blooming again with that charming color. She shot a furtive glance at the camera, and Tyler and the rest of the viewing public received an eye full of scowl.

"You said you like to dance." It sounded like an accusation.

"Now that sounds like a judgment," Josie said. "She's gonna deck Nolan if he's not careful."

"I work at *Maxwell's*, a burlesque club on K' Road in Auckland," Susan said in a firm voice while staring straight into the camera. "I take care of the accounts and wages and also dance on stage several nights a week."

"You're a stripper," Nolan said.

"Well," said Josie.

"I didn't see that coming," Eric said. "She looks like such a goody-two-shoes."

The frisson of interest in Tyler grew and he couldn't tear his eyes off the screen. This was the first woman to attract his curiosity since Rebecca stomped all over his heart. A snort escaped him, attracting a quizzical glance from Josie.

"Do you disapprove?" she asked.

Tyler shook his head, ears peeled to hear every word from the little lady.

"You really need to educate yourself about burlesque," Susan said. "Burlesque is not the same as stripping."

"But you do perform on a stage."

"Yes, I do, and I'm rather good at it. *Maxwell's* is a very busy place." Her chin lifted and she spoke with pride.

"I like this woman," Eric said. "I like her backbone. She's a bit flustered, but she's holding her own."

Nolan stared at her for a long moment, and Tyler almost wished he was watching the show in the presence of his mother. She'd made her disapproval very clear when he'd announced Rebecca was pregnant. He could only imagine what she thought about this Susan's announcement. His mother was concerned with appearances and still didn't speak to Tyler, even though he and Rebecca had ended up getting married.

"I wonder if you'd find the countryside a little quiet," Nolan said. "We don't have shops or movie theatres or clubs."

"I'm open to trying new things," Susan countered. "I've never lived in the country, but I'm sure I'll find things to keep myself amused."

The *Farmer Seeks a Wife* went to an ad break, leaving Tyler's mind free to wander. He could think of countless ways to help keep Susan amused, and none of them included his older brother.

"I like her too," Josie said. "I'd love to meet her in person, although I don't suppose we'll get a chance after her bombshell." She darted a quick glance at Tyler.

"Just say it," he said. "Mum is probably having conniptions and stressing about what Reverend Jacobs and the rest of the churchie people are going to say."

Eric let out a rude snort. "Clare's morals police will get good mileage, that's for sure."

"My lips are sealed." Josie made a lip buttoning motion. "I'm staying far away from the gossip vine. I'm not even going to give into the temptation to prune, although I hate to think about the character assassination of that poor girl. Anyone for more tea?"

"Not for me, thanks," Tyler said. "I'll just look in on Katey and make sure she hasn't snuck out of bed to play with her doll's house again."

"I'll pause the show if it starts before you come back," Eric said. "We don't want to miss a thing."

Tyler strode down the dark passage leading to his daughter's bedroom and pushed open the door. Katey's nightlight, resplendent with unicorns, lent a warm glow to the room. His heart twisted on seeing her amidst a herd of soft toys and one semi-bald doll. Katey's golden blonde hair—Rebecca's hair—spread across her pillow and a quiet whistle sounded each time she breathed.

Rebecca.

The woman was everywhere even though she'd died two years ago now.

He sighed and backed out of his daughter's room. So many memories...

"The show has just started," Eric said when Tyler skirted the glass-topped coffee table to reclaim his seat on the couch.

"There are some attractive girls," Tyler said as they watched the segment featuring a farmer from Otago and his group of women. "The city men must be doing something wrong."

"Which ones do you think he'll choose?" Josie asked.

"A blonde one," Tyler said promptly and laughed when Josie prodded him in the ribs. "What? You haven't noticed most of the women in his group are blonde?"

"Of course I noticed," Josie said. "Which blondes will he choose?"

"If he's smart, he'll go with the girl who was brought up on a farm. A fish out of water is very well for a short time, but some of those women wouldn't like the isolation of his farm. It's damn cold down there in the middle of winter. Lots of snow. At least the woman Nolan chooses will only have to face rain and mud," Eric said.

"When we come back, each of our farmers will choose eight women from his group to go forward to the next round. Who will it be? Ladies and gentlemen, the tension is palpable here, and I'm as anxious as the girls to learn who our farmers choose," Hailee said in a confidential manner.

"So who is Nolan going to pick?" Eric asked.

Tyler knew who Nolan wouldn't select. "Of the ones we saw, I think he liked the woman who owned the dog and a tea shop. She seemed nice and she was subtle yet sexy. Mum would approve of her."

Josie nodded. "The woman who worked as admin at the

fast-food restaurant. With her farming background, she'd be a good candidate."

"Quiet, the show is starting again," Eric said.

Tyler smothered a grin. He'd take a safe bet that most Clare residents were glued to their televisions tonight.

"Oh dear," Josie said, her tone sympathetic when the first farmer read out his eight picks. "Some of the women look as if they might burst into tears."

"At least the women they showcased tonight might get a little attention from the single men in their area—one's they haven't met before," Eric said.

Tyler didn't comment, instead wondering how he could get up to Auckland to meet Susan in person. He had a starting point—the club on K' Road and her name—but he figured a lot of other men would have the same idea. He thought about their work schedule on the farm and acknowledged the truth. He couldn't leave Eric to cope with the haymaking on his own. The sheep were due for crutching too.

"It's Nolan's turn," Josie said.

They listened to Hailee ask Nolan several questions.

"He's good," Eric said. "He comes across as confident yet not arrogant."

"Shush," Josie said, her eyes glued to the screen.

Tyler watched Nolan scan the line of women, his expression suitably somber. "Hailee, the ladies I have chosen for the next stage are Maxine, Elle, Tamara, Lucy,

Anna, Cherry, Jasmine and Susan."

"He picked the stripper," Eric said.

Shock rioted with excitement in Tyler as Hailee informed the viewing audience that the chosen women plus the men would be blogging about their experiences on the show. "If anyone has any burning questions for our farmers, there is a forum to post your queries and you can also comment on the blog posts. During the next show, our farmers are taking their eight women on a group date so they can assess the women in a social situation. Tune in at the same time on Thursday to learn what happens," Hailee said.

The closing credits rolled over her smiling face before the camera panned across the room to show each farmer surrounded by his chosen women.

"Well," Josie said. "I didn't expect that."

"No." Tyler stared as the camera plucked Susan's face from the group and highlighted her for the viewing audience. Their mother was probably frothing at the mouth right now. Nolan never upset her intentionally. He was the doting son who always did the right thing while Tyler was the bad boy who messed up—according to their mother, at least. What the hell was Nolan playing at?

Tyler couldn't wait to discover the fallout.

CHAPTER THREE

SUSAN STARED AT THE blank computer screen then glanced at the written instructions provided by Jennifer's harried assistant.

"What are you doing?" Maggie halted beside Susan's desk in the office at *Maxwell's*.

"I'm trying to decide what to put on my blog. I was going to go ahead with the post on burlesque, but I checked out the posts written by other entrants and they've all written introductory posts about themselves and their interests."

"So?" Maggie said.

Julia popped her head into the office. "Susan, it's only half an hour before you're due on stage."

Susan glanced at the clock on her screen. "Bother. I'm on my way to the dressing room."

"Connor brought his camera. We'll get some shots

tonight. I thought we'd take a few of you getting ready, if that's okay."

"Sure," Susan said, already shifting to show-mode. "I'll take care of this later."

It was almost three when Susan unlocked the front door of the apartment she shared with Christina. Although the first day of filming had taken place two days before, her mind still whirled with astonishment. Nolan Penrith was playing games and doing it in a public arena. How to react—that was the problem.

The answer popped into her mind like a magical genie.

Act like herself.

If Nolan didn't like the person she was, that was his problem. No way did she intend to change her natural personality to please a man. Been there and hadn't liked the T-shirt.

She powered up her laptop. Time to write her post and stop stressing about the contents. No sheep behavior for her. Yes, she'd do her own thing. She took a deep breath and started writing.

Last year, I worked for an inner city accounting firm. My best friends worked there too, but now we've gone on to do other things. Julia took over the management of Maxwell's *when her mother's health deteriorated. All of us helped her while she rebranded the club and reopened. That was when I discovered I have a talent for dancing. I not only enjoy performing, but it helped me to climb out of the deep rut I'd fallen into. It turns out dancing and physical exercise is character building too, and I've changed for the better.*

A win-win situation all the way around.

Yes, I'm a burlesque dancer. Yes, I wear skimpy costumes and sometimes I take off my clothes. Some people will call what I do stripping. Their problem, not mine.

Burlesque has been around for a long time with some saying the art goes back to Greek times. During the 19th century, dancers performed burlesque for the lower classes, and the management and choreographers used the form of expression to poke fun at those in the upper classes. Nothing like thumbing your nose at the rich and getting paid for it! When audience numbers dwindled, the women donned skimpy costumes to attract a larger crowd. Really controversial during staid Victorian times where even chair and piano legs were covered so as to avoid offense, although it made good business sense.

Give the men something they don't get at home. A simple demand and supply situation.

Susan's computer let out a beep, indicating the arrival of an email. She clicked the icon and spotted a message from

Maggie. Her friend had attached several of the photos Connor had snapped during the night. A slow grin spread across her face. The pictures were perfect and a step up from the cat and dog photos the other participants had posted on their blogs.

Susan resized a photo of her in the dressing room, applying her stage makeup and another of her onstage. Connor had caught her saucy smile as she looked over the top of her feather fans.

It's no secret that Maxwell's, *in its former guise of* The Last Frontier, *used to be a strip club, but what most people don't realize is that originally, the club offered burlesque performances, and Julia Maxwell, the manager of* Maxwell's, *has taken things full circle to the beginning.*

We still do pole dancing, but I challenge you to come and watch our show. There is nothing tacky about the acts. Maxwell's *is class all the way. The pole dancing is very popular for hen's parties, and everyone joins in, learning the basics and having a lot of fun.*

Maxwell's *is a place where both sexes come to relax, have a few drinks and enjoy the nightly entertainment.*

At first, I was dubious about dancing, but most of you wouldn't recognize me on stage. You could pass me on the street and not see me as the woman who danced in front of you the previous evening. Well...that is until I appeared on national television. I figure you might notice me now.

I started dancing to help my friend save her mother's club. I did it out of friendship and because I know she'd help me if ever I needed her. Julia is a stern taskmaster. Every muscle in my body ached the day after our first practice session. I walked like a duck for a week before finally, my muscles adapted to the exercise and my fitness levels increased. Slowly, dancing began to feel like second nature.

These days I find burlesque an excellent form of stress release. I'm fitter, healthier and a dress size smaller. Score! But I'm also happy. I've found my niche at the club. Some people might judge me—believe me, in the past I would have numbered amongst you—but I've grown during the last year. I've learned doing something that makes you happy is as important as finding someone to share your happiness.

One of my friends took some photos for me to include with my post. The first photo is of me getting ready to perform. The makeup and costume is a huge part of burlesque, and after much practice, I've managed to become an expert. The second photo shows me in action on stage, doing a fan dance. I dare you to tell me this picture is disgusting.

The next step in the Farmer Seeks a Wife *competition will prove interesting. I sent in my application because I was lonely and wanted to find a man who accepted me and my quirks.*

Despite my occupation, I'm pretty ordinary. I enjoy moonlit walks, days at the beach and dinners out. Expensive meals aren't necessary, since fish and chips on the beach can be just as enjoyable as the most expensive five-star meal at a top restaurant. Togetherness and common interests are important, and that's what I'm looking for in a husband. I want a man to make me laugh, to hold me when I'm sad and to support me in everything I do. In return, I'll look after him, shower him with love and honesty. I'll give my everything.

If you have any questions about burlesque, have at it. I'll be happy to chat with you.

Susan's lips twisted, mocking herself, as she proofread her post. She'd receive rude messages and, no doubt, a few crank emails. At the very least, Julia would garner publicity for the club. She read her post a final time, made a few small adjustments and hit send.

Her area of the forum remained empty, but she saw she'd received emails already. The first message made her stomach buck and not in a good way. With a shaky hand, she hit delete. She shuddered and rubbed her hands together, imaginary cooties crawling over her arms and legs.

Her trembling fingers communicated with the cursor, and she had to concentrate to hit the next email in her inbox.

Dear Susan,

My name is Tyler Penrith, and yes, the name should be familiar to you—I'm Nolan's younger brother.

I want to apologize for my brother's rudeness, and I can't believe the numbskull flashed your butt to national television viewers. While most men—if they are gentlemen—would apologize and assure you they didn't peek, I'm gonna hit you with honesty. I looked and loved the view. You're an attractive lady. Learning about your job just intrigued me more. You possess layers and are like a complex perfume and I find myself wanting to learn more.

Susan found herself grinning. No one had ever compared her to a perfume before, and she rather liked the contrast.

If my idiot brother doesn't choose you during the next elimination, would you consider me?

I am a widower with a four-year-old daughter. My wife died of cancer over two years ago now, and as much as I love my daughter and have incredibly supportive in-laws, I find myself wanting more. Sure, I have friends in Clare, and I get out occasionally, but seeing you on television tonight was the first time I've found myself attracted to a woman. Go figure! The woman I'd like to get to know better is out of bounds because of my brother.

If you'd ever like someone to talk to, I'm here. I'm not a gossip and would never pass on any confidential information should you care to use me as a sounding block. I'm including my phone number along with my private email address if you'd like to contact me. If you're as savvy as I think you are, you'll want to check me out. The number is in the phone directory under my in-laws name. Katey and I live with my in-laws, Eric and Josie Murdoch.

Eric and Josie own a farm and I work as a general hand for them, doing a bit of everything. I'm twenty-five years old—yeah, a little younger than you, but don't let that put you off. In life experience, I'm older. I grew up quickly with a child and a sick wife because I had to. In my spare time, I enjoy rugby and like to draw and paint. Like you, I'm looking for that special someone who gets me, despite my flaws, someone who is sexy and honest and not afraid of the hard work necessary to make a successful relationship.

I hope you'll take my offer seriously, and at least take pity on me, letting me down gently if you're not interested. I won't like it, but my ego will no doubt recover. My daughter is a handful and keeps me busy. I won't have time to sulk.

Since I know what you look like, I've attached a snapshot of me and Katey. Nolan and I don't look much alike. My mother says I take after my father's side of the family.

Best wishes,

Tyler Penrith

Susan found herself holding her breath as she clicked on the attachment. The photo appeared on the screen and her breath whooshed out. Tyler Penrith was a cutie with dark chocolate brown hair and brown eyes. One dimple flashed at the right side of his impish grin. The child in his arms had the same mischievous smile twinkling in her brown eyes but had blonde hair. Their heads were close together, and they were both staring into the camera.

Tyler didn't look anything like Nolan. Together, the two brothers would be like night and day. A cliché—sure—but Nolan was a burly man with brown hair and sun-streaks of blond from working outdoors while Tyler brought to mind dark nights, silky sheets and...

Stop right there, Susan. She was committed to the show. Yet every instinct told her to email Tyler back. No, she needed to think about her next step first. She'd jumped too soon before and landed in a pile of steaming crap. She'd talk to her friends tomorrow, show them the email and hear their thoughts.

To distract herself, she clicked on the next email. *Eew!* That was disgusting. She hit delete and steeled herself for the next one. Hit delete. The last two emails were from church groups, decrying her profession. They went into the trash.

Unable to help herself, she clicked on Tyler's photo again, smiling in response to his happy expression. The humor in his eyes and the echo in his daughter's face wiped away the filth from the other emails and brought a surge of hope. She wasn't a lost cause, despite what her family thought. Her friends believed in her, and even better, she believed in herself.

SUSAN WAITED UNTIL AFTER their usual Saturday dance practice. She, Christina and Julia were relaxing with a cup of peppermint tea when Maggie and Connor breezed into the club.

"Do you guys have time to watch Connor's game?" Maggie asked. "It's a beautiful day outside and I could do with the company."

"I'm in, but I'll have to bring Alex with me," Julia said.

"We can help keep an eye on him," Maggie said.

"Count me in," Christina said.

"Are you okay?" Susan asked. "You look tired."

Christina gave a heartfelt sigh and took off her glasses to rub a smear from the lenses. Without the disguise, it was easy to see she wasn't sleeping. "I've been staying with my godmother. She's not well again, and I'm worried about her. She refuses to go to the doctor."

"Anything we can do?" Maggie asked.

Christina shoved her glasses back into place. "Not really. I need to persuade her to make a doctor's appointment. I'm working on it. I'd like to go to the game. The fresh air will probably do me good."

"I did my first blog last night," Susan said. "And I've already had half a dozen emails." She screwed up her nose. "Most weren't very polite."

"Most?" asked Connor.

Susan grinned and picked up her phone. She thumbed to the photo of Tyler and his daughter and handed it to Christina. "This is Tyler, Nolan's younger brother. He wrote me a really nice email offering himself as a prospective candidate if his older brother rejects me at the next stage."

"Cute," Christina said, passing Susan's phone to Julia. "What happened to the kid's mother?"

"He said his wife died of cancer a few years ago," Susan said.

"Are you sure he's who he says he is?" Connor demanded.

"He gave me his phone number and his email address, told me his name and gave me personal details. He didn't come across as a creep, but he told me I was welcome to check him out."

"Send me his details," Connor said. "I'll do it for you."

Susan nodded, happy to accept the offer. Connor was the computer wizard, and he'd know exactly where to look.

Julia cocked her head, her blonde curls swinging against her cheek with the action. "You like him."

"Yeah. I shouldn't. He's three years younger than me," Susan said.

"Three years is nothing," Maggie said. "You seem more excited about him than his brother. I say go for it."

"After I've checked him out," Connor said in a stern voice.

Susan gave him a cocky salute. "Yes, sir."

"I'll do my searches tonight and let you know by tomorrow at the latest."

"Thanks," Susan said. "I appreciate it."

"You're going to cheer my team on this afternoon," Connor said. "It's the least I can do in return."

"Tyler Penrith is who he says he is," Connor said the next day after yet another dance practice. "Nothing bad jumped out at me during my searches."

"So what are you going to do?" Maggie asked.

"I'm not sure. I have my group date on Wednesday afternoon. We have to meet Nolan at Downtown and were told to wear comfortable clothes and footwear."

Julia frowned. "You don't know what you're going to do or where he's taking you?"

"No, which makes it difficult to know what to wear," Susan said.

"Do you know where the other farmers are taking their dates?" Christina asked.

Susan jumped to her feet and started pacing. "No, I asked, but they're not telling us anything."

"The comfortable shoes direction makes me think there will be walking," Connor said.

"Wear your runners—the black ones or a pair of comfy boots," Christina said. "The weather could do anything but check the forecast. I'd go for layers. Jeans and a shirt with a vest and a waterproof jacket. A colorful scarf and maybe a hat."

"Take a small daypack instead of a purse," Maggie suggested. "That way if you need to peel off layers, it will be easier to carry them."

Susan discovered the women's idea of comfortable dress varied considerably when she joined Nolan's group at

Downtown, not far from the Britomart train station. Only three of them wore flat shoes. Susan had kept her makeup light and natural and wore a sage green beanie to counteract the wind whistling along Quay Street.

A cameraman—the same one who'd delighted in her mishaps—stood beside Nolan, his camera already panning their faces and recording their reactions to Nolan. Susan stood quietly, surveying her competition.

"Put us out of our suspense," one of the women demanded.

"We're catching the ferry to Rangitoto and will do some exploring," Nolan said. "I've organized water bottles and a snack pack for us. When we come back we're going to the top of Sky Tower for dinner."

The woman standing next to Susan gave an audible groan. "I hate walking. I'm gonna freeze my butt off."

Susan snuck a glance at the woman's shoes and mentally added sore feet to the equation. She listened to the other comments and smiled inwardly. This outing was a clever way of weeding out the candidates who wouldn't cope with living in the countryside. If they couldn't handle a little walking, they sure as heck wouldn't hack it in Clare where Nolan lived and farmed.

"The ferry is this way," Nolan said.

Susan followed the group with a sense of anticipation. She hadn't visited Rangitoto Island for years, not since a long ago school trip. The views of the city from the summit were wonderful, and she was glad she'd listened to Connor and packed her camera. A few snapshots would make a welcome addition to her blog.

Nolan made a point of speaking with all of them individually and did well with recalling their names.

"Susan," he said. "It's good to see you again." His gaze took in her clothes and she thought she caught a flash of approval. "You've created a tempest in Clare. Most people think I should give you a wide berth."

And just like that he dispelled her happy bubble. Susan lifted her chin and met his gaze with a glare. She was trying hard not to slip into her old judgmental ways, but this man poked holes in her confidence.

"You'll have to decide if you agree," she said. "This is a nice treat. I haven't set foot on Rangitoto in years."

His direct gaze sliced and diced again until one of the other women claimed his attention. Susan fell into step with Cherry and offered her a smile.

"You're the dancer," she said.

"That's part of my job description." Susan could feel her good mood taking a wet 'n' wild slide toward insecure.

"I couldn't do what you do. I'd feel so exposed."

"Dancing is a rush, and I've never been in such good shape in all my life." Enough about her job. "Have you always lived in the city?"

"Yes. At least Clare doesn't seem too isolated. Some of the farmers live and work in really remote areas."

"Nolan said the farm is still half an hour from the township."

"That far?" The woman frowned. "He told me about the beautiful scenery. I assumed the town was closer."

"Is that a problem?" Susan asked.

"I guess not. I mean Nolan is gorgeous. His boots are welcome under my bed any time." The woman whispered the last and cast a sidelong glance in Nolan's direction.

"Yes, he is attractive. I'm looking forward to learning more about him." She wondered if she could slip in a few questions about his family. Connor had given Tyler a genuine stamp. The information on him was patchy, though, and not enough to quench her curiosity.

The ferry ride was a short one, and Susan stood at the stern, enjoying the fresh sea air and watching the flit of yachts as they zapped back and forth across the waves, their colorful sails billowing in the gusts of wind. The panoramic view of the city buildings, bathed in autumn sun, caught her eye and she fumbled inside her pack for her camera.

"I have to say," Nolan said, coming to stand beside her, "that the city looks good from this angle."

"As nice as the view from your house?" Susan asked.

"They're each pretty in their own way."

There was a moment of companionable silence between them.

"Do you have brothers and sisters?" Susan asked finally.

"A younger brother. Tyler."

"Does he work on the farm with you?"

"No, he lives with his in-laws and works on his father-in-law's farm."

"He's married?"

"A widower. His wife died a few years ago."

Susan nodded. "That must have been rough."

Nolan shrugged, and Susan knew she couldn't ask more questions without him asking questions in return.

"I have two sisters, both married."

His expression sharpened. "Older or younger?"

Susan sighed, knowing exactly where this conversation would head. "Both younger than me, married with children."

"But you're not married."

"No." She'd come close, thought she'd found the one. Twice. And both times she'd regained possession of her trampled heart with her confidence in tatters.

His brows rose, a silent prompt for her to continue. "If I were married, I wouldn't be on *Farmer Seeks a Wife*," she said. "What do your parents think about you being on a reality show?"

"What do yours think about you?"

"Snap," she said. "My mother loathes the publicity caused by her delinquent daughter."

"My mother, on the other hand, is following proceedings closely since she was the one who sent in my application." His dry tone filled in some gaps. Namely, that he hadn't come willingly.

"You don't want a wife?"

"I'm not averse to the idea," he said. "But I like to do my own choosing."

"I hear you. My mother and sisters are always trying to fix me up with suitable men when I go home to Hamilton. Blind dates are awkward."

"On that we agree."

"I'm like most of the women who applied for the show. I'd like someone to share my life, but if it doesn't happen I've realized that's okay too. I have great friends—ones who'd go the extra mile for me if I asked for a favor. Settling for second best to make my family happy won't do much for my contentment."

He nodded and moved out of the way of a deck hand as the captain backed the ferry up to the wharf. "That's true."

Susan disembarked with the rest of the women and moved aside to take photos. She strode back to the hovering group. "Can I take a group shot?"

The women clustered around Nolan. "Say sexy farmer," Susan said and clicked the shutter when everyone laughed. She examined the shot. "Nice photo."

"Everyone ready to walk to the summit?" Nolan asked.

"I'd like to catch the cute train," one of the women said.

A couple of the others agreed and went off to buy tickets. The rest of them started the walk along the scoria paths. Weird lava shapes studded the landscape, remnants of the eruption over six hundred years ago. Native pohutukawa trees poked from crevices and Susan snapped a photo of a rock that reminded her of one of the *Lord of the Rings* movie characters.

Gradually their group broke into twos and threes with a couple of the women sticking to Nolan and peppering him with flirtation. Susan didn't bother to compete, merely enjoying the walk and stopping to take photos whenever tempted.

But the giggles of the other women eventually intruded and tumbled her back into the present. She shot a glance to her right and saw Nolan grinning down at a shapely blonde—Cherry or Anna. Susan couldn't remember her name. While the man was smiling, he managed to distance himself as well. Despite putting on a good game face, he didn't want to be here, she thought. Yet he'd gone ahead with the reality show anyway to please his mother.

Another reason to avoid him.

She did *not* want a mommy's boy.

Frowning at her discovery, she took a moment to stop and capture the view of the central city and the thrust of the Sky Tower. A penis-symbol for sure. The tower jolted her mind in the direction of men and her current man-drought. There came a time when a vibrator wasn't enough and only the solid weight of a man moving against her body would dissipate her hunger.

Since she seemed to put her foot in her mouth every time she spoke with Nolan, she'd have to look elsewhere.

But where?

Tyler.

Her inner rebel came out to play. Tyler's face floated into her mind, his grin, his protective arm around his daughter. Connor vouched for him, and Nolan had confirmed some of the details. Still, she hesitated. He was Nolan's younger brother, and that felt weird.

They'd continued to correspond—just friendly notes about their interests and their daily routines. Tyler worked hard on his father-in-law's farm and seemed to be fully involved in his daughter's life, although he admitted that if it wasn't for his mother-in-law, he'd be in trouble. He spoke fondly of Eric and Josie, and it was obvious he liked and admired his in-laws.

More telling perhaps was that he seldom mentioned his own parents or Nolan. Instead she learned about fencing, sundry farming chores and Tyler's painting. He seemed passionate about art.

Aware she was lagging, Susan put on a burst of speed, jogging up to the crest of a small hill. At the back of her mind, she realized she wasn't even puffing and pride surged with an inner cheer. Julia might act the stern taskmaster when it came to dancing, but all that training was paying off big time.

Finally, their group reached the spot where the train was

parked, ready to make the return journey. Susan wandered in the rear, the gravel path crunching beneath her boots. The gravel gave way to a boardwalk, which led up the last rise to the summit. Since it was the middle of the week, most of the other visitors were tourists. Nolan and his harem didn't attract attention.

"This way, ladies," Nolan said. "We have lunch boxes for everyone in the clearing over here."

An assistant—a pencil-thin Asian male—appeared from the direction Nolan indicated and had a muffled conversation with the cameraman before turning to face them. "Ladies, before you eat, Jennifer wants me to organize one-on-one chats for each of you with Nolan. These will be filmed and some shown during Thursday's show. This will also give Nolan an opportunity to get to know you better and help him to decide who to choose for the next stage."

"How many of us are eliminated this time?" a blonde asked.

Susan frowned when she realized most of the women were blonde. Interesting.

"Nolan needs to eliminate two today and another three next week," the assistant said. "We'll do your interviews in alphabetical order." He consulted his clipboard. "Elle, you're up first. We have a private spot set up over here. If you'll follow me."

Nolan gestured for Elle—a strawberry blonde—to

precede him and the pair followed the assistant.

"Are you nervous?" one of the women asked Susan.

"Not really," Susan said. "After flashing my butt at the camera, I figure things can't get much worse."

The woman chuckled. "I saw that. I felt bad for you and at the same time I was glad it wasn't me."

Susan clicked a photo of the women as they opened their lunches. "I wonder what sort of questions Nolan will ask us."

"I hate to think," the woman said.

Elle appeared on the track and ambled over to the group. "Cherry, you're next."

"What were the questions like?" Susan asked.

"You have to pick a sealed envelope then Nolan opens it and reads out the three questions." She giggled. "He asked about my first kiss."

Cherry went off and came back, her cheeks scarlet. "He asked if I enjoyed sex. If that portion airs on television, I'm going to be mortified. My parents watched the first show. My grandparents. Oh, Jasmine. It's your turn."

Susan's gut did a nasty buck, her confidence sailing in an arc to fall to the pit of her stomach with a crash. Oh, goody. She had a sex question to look forward to, and she'd have to wait until the end because her surname was Webb.

Jasmine returned, grinning. "Your turn, Maxine. He asked me to tell him about my favorite sexual position."

Susan felt her mouth drop open and snapped it shut.

The questions seemed to becoming more personal. "What did you say?"

"Reverse cowgirl," Jasmine said. "That's what the couple in the erotic romance I'm reading was doing, so I went with gut instinct and lied. I'd better warn my parents about this next segment of the show, but I guess they did say the show would be adult rated."

"As long as they don't expect to film us having sex," Susan muttered.

Maxine returned, shaking her head. "Lucy, you're up."

"Tough question?" Susan asked.

"He asked me if I'd be willing to let a man tie me up. I said no way, no how. If there was any tying up, I was the one who was gonna be doing it. With all the hype about that BDSM novel, he was probably disappointed with my answer," Maxine said.

"Wow," Elle said. "I think I lucked out with my question. Talking about a first kiss is much easier."

Foreboding shot to new heights in Susan. She watched the remaining girls disappear to meet with Nolan then it was her turn for questions.

"Why do I feel as if I'm about to appear before the firing squad?" she asked Nolan before she remembered that blasted cameraman. She shot a quick glance at the camera and sure enough, she saw a smirking mouth beneath the camera housing.

She sank onto the picnic blanket, relieved when she

didn't suffer any clothing malfunctions.

"Are you nervous?" Nolan's eyes laughed at her.

"Should I be?" she countered.

His mouth twitched. "Since there was only one envelope left, I opened it before you arrived."

Her gaze narrowed. "Bring it."

The cameraman sniggered.

Nolan flashed a grin before his gaze went to a single sheet of white paper. From where she sat, she couldn't read the questions. *Blast.* "Question number one: do you prefer your men to wear boxers or briefs?"

Okay, that wasn't so bad. "Neither," she said.

There was a moment of startled silence. The cameraman made a choking sound behind his camera.

"You prefer commando?" Nolan asked.

"Well, I can live with commando some of the time because, I mean, it's *so* convenient when you're in a hurry." Where on earth was this coming from? She was channeling her inner bimbo—that was clear. "But mostly a man should wear boxer-briefs. You get great support plus you look good," she said, her sugar-sweet tone daring him to take umbrage at her reply.

Nolan's lips quivered again, and he cleared his throat. "Great answer. Uh, the next question—this one is mine because I'm curious. I've done some research on your burlesque. I know your dancers do the fan dance at the club. How many garments are you left wearing at the end of the fan dance?"

"Are you trying to get me to admit I'm a stripper?"

"Answer the question, please."

"The object of the fan dance is to titillate and make those in the audience wonder if they'll catch a glimpse of the dancer's body. Part of the dance is removing the top without revealing extra skin to the audience."

"Do you do the fan dance?"

Susan sucked in a quick breath. Curse the man. "Yes, I am one of dancers at *Maxwell's* who do the fan dance."

"Which means you're technically a person who takes off their clothes to entertain," he said in a silky voice.

Why bother arguing? "That is correct."

"How do you get off the stage without anyone seeing your scantily clad body?"

"I've answered more than three questions, but for your information—I leave the stage when the curtain comes down. The only people who are backstage are the other dancers and my friends. I do not flaunt my nudity. *Maxwell's* is a decent club with a good reputation, and we have so many applicants to join our dance team we don't have to advertise."

"Hmm," Nolan said. "I still don't understand why you'd want to live in the country when it's obvious your job skills require an urban setting."

Susan bit back the tumble of words that battered her brain in a demand for freedom. She took a deep breath.

"Smug, arrogant men are not a turn on."

The cameraman let loose one of his chuckles and kept right on filming.

"Is that all?" Susan demanded. "I want to take more photos before we have to leave to catch the ferry."

"One last question," Nolan said. "What is your biggest sexual fantasy?"

She cringed a little inside. Her mother would watch this. She'd probably laugh, but that wasn't the point.

"Cat got ya tongue?" The daredevil gleam in Nolan's eyes told her he expected her to balk.

"I think sex should express the love between a man and a woman. There should be passion and lust, but those emotions should be tempered with honesty, caring and laughter. If I were honest, I'd have to say that my biggest sexual fantasy would be to please my partner in bed. The pleasure should flow in both directions."

"But that's not a fantasy, is it? You're sidestepping the question."

Susan's hands clenched in her lap and heat layered on top of layer in her face. "All right. I fantasize about being alone on an island with one special man. We play hide and seek, but there's an edge to the game because if he captures me within half an hour he gets to spank me and tie me up so I'm at his mercy. That's his favorite kink," she added. "Me, I'm determined to outwit him because in return I get a sexual slave for the rest of the day who will do whatever I want, get me off how I want. Would you like more detail?"

"Yes," said the cameraman.

Nolan gave a curt nod.

"It's really a win-win situation for me," Susan said. "Because I get off on my lover tying me up and spanking makes me so hot I start creaming at the first love tap. But I don't like to make it easy for my lover. I creep into the forest and find a hiding place. In the distance, I hear a shout, the signal the search has commenced. My heart is thumping so loud I wonder if he'll hear. My nipples are hard—did I mention I'm wearing an itty-bitty bikini? No? Okay, that's what I'm wearing and it's not doing a good job of hiding my sexual response.

"Time ticks away. Ten minutes. Fifteen.

"My muscles are cramping from crouching in position for too long. I shift my weight and then it happens. In my uncomfortable shifting, I put my weight on a stick. A sharp crack rings out. My heartbeat goes crazy. I swallow. Maybe he hasn't heard?

"Another five minutes pass, and I become aware of insects. They're biting my skin in tender places. A cramping pain starts in my foot. I bite my tongue and stand carefully. I shift my weight, and this time I'm careful of foot placement. Then there's a whisper just behind me."

"Why don't you run, little girl?"

CHAPTER FOUR

"It's him! Instinct makes me bolt, but of course, it's too late. He's bigger, stronger, and before I take half a dozen paces, he grabs me by the hips, drags me to a stop. The next minute, I'm draped over his shoulder and watching the ground." Susan paused to judge Nolan's reaction.

"What happens next?" His gaze held a hint of challenge and an irritating smile played around his mouth.

Susan flexed her fingers and rearranged her hands. She would *not* resort to violence. "He carries me back to his camp and ties me to a tree. Then, he gets his big knife. Fear makes me whimper as he approaches, and I beg him not to hurt me. His dark eyes glitter, and he sticks the blade under the shoulder strap of my bikini. It's a relief when he cuts my clothing from my body." Susan stopped talking and frowned. "How long do you want this fantasy? We'll have to leave to catch the ferry soon."

Nolan's glance held speculation. "One last question. Did you get off on him tying you up? Was the sex good?"

Susan stared right back, not flinching. "That's two questions." She was proud of her even tone.

"Pick one and answer," Nolan ordered.

Susan cocked her head to the side and stared straight into the camera. She let her tongue moisten her top lip in an unhurried swipe. "Oh," she said. "It was very, very good. The best sex I ever had."

Hey, Susan.

I have a few minutes before I need to collect Katey from a birthday party. How did your second date go? If you're falling for my big brother, I'm going to need to put a contract out on him or something. Maybe you could give me a couple of hints about what happened on your date since the suspense is killing me. Thursday night has become my favorite night to watch TV.

One other thing. I'd like to meet you in person. Would you consider that? My in-laws will babysit Katey for the weekend if I ask. They're always telling me I need to get out more with people my own age. The drive to Auckland isn't too bad—about five hours, or I might be able to get a flight. I know you have to work, but maybe we could spend a few hours together. No pressure, but it's difficult to get to know a person via email. You don't know me well, and if you'd feel better going out in a group situation—maybe drinks and dinner with your friends—I'm fine with that. More than fine. It would be great to meet some of your friends, since they sound like a fun bunch.

Let me know what you think.

Best wishes,

Tyler

A shiver worked through Susan, not fear, but something resembling exhilaration. Grinning, she went in search of Julia.

"Tyler wants to meet. He suggested coming up to Auckland and said if I was nervous about meeting him alone, we could go on a group date with my friends. Will you do it? Will you be my chaperone?"

Julia let out a shriek.

Christina came running from the direction of the dancer's dressing room. "What? What's wrong?"

"Tyler has asked Susan out on a date," Julia said.

"The hot younger brother." Christina fanned her face, her flapping hand doing nothing to hide her grin. "When?"

"He hasn't mentioned any particular dates. I think he's floating the idea."

"What are you going to do?" Julia asked.

Susan thought about it for two seconds. The answer was easy. "I want to meet him."

"What about Nolan?" Christina asked.

"I doubt he'll pick me again. For one, he seems to have a thing for blondes since I'm the only brunette in the group. And two, we seem to strike sparks off each other and end up bickering like kids. He's attractive, but I think we'd make better friends."

"I wish you'd give us some hints about the show," Julia said.

Susan made a buttoning motion across her lips. "Not gonna happen. You'll have to wait until tomorrow night to see it with everyone else." A full day of peace before the teasing commenced. "At least the club is getting good publicity. Numbers have been up since last Thursday."

Julia arched her brows. "Will the numbers increase again this week?"

Susan felt the color sweep into her cheeks. "Quite possibly."

"*Ooh*." Christina rubbed her hands together. "Tell us more."

Susan ignored the demand. "Do you think Maggie and Connor would come for dinner with us?"

"What am I? Chopped liver?" Julia demanded. "Ryan and Caleb are due home in two days. What if I organize Christina and Caleb to look after the club? Ryan and Connor would love to help chaperone."

"I demand a secret in exchange," Christina's eyes twinkled behind her glasses. "That's fair. And I get to tell Caleb the secret too."

Susan huffed out a sigh. "Deal," she said. "But you don't get your secret until Tyler confirms he's coming up to Auckland. I'll email him back and see if he can visit next weekend. That will give him time to arrange a sitter, and we'll have time to sort things out here."

"Tell him not to book a hotel," Julia said. "Caleb won't mind Tyler bunking at the apartment with him. I think Caleb gets a bit lonely now that Ryan and I are renting our own place."

"Go and email Tyler back right now," Christina said. "I want my secret tonight, so I can gloat to Julia and Maggie. If I have to put up with the handsome, sexy Caleb, I want compensation."

Her friend's comment had Susan chuckling as she hurried back to the office. Christina and Caleb had become good friends, and they were continually trying to fix each other up. They entertained themselves and everyone else by telling outrageous stories about their blind dates.

Dear Tyler,

I'd love to meet you in person. Would next weekend work for you? My friend Julia said you can stay at Caleb's apartment—that's her husband's best friend—so don't bother booking a room anywhere. Julia and Maggie plus their husbands have offered to chaperone me. You'd better be on your best behavior because both Maggie and Julia are protective mother-hens. Don't tell them I told you that or I'll have to break a part of your person. I've done a self-defense class, so you've been warned.

The date was another disaster. I embarrassed myself, yet again. When it comes to your brother, I seem to develop foot-in-mouth disease. It was a bit different this time though. I mislaid my verbal filter. I hope the director decides to cut my portion because I'm still cringing at the memory. Yeah...are you sure you want to meet me?

Anyhow. Movin' on... Does your brother have a thing for blondes? I wondered because I'm the only woman left with dark hair.

At this stage, I'm not sure who made the next cut. Jennifer decided to up the suspense and film the guys making their choices at a separate location. She said she didn't want to take the chance of a leak and it gave them a bit longer to weigh the pros and cons of each woman. Her assistant is going to ring the successful applicants a couple of hours before the show airs.

I hope next weekend works for you because I'm looking forward to meeting you.

Susan

THURSDAY WAS SALE DAY, and Tyler rose early to check on the cattle they'd mustered the previous afternoon. The truck to cart them to the sale grounds arrived half an hour late. A puncture, the harried driver explained.

With the cattle safely loaded, Tyler took care of shifting a paddock of ewes and fed the chooks for Josie. Katey had already departed for kindergarten when he arrived back at the house for a quick breakfast.

"Trouble?" Eric asked. "I was about to come looking for you."

"The truck had a puncture. No point both of us getting up so early," Tyler said. Eric and Josie had done so much for him. Taking care of the early morning chores was nothing in exchange.

Eric checked his watch. "I'm going to head off and meet

Jock and Buck for a late breakfast before the sale."

"Sorry, Tyler," Josie said. "You'll have to eat on your own. Eric is dropping me at Janet's. We're going shopping."

The elderly couple departed with hurried farewells, leaving Tyler to himself. He'd catch up with them tonight and ask about looking after Katey during the weekend.

Hours later, Tyler settled in front of the television alone. Katey was in bed and Eric and Josie had decided to have dinner with friends before heading home. The opening credits came on for *Farmer Seeks a Wife* and anticipation swirled within him.

"Welcome to the second installment of *Farmer Seeks a Wife.*" Hailee bubbled, her words punctuated by her trademark bright smile. "I don't know about you, but I'm eager to learn what happened during our farmers' second date. Let's see, shall we? Over to our first farmer, Ray."

Tyler watched impatiently. He heard a car outside, hit live pause and jumped up to make a pot of tea.

"*Farmer Seeks a Wife* is on now if you want to watch," he said the moment Josie walked into the kitchen. Tyler reached for her shopping bags, several of which were emblazoned with the emblem of a local department store, and relieved her of their weight. "Where do you want these? In your bedroom?"

"Yes, please," Josie said. "Oh, good you've started to make tea."

"Does Eric need a hand?" Tyler asked on his return.

"Yes," Eric said, depositing a box of vegetables on the counter. "This woman shopped today."

Josie elbowed her husband. "Shush. Stop complaining. We received top dollar for our beef at the sale."

Grinning, Tyler trotted out to the garage to grab the rest of the shopping. It took two trips and by the time he'd finished, the tea was ready to pour.

"Come and watch the show," Tyler said. "I'll help unpack the groceries once it's over."

"Good idea," Eric said. "I'm exhausted. Need to build up my strength."

Josie elbowed her husband again. "Shush. I can't hear."

"Do you want me to rewind to the start?" Tyler asked.

"Don't let Eric do it," Josie said in alarm. "He'll push the wrong button and we'll miss the entire show."

Eric grumbled under his breath, and Tyler bit back his amusement. No way was Eric getting his hands on the remote. Lesson already learned.

Tyler let his mind drift while Eric and Josie caught up with the show. He shifted his weight, sprawling out, only to shift again and fold up his legs.

"What is wrong with you, Tyler?" Josie demanded when a commercial break started.

Eric grinned over the rim of his tea mug. "Easy to see where Katey gets her fidgety nature."

God, he couldn't wait any longer. "Josie, I wondered

if you and Eric would mind looking after Katey next weekend. I want to go up to Auckland to visit friends."

Eric and Josie shared a quick glance before making him the center of their attention.

"Of course we'll look after Katey," Josie said. "You haven't visited your friends before."

Tyler sighed inwardly. He'd known nosy questions would come, and he couldn't be rude to this couple who'd treated him better than his own parents. "I've met someone on the internet. I'm going to meet her and her friends."

Josie frowned. "But what if she's spinning you a line?"

"I don't think so, but meeting her in person will let me know either way," Tyler said.

"Where are you staying?" Eric asked.

"With a friend of hers," Tyler said. "The show is starting again."

Eric and Josie exchanged a concerned look before focusing on the television.

"It's Nolan," Josie said. "Good gracious. Look at that girl's shoes. How does she expect to tramp to the top of Rangitoto in that footwear?"

They watched as she plus a couple of the other girls headed straight for the land train and climbed aboard.

"She's suitably dressed," Tyler said, his eyes feasting on Susan. She'd dressed for the day and wore a pair of sturdy boots. She looked just as appealing in her casual jeans, jacket and beanie as she had in her red dress.

The show continued with snatches of conversation, a panoramic view of the city and then the questions started.

"Oh my," Josie said. "The kissing one wasn't too bad, but the questions seem to becoming harder and more difficult for the girls to answer."

Susan appeared on the screen—at long last—and Tyler's heart beat a little faster.

"She's my favorite," Josie said. "But I thought Nolan preferred blondes. Every woman I've seen him with has been blonde."

"The rest of the women look like blondes," Tyler said.

"I hear your mother is outraged at his selection of women," Eric said. "I caught up with the gossip at the sale."

"I haven't seen her for a long time," Tyler said, the pain of his mother's rejection having faded into a dull ache.

"I know she's your mother, but she's a judgmental old bat," Eric said.

"Oh my. Good answer," Josie said. "Well at least Susan's question wasn't too bad."

Nolan appeared on the screen and asked a second question.

"He's baiting her," Eric said.

Tyler's hands clenched around his mug and he fantasized about punching Nolan. His brother was needling Susan.

Susan answered the question and the camera shifted back to Nolan. "What is your favorite sexual fantasy?"

"Oh my." Josie shot a quick frown at both of them. "That's a horrid question. If she answers people will slam her for it, and if she doesn't answer she'll receive the same amount of flak."

Tyler stared at the screen, his chest tight with apprehension. She'd said she'd lost her verbal filter. Susan started talking, painting pictures with her seductive words.

When she finished, Josie clapped her hands together in delight. "I like this girl. She has gumption and sass."

Tyler liked her too. Very much. The weekend couldn't come quickly enough.

The segment with Nolan wrapped up, and Hailee appeared on the screen. "Wasn't that exciting? That last question—wow!" She beamed at the camera. "Tune in next week to meet the rest of the farmers and their ladies, plus we'll have the announcement of who goes through to the next round. I think we're in for a treat. Don't forget to check out the blogs on the station website. Feel free to enter the online polls and chat on the forum. See you next week!"

"Well," Josie said. "Who do you think Nolan will choose?"

Chapter Five

Tyler caught a cab from the airport to the hotel Eric and Josie had insisted on booking. *For peace of mind*, according to Josie when she handed over her credit card.

Tyler wasn't worried about Susan or her friends murdering him in his bed. He'd learned a lot from their exchange of emails.

After checking in, he shot Susan a text to tell her he'd arrived. His phone beeped a few minutes after he'd hit send.

Meet at Maxwell's on K' Rd. Bang for entry on arrival.

Tyler decided to walk from his hotel at the bottom of Queen Street. He strolled past the cruise terminal where a huge ship hugged the wharf. Passengers and crew scurried up and down the gangway.

An Elizabeth Square flower seller snagged his attention and he bought four bunches—for Susan and one for each of her close friends. He was looking forward to putting faces to names.

Tyler wandered up Queen Street and tackled the hill leading to K' Road at a fast stroll. Buses, cars and taxis choked the streets and workers spilled from offices and shops, ready for their home comforts and a weekend of freedom. He paused at a crossing, taking a rapid step back when a huge bus lumbered around the corner. It lurched to a stop and passengers piled on board.

When he reached K' Road, he took note of the clubs, the adult stores interspersed with a small convenience store, a shop selling saris and a café. The door of *Maxwell's* was closed and after a quick breath, Tyler knocked for entry.

An elderly man opened the door a crack and peered at him. "We open at six."

"I'm here to see Susan. She told me to bang on the door."

"You're Tyler." An attractive blonde appeared behind the man. "Let him in, Stan. This is Tyler, Susan's friend."

"Hi." Tyler smiled, his nerves settling until he recalled the rest of New Zealand thought Susan was Nolan's girl. His brother—blast him—had included Susan in his latest pick. "I bought some flowers." Tyler handed over a bunch to Julia.

"Aren't you sweet?" Julia sniffed at the bouquet of mixed flowers. "Susan is sorting out the change floats." She took his arm in a friendly manner. "I'll show you to the office. We can't leave for dinner until after the first dance sequence."

"That's fine," Tyler said, taking in his surroundings with interest. The room was huge, the walls the deep blue-black of dusk before real dark stole in to mute the landscape. Borders of intricate golden scrolls contrasted with the blue to give a classy air. "You have a nice place here. It's...elegant."

"We like it," Julia said. "If it weren't for Susan and the rest of my friends, my mother would have ended up selling the club."

"It's a family business?"

"I'm fourth generation." Julia steered him toward the bar, past gleaming tables to a group of men and women. "This is Maggie and Connor. This is Caleb and Ryan, my husband." She released Tyler and winked at her husband.

Maggie was a curvy woman with brown hair and large breasts, although after his first glance, Tyler focused on her husband. Connor was a big man, a few inches taller than Tyler and he bore the fit build of a rugby player. Tyler would've picked him as a rugby man even if Susan hadn't told him about her friends.

Ryan and Caleb were as alike as Susan had said with dark good looks—at least from a female perspective—and the wiry strength and grace of runners.

"I recognize the names. Susan has mentioned you in her

emails." Tyler handed flowers to Maggie and shook hands with everyone, despite his impatience to meet Susan. They were vetting, checking him out because they cared about their friend, and he couldn't blame their caution. He'd do the same if he were in their position, and the size of the three men, their assessing gazes, didn't faze him in the slightest.

"Is he here yet?" A woman's voice came from up on stage.

Tyler straightened, admitted to nerves and did his best not to show his anxiety.

"Yes," Julia said, amusement coloring her tone.

The woman with golden brown hair popped from behind the curtains, and Tyler relaxed. She wore glasses and each time she moved, her bracelets jingled.

"Oops. I'll go and tell Susan," she said.

"Not so fast," Maggie said.

Tyler shifted to stare at her impish face.

Maggie winked and the big, husky man at her side growled. "We haven't had time to interrogate him yet."

"Excellent. I haven't missed the good stuff," Christina said, careening to a halt beside him. "Hi." She stuck out her hand. "I'm Christina. Are you playing our girl?"

"No," Tyler said, sharing his glare around. He got their protectiveness, but surely he deserved a chance. "I haven't told Susan a single lie." He offered flowers to Christina when instinct prodded him to use them like a sword and smack her over the head.

"What about your brother?" Julia asked.

Tyler met her slightly accusing gaze. "I don't know anything of Nolan's plans."

"Does he know you're up here?" Connor shifted his weight and Tyler got the idea the men were waiting to pounce if he screwed up in his replies.

"I haven't spoken to Nolan for weeks."

"Why not?" Christina's gesture set her bracelets jangling. "Aren't you close to your family?"

"We're polite," Tyler said. "I'll discuss my family situation with Susan." He'd intended to tell her of the sordid past anyway, since he wanted to start with honesty.

Julia scowled. "Why—?"

"That's enough, sweetheart," Ryan said. "Give the man a break and take him to meet Susan."

She nodded. "Come on."

"Leave them alone," Ryan added. "Susan knows we're here if she needs us."

While they'd been talking, two women appeared behind the bar. An elderly man prowled from behind the curtain. Although he was older, he looked alert and fit in his white shirt and black trousers.

"Should I tell Stan to open the doors, Julia?" the man asked.

Julia glanced at her watch. "Please, Curt. Come on, Tyler. Susan won't have much time until she needs to change for her routine."

Tyler went with Julia, aware of the murmur of voices behind him, the silent speculation. No doubt he'd face more questioning during the weekend. No problem. Susan's friends cared for her, which only made her more attractive to him. A woman who inspired loyalty beat his wife, hands down.

"Susan, you have a visitor," Julia said, standing back to usher him into the small office. She checked her watch and grinned. "Sorry, but you only have ten minutes. Inconvenient for us too, since we had to cut our interrogation short. See you soon."

Susan groaned, her blue eyes settling on him as Julia left them alone. "They didn't?"

"They care about you," Tyler said, drinking her in. With her long straight hair and freckles, her bright blue eyes, she was even prettier in person. "I know this is forward since we haven't met before, but I want to kiss you."

"Yes," she whispered.

He set his last bunch of flowers aside and closed the space between them. She glanced up, a tiny smile playing on her lips.

"I'm so glad you agreed to meet me in person." Unable to resist, he ran the tips of his fingers over her cheek. It was soft and silky and immediately he wanted to experience more of her—preferably while she was naked. He breathed in her scent, soapy with a blast of citrus, and his craving intensified. In person, her freckles stood out—charming cinnamon-colored dots that tempted him to taste. "You're beautiful."

Her dark lashes lowered to screen her blue eyes but the curve of her lips told him she found the compliment pleasing.

"It's hard to judge height on television." It was difficult to judge a lot of things while watching the screen. Seeing her in person let him indulge his senses.

"What's wrong with my height?"

"Not a thing." The six inches difference worked for him. His head dipped and he took her lips. Gentle at first, he explored, tasted, then her arms wrapped around his neck and she pressed closer. Given her encouragement, he took the kiss deeper, tangling their tongues and doing some of the things he'd dreamed of when he first saw her on television. He stroked his tongue against hers then bit her full lower lip. Her soft breasts pressed against his chest and her encouraging sounds went straight to his cock.

He let his hands wander down her back and come to rest on her butt. He pulled her against him, groaning against her mouth when his cock came into contact with her lower body.

"Ahem!" Julia said from the doorway.

They sprang apart, both breathing hard and emotionally off-balance. At least he was teetering, the rush of lust almost taking him out at the knees. He found he wanted to possess her, to mark her, take her in every way so no one was in any doubt she belonged to him and he belonged to her.

"I thought you'd be talking," Julia said, a wicked gleam in her eyes. "I can't wait to report back."

"I don't suppose I can bribe you to keep quiet?" Susan asked.

Tyler shot her a quick glance. Nope, she didn't look as if she regretted their close encounter. Oh, her cheeks were flushed, but she'd moved close again, the heat from her body searing his hip through his clothing.

"Not a hope." Julia had changed into a figure-hugging blue dress with a slit up one side. "I'm going to do the intro thing because we're packed already. You're on soon." She started to leave before strolling back into the room. She grasped Tyler's arm. "Since I can't trust the two of you alone, you're coming with me."

Giving in gracefully, Tyler blew Susan a kiss. The smile that spread over her face pumped lust afresh. Once Susan finished work they'd have the rest of the night to talk and get to know each other, and hopefully most of Saturday and Sunday morning before he caught his flight back to Napier.

Julia towed him back to her friends. "I found them in a lip lock," she announced.

In the short time he'd been away, the club had filled with both men and women. Soft music played in the background and waitresses scurried to and from the bar with trays of drinks. Two female bartenders moved with practiced efficiency behind the bar.

The group of friends exchanged glances before focusing on him. Tyler stared back, determined not to speak first. He didn't owe them explanations. This was between him and Susan.

"Do you play rugby?" Connor asked.

Tyler blinked. "I played at high school and university, but I don't get much free time on the farm."

"Position?" Connor asked.

"Occasionally winger but mostly a back."

Connor grunted. "We're a man down for our game tomorrow afternoon. Are you interested?"

"It depends on Susan," Tyler said. "She might have other plans."

"We're all going to watch the game," Julia said.

Another thought occurred. "Are you intending to beat me into a pulp on the rugby field?"

Julia's husband laughed and the other guy—Caleb—joined him. "You catch on quick, country boy," Ryan said.

"Are you playing?" Tyler asked him.

Ryan shook his head. "Caleb and I don't play. We have more sense than Connor."

Why not? Tyler decided. Fitness wasn't a problem. "Sure, I'd love to play."

Connor nodded.

"You'd better grab your table before someone decides to ignore the reserved sign," Julia said. "What would you like to drink, Tyler? A beer?"

"That would be great."

Julia nodded. "Everyone else want their usual?"

Minutes later, Tyler found himself seated at a large circular table, hemmed in by Connor and Christina, and waiting for character assassination, for potshots, for concern.

"I hear you have a daughter," Connor said.

Tyler relaxed at the non-confrontational question. "Yes, Katey is four."

"A similar age to my son, Alex," Ryan said. "Who's looking after her this weekend?"

"My in-laws," Tyler said. "Josie—that's my mother-in-law—she's taking her shopping and for afternoon tea. She wasn't happy about me going on a plane without her, but the promise of afternoon tea smoothed the path."

"Susan said your wife died a few years ago," Maggie said. "I'm sorry. That must have been rough."

It had also been a relief, but Tyler didn't intend to share that particular snippet. He'd get to the dark details of his past with Susan, once they knew each other better.

The drinks arrived, interrupting his need to reply straightaway. He gripped his beer bottle, tension sliding across him to settle in his shoulders. When the waitress departed he said, "Yes, she died way too young. My in-laws were great and they continue to support me. I'm lucky."

"Do they know you've come up here to meet a woman?" Caleb asked.

"Yes."

"Do they know her identity?" Maggie asked, shooting to the heart of the line of questioning.

"No. I told them I met her on the internet."

"They were okay with that?" Ryan asked. "My parents would have asked a hundred questions, given me a hundred lectures."

Tyler smiled. "Oh, they asked nosy questions but I told them I didn't intend to answer any until I knew if things were going to work out."

"Do you do this sort of thing often?" Connor demanded.

Tyler met his gaze without flinching. "No, I haven't dated anyone since my wife died." He'd gone out to town socials and danced with women, but after his wife trampled his feelings, he'd needed time to heal plus he'd had responsibility for Katey. "My concern was for my daughter, not my love life."

"Why Susan?" Maggie asked.

Tyler scowled. "Why not? She's beautiful."

The music changed to a vocal track and the lights dimmed—a signal of some sort because club patrons straightened to attention and the buzz of conversation died. Up on the stage, a spotlight appeared and Julia walked into it, stunning and attention grabbing in her blue gown.

"Good evening," Julia said, a mike amplifying her voice. "Welcome to *Maxwell's*, and thank you for coming out so early on a Friday night."

Cheers rang out.

"We want Fantasy Girl," a male voice shouted from the rear.

"Fantasy Girl!" others picked up the chant.

Julia smiled and gestured for silence. "We have a chorus of dancers first out, and Susan is one of the dancers. She'll be doing a couple of dances, so stick around and enjoy the fun!" She gave a theatrical flourish with her right hand, the music shifted to sultry and flirty and the curtains opened with a swish. The spotlight on Julia faded and whoever was in charge of lighting started off a sequence of illumination that picked out a row of long legs. Fishnet stockings. Sexy.

Expectation pulsed like a live thing, bouncing from the men and women eying the stage. Tyler leaned forward, eager to see this side of Susan. The women wore identical dark wigs and slim black masks. Their lips were painted a sultry red, and they wore sexy maid costumes with panache.

He watched the sequence, mesmerized by the athleticism and the sensual nature of the tease. He wasn't sure what he'd expected, but Susan was right to take issue with people calling her a stripper. This dance highlighted sensuality with the slow reveal of long limbs and bare shoulders. Sexy and breathtaking, the dance raced to an end almost too quickly. The music crashed to a climax. The women froze in position. Silence fell. Each of the women straightened, blew a cheeky kiss at the audience, then the curtains closed, breaking the audience's spell. Applause and cheers rang out along with a few rude suggestions about maids.

"Is the routine new?" Caleb asked. "I don't remember seeing it before."

"We've been doing it for about a week," Christina said.

Tyler lifted his beer and took a long sip to temper the heat roaring through his veins. The dance had been...intense. Definitely sexy. But which one was Susan? He had no idea.

The spotlight bloomed again and the crowd quieted. "Since you're such a great audience, we're going to change things up tonight," Julia said. "In ten minutes, we'll have a fan dance for you."

"What about Fantasy Girl?" a man shouted from the rear.

A flurry of ribald comments shot at Julia like bullets from a paint gun, each more colorful than the last. Grinning, she raised her hand for silence. "You know this club is about whimsy and imagination. All our dancers fuel fantasy. Yes, Susan is dancing tonight, but I'm not about to point her out. That's what we have brains for—to fantasize!"

The crowd stomped their feet and pumped their fists in the air. Tyler scanned nearby faces. The men lusted after the dancers and the women aspired to be the dancers.

"Does Julia dance too?" he asked.

Ryan gave a curt nod. "All the dancers wear masks, so most people never know their identities, but I know my wife's body."

"Maggie and I dance on occasion," Christina said. "It's a real rush. Susan is a natural though. She's good—almost as talented as Julia." She placed her hand over his and leaned closer. "You don't need to feel jealous. Susan hasn't dated anyone for ages. You're the first man she's brought to meet us. She's not interested in anyone else."

"Thanks," Tyler murmured, her words settling the tension roiling in his gut.

The chatter at their table became general, ranging from the rugby game tomorrow to where they were going for dinner after Susan's next dance to the management of *Maxwell's*. Tyler listened with half an ear and nursed his beer. No way did he intend to drink past his quota. If things proceeded the way he wanted, he'd manage to talk Susan into returning to his hotel. He wanted to explore her—both mind and body—with an intensity he'd never experienced with another woman.

The lights shifted, softened, and the chatter died. This time Julia didn't introduce the act, but remained behind the scenes.

The curtains glided open and Ryan let out a soft groan. "In a minute, mate, you'll know exactly how I feel every time my wife dances."

Two masked dancers—both redheads—stood in the middle of circles of rose light. Large pink feathers flickered enticingly in front of their bodies, revealing and concealing, never ceasing their graceful arcs. The dancers' mirrored each other.

"Susan is on the right," Christina whispered.

Immediately Tyler's gaze settled on her, his emotions swinging wildly from conservative to radical. He couldn't take his eyes off her yet part of him wanted to jump on stage and whisk her away. His eyes only.

As one, the dancers reached behind their backs. Two flamingo pink bra tops flew into the audience. Eager hands grasped the tops and cheers rang out from the victorious recipients.

On stage, long legs flashed and the next minute two pairs of neon pink panties flew in their direction. Ryan caught one pair and grinned while the other pair landed right in front of Tyler.

"You'd better grab those or Caleb will beat you to them," Connor said with a knowing smirk.

Tyler reached for the pink panties, briefly wondered

what to do with his prize. Finally, he stuffed them in his jacket pocket while he kept his gaze glued to Susan. Pressure grew in his chest—apprehension. He waited for the fans to go in the wrong direction, waited for the flash of a butt or bare breasts. Susan's naked body.

"Don't worry," Christina whispered. "They've done this dance heaps of times. No one will get a peek."

Tyler hoped she was right. He found himself mesmerized by the flirty movements, the arch of bodies and the sexy smiles beneath the black masks. The music crashed to a finale and the spotlights flicked out, leaving a black stage and silence. Then enthusiastic applause broke out and Tyler slumped back in his chair.

Both men and women gave an enthusiastic response to the dance. There were a few wolf whistles, more lewd comments.

"I bet those two women are horny after all that teasin'," a man at a nearby table said in a loud voice.

Tyler tensed.

"I think I might head back to the dressing room and take on both of them. My big cock is more than capable of the job."

Tyler half stood, but Ryan reached out to grasp his arm. "Don't bother wasting your energy."

Christina wrinkled her nose. "Yeah, guys who mouth off like that usually have dicks the size of walnuts."

Tyler half spluttered at the insult and sank onto his

chair. Ryan was right. Creating a scene wouldn't solve a thing. "How do you cope with other men lusting after your wife?"

"She's not interested in other men, and she comes home to me." Ryan hesitated and seemed to consider his words carefully. "I do a lot of traveling with my job, so the trust needs to go both ways. Besides, Julia loves working at the club and enjoys dancing. No one recognizes the dancers when they're dressed in their normal clothes. The costumes and masks do the job of concealing identities."

Tyler gave a swift nod of acknowledgment and picked up his drink to swallow the last mouthful. Even though he hadn't known Susan long, their exchange of emails had covered a broad gamut. She loved to dance, and trying to change that—take dancing away from her—simply because he couldn't handle audience comments would shoot this budding relationship to the no-way-in-hell pile.

He needed to work past his possessiveness. Besides, he didn't have the right to quash talent. It would be like someone telling him he could never paint again, could never pick up a pencil to sketch a portrait of his daughter.

"They were incredible," he said. "*Maxwell's* is a slick operation."

"Thank you," a soft voice said. "Susan is taking care of a last minute panic with the change. She won't be long and then we can go." Julia turned to Christina. "You have our number if you need us."

"Here's Susan now," Christina said, making shooing motions with her hand. "We've got this. We can't do much damage in one night. Go. Go."

Susan stopped beside Tyler. "What did you think?"

"You were great. I'm going to frame that pair of pink panties." He grinned at her, his protectiveness easing now that she stood at his side. He had more important things to worry about, such as his brother's unpredictable antics. "How did you manage to land them in the right place?"

She grinned. "Julia and I have a lot of practice. Plus we have a private competition, an incentive. A poor throw means I have to buy a round of margaritas the next time we have a girl's night out."

Tyler grinned down at her and unable to resist, bent his head to snatch a quick kiss.

Maggie poked him in the ribs. "That's enough of that. The pair of you can cuddle on the dance floor. Besides"—she lowered her voice—"someone will recognize Susan and wonder what's going on with her kissing a man who isn't Nolan."

Fuck, she was right. Tyler drew back sharply. "I'm sorry."

"It's okay," Susan murmured.

"Would you and Susan like to ride with us?" Julia asked.

"That would be great," Tyler said. "I didn't bother with a rental car since I figured I wouldn't get much use out of it this weekend. Where are we having dinner?"

"At the Grant Hotel."

"That's where I'm staying," he said.

"How convenient," Julia said, wriggling her eyebrows at Susan.

A HOSTESS SHOWED THEM to a private table at the rear of the restaurant. Tyler trailed Susan, noting both the stunning night panorama out the floor-to-ceiling glass windows and the way several diners recognized her. Maggie had been right to remind him of observers in public places. Public shenanigans might create an unfavorable backlash.

His mind circled back to his brother. Damn, he wished he knew why Nolan had suddenly stepped out of his good-boy good-son persona. It wasn't his normal behavior.

"She's a charming and sexy woman," Nolan had told Hailee during an onscreen interview. Although they didn't talk much these days, Tyler knew his brother. Something else ran beneath his glib public reasons.

Undercurrents.

Tyler pushed aside his unease to focus on the woman who'd brought him to Auckland. "What are your favorite foods? We haven't covered food likes and dislikes yet."

"I love roast beef with all the trimmings, but since I started dancing I've cut back on red meat. I eat mainly fish and lots of vegetables and fruit with an occasional foray into the naughty stuff."

Tyler paused to accept the menu from the waitress. "No huge sweet tooth?"

"I have a fondness for anything lemon and chocolate. What about you?"

"I like cinnamon and spices," he said and reached over to tug a lock of her glossy brown hair. "Your freckles remind me of cinnamon drops."

"Cut out that flirting," Connor said in a stern voice. "We don't want to attract attention."

"Hell no," Ryan said with a quick glance at Julia. "That's the last thing we want."

"I guess I should behave," Tyler said.

Susan winked, leaned closer. "We can play footsie under the table."

Her casual manner quashed Tyler's stirring apprehension, made him relax and enjoy the treat of adult company his own age.

The dinner was full of spirited conversation and laughter. Tyler liked Susan's friends, but he craved alone time with his lady. He'd never talked to a woman before, not like he did with Susan. Their frequent emails seemed to have cut through the awkward getting-to-know-you conversations. Now Tyler was impatient to get to the physical stuff—if Susan agreed.

He caught her frequent glances, shared smiles and under

the table they held hands for an all too brief moment.

"Hello."

Tyler glanced up to see a young couple from a neighboring table. They looked straight at Susan.

"You look like the girl on the farmer reality show. Are you Susan?" the female of the couple asked.

"Yes, I am," Susan said with a smile. "Are you enjoying the show?"

"It's great. We hope Nolan chooses you," the woman said. "Can we have your autograph?"

Tyler bit his tongue, bit back his protest, bit back his inner fears. Nolan bloody better not pick Susan again, not now that Tyler had met her in person.

"Sure." Susan smiled again and accepted pen and paper from the woman. Tyler watched her scrawl a message and a signature before she handed back the autograph.

"Thanks!"

"Good luck," the man said, and he ushered his lady back to their table.

"You're famous," Tyler said.

"I've had a few requests for autographs. A teller recognized me at the bank and a group of teenagers noticed me in the café. I get a lot of messages on the website. Some are creepy."

"The price of fame," Maggie said with a loud sigh.

A solo male guitarist started on another bracket of songs, the music soft and dreamy and perfect for lovers.

"The guy has a good technique," Ryan said. "Julia, do you want to dance?"

"Do you play?" Tyler asked.

"A little," Ryan said.

Susan laughed. "He's actually being modest. He's a pretty fair musician."

Connor and Maggie joined Julia and Ryan on the dance floor, leaving Tyler alone with Susan.

"What would you like to do after dinner?" he asked.

Susan groped for his hand under the table and their fingers entwined. "I'd like to be alone with you."

Tyler's pulse jumped on seeing her expression. "In my room?"

"Yes." She glanced across the room at her friends. "I'd better let Julia know I'm leaving. What room number are you?"

"I'll wait for you."

"No," Susan said. "People keep looking in this direction. We'd better leave separately or else we'll start a gossip blitz."

"How about if I say goodnight to your friends first and pretend I'm leaving?" Susan was right to act with caution. Josie had mentioned the stories in the ladies' magazines. If an enterprising reporter got hold of the fact Susan was dating someone other than Nolan, they'd shout the news across the media.

And his mother would create merry hell. She barely spoke to him as it was...

"Tyler?"

"Sure." He pushed aside his past to concentrate on Susan. "Good plan. I'm in room 612. Will you stay the night?"

"Yes." She didn't hesitate.

"What about Nolan?"

Her nose crinkled in a cute manner. "Your brother and I are not a good match. He doesn't approve of me, and I'm still trying to figure out why he picked me during the last round."

"See you soon," Tyler said, standing. Without a backward look, he strode between the tables, most of them still full despite the lateness of the hour. He tapped Ryan on the shoulder. "Sorry to interrupt. I'm off now. It was great to meet you all."

"You're still gonna play rugby, right?" Connor asked after he steered Maggie over to them.

"Sure," Tyler said. "What time do you need me and where is the game?"

"Have you got a phone?" Connor asked. "I can text you the details. Is Susan not going to go with you?"

"We're leaving separately," Tyler said, after giving Connor his number.

"Good idea," Ryan said, offering his hand.

Tyler left with a final wave and hoped like hell Susan wouldn't keep him waiting too long.

SUSAN TOOK HER TIME, not wanting to make their planned meeting seem obvious to anyone taking notice.

"Why are you checking your watch every few seconds?" Maggie asked.

"You should have another glass of wine first," Julia said. "You don't want him to think you're too eager."

Susan tossed her head and shared around her scowl. "Easy for you to say. You have husbands. I have to rely on my battery operated boyfriend. The real thing would make a welcome change."

"But that doesn't mean you have to jump into bed with him," Julia said.

"Stop." Susan held up her hand. "We've been emailing back and forth for two weeks. I know more about him than I knew about any of my previous boyfriends. Connor checked him out. Everything he's told me is the truth. I didn't get any weird vibes tonight. Did you?" Her challenging gaze slid from face to face, measuring her friends' reactions. "I want him. Don't judge."

Julia sighed. "I want you to be careful. Where will you be?"

"He has a room here." Susan lowered her voice in case the loitering waitress was eavesdropping. "Room 612. That's where I'm spending the night."

"Don't tire him out too much," Connor said. "We need him to play rugby."

"You and your rugby." Susan stood and kissed him on the cheek. Ryan received the same treatment, and she gave Maggie and Julia a swift hug. "Don't worry. I'm not a kid. I'm not a virgin either," she whispered. "Although things might have sealed over because it's been a hell of a long time."

Maggie grinned and Julia chuckled.

Susan made her way to the elevator and hit the call button. The lobby was empty. She stepped into the car and waited for the door to slide shut. Nerves swirled in the pit of her stomach, but they were the good kind. No second guessing. She really liked Tyler, and at least he wasn't married.

She tapped on his door, and it opened abruptly.

"What took you so long?"

CHAPTER SIX

"I DIDN'T WANT OUR disappearance to look too obvious." Susan stepped inside and the door clicked shut, closing down outside distractions. "I'm here now. What are you going to do with me?"

Tyler prowled toward her and backed her up until the wall hit her spine. His mouth covered hers before her startled cry could emerge. Then he was all hands, mouth, teeth, dragging her into temptation, tossing her into lust and passion and shoving aside every single bit of past history with other men.

Her mind and body focused on him, the enticing rasp of his callused fingers against her collarbone. The ravenous hunger of his mouth. A shiver worked down her body, her nerve-endings singing. Each pleasurable blast from his attentions, the press of his lips, the stroke of his tongue, pooled at the needy spot between her legs.

The contact gentled, and she moaned, clutching his broad shoulders in case he decided to do something stupid, like lift his head to breathe.

Oh yes. She had to kiss him again, let him kiss her. Feed the simmering passion gathering inside her like one of those romance novel infernos she'd started reading after Maggie introduced her to the erotic romance concept.

Finally, Tyler lifted his head. "I thought I'd never get to kiss you again. The one taste in the office wasn't enough."

"More," she demanded.

"Don't you want a drink? I arranged room service to deliver a nightcap."

Susan raised her hand and ran her fingers over his jaw. She liked the rasp of sound and repeated the move, petting him like a cat. "I've had enough to drink. I want to remember everything we do together."

"I have a rugby game tomorrow. I'm under strict instructions to get plenty of sleep."

"If you want to sit back and let me do the work, I'm up for that." Susan tried to keep a serious expression, but her twitching lips spilled her lurking jocularity. If he called her on this, she might muck up the seduction process. Maggie might think sex was like riding a bike. Susan wasn't so sure. Those memories lived in the dim recesses of her mind.

Heck, maybe it was best if she went on instinct anyway. Just strip away his clothes and explore his lovely, muscled body to her heart's content. She could take him into her body or impale herself on his hard cock and grasp pleasure. Humor spurted forth, and she pretended to ponder. "What do you think about me tying you up?"

"As long as I get my dick inside you soon, I don't care what you do."

She blinked. Not the response she'd expected.

Someone knocked on the door. "Room service."

Tyler tugged Susan away from the wall and held her to his side as he opened the door.

"Room service, sir," the young male attendant said.

"Thanks," Tyler said, standing aside to let the lanky employee wheel his cart into the room.

Susan took the opportunity to take in the details she'd missed when she'd first entered. It was a standard room with a huge bed. Pillows in various shades of green, cream and brown festooned the end nearest the headboard. A sage green cover spread across the king-size mattress while a chair and desk sat against another wall. It was the view that drew her, and she moved away from Tyler to kick off her heels. Her bare toes sank into thick carpet as she made her way over to the huge window.

During the day, Tyler would have a gorgeous view of the harbor and the bridge that spanned the water. Now, she could see the lights from the buildings hugging the coast and those of vehicles driving over the bridge, but the actual water was dark. A lone ferry bobbed across the expanse, one of the many night charters full of party people.

Behind her, Tyler closed the door and she turned to him. "I never tire of the harbor. It's so pretty in all its moods."

"You'll like Clare. The sea isn't too far away. Eric's farm is partly flats and the rest is hills. The views over the valley toward the town are spectacular. We're about twenty minutes drive from the township. We have nearby vineyards and lots of places to walk."

"You like it there," Susan said.

"I like it here too." And the expression in his gaze told her why.

Her stomach turned to pudding, the burst of lust taking her by surprise even though it shouldn't. She shifted her weight, trying to ease the heat surging through her. "You're younger than me."

"So?" He crossed the room and wrapped her in his arms. "A few years younger. It's not a major difference." His fingers traced across the throbbing pulse point at her neck. He stared for an instant, then reached for the zipper at the rear of her dress. This one was blue and she knew it suited her, making her eyes look like the tropical sea on a sunny day. At least that was what Christina had told her when they'd gone shopping for outfits.

He slid the zip down slowly, as if he were waiting for her protest. Not gonna happen. She lifted her hand and stroked his biceps beneath the cotton of his gray shirt. Warmth seeped to her fingertips and impatience tore through her. "Race you to get undressed."

"No, you don't." He grasped her shoulders to halt her retreat. "I've fantasized about undressing you ever since I first saw you on TV. It would be plain mean of you to deprive me."

Susan swallowed, her knees threatening to buckle. "Okay."

She quivered as he peeled the blue material from her torso and let the dress slide over her hips. Earlier that night, she'd donned a brand new set of lingerie in a shade a fraction lighter than her dress. The bra cupped and lifted while the high cut panties did wonders for her legs.

He blew out a breath that came close to a whistle. "Way better than the vision I'd conjured." His fingers traced the swell of her breast before moving to the other. She gasped when he followed the same path with his mouth. Her breasts prickled and her nipples pulled to hard points beneath her bra.

Without warning, he lifted her from the circle of fabric and carried her to the edge of the bed.

"It's been a while for me," he said. "The first time is gonna be fast and hectic. If I come first, I'll make it up to you."

She nodded, part of her comparing her last lover to Tyler. The married man who'd squeezed her in for quickies. Quick on his part. Not such a big reward for her since she'd missed orgasms and later discovered he possessed a wife, tucked away in the suburbs.

He unfastened her bra and slipped the straps down her arms. Immediately, his fingers stroked her aching flesh.

"That feels good."

"I can do better yet." He gently pushed her down onto the mattress.

"Don't make rash promises," she said. "I'll expect you to prove any statements about your abilities."

Laughing, he gave her a quick kiss on the lips. With another fast move, he whisked off her panties then straddled her naked body, his black trousers abrading her skin in a promising manner. She couldn't wait for him to get naked too.

"First, I get to play, otherwise it will be all over in minutes." His rueful glance at his groin pulled a delighted chuckle from her dry throat.

This was something else new to her—the playful teasing. So much fun. Another mark on the plus side for Tyler.

His fingers plucked one nipple, and he avidly studied her reaction, the arch of her hips pleading for a more intimate touch.

"Yes, please."

"Oh, I please very much," he said in a husky tone. Eyes glinting with promise, he leaned over her, replacing his fingers with his mouth. Hot, wet pulls ricocheted through her body, settling in an ache in her pussy.

"Tyler." Her hands slid across his skull, the bristles of his dark hair soft beneath her fingertips. Everything he did felt good, pushed her in the direction of desperation. "I want you to hurry."

"I can do that."

"Oh. Did I say that aloud?"

"You did."

His tongue dipped into her navel.

"You're good at this." Almost too good. The achy spot in her pussy swelled, her hips lifting in another silent demand.

Tyler rose off her, allowing her room to move. "Spread your legs for me."

A blush washed into her cheeks, the rush of heat tumbling her into panic. What if—?

"Stop thinking so hard," he whispered, amusement twinkling in his eyes. "I know what to do and I've seen women before."

Heck, she didn't mean to be such an idiot. "I have no idea where this is coming from. The sudden insecurity, I mean."

Tyler repositioned his body so he knelt between her legs. "You think I'm not worried about screwing up the first time between us? It's when your partner isn't concerned that you need to worry. From where I'm sitting, you have nothing to lose sleep about." One single finger blazed a path from her navel to the fold of her leg. His eyes gleamed. "Do you want to know what's gonna happen next?"

"I think I know."

Tyler slid his hands beneath her butt and lifted her to his mouth. Heat enclosed her clit, the quick flick of a tongue making her gasp. He explored her slit with a slow, luscious lick, lifted his head to grin and started the sensual torture. Again.

Susan gripped his head, attempting to hold him in place. Instead he teased her, laving her folds and nipping hard enough to make her wince. His tongue soothed the ache, transforming the pain into something more. He sucked on her swollen nub, tormenting it incessantly until she was so tender it was almost painful.

Her muscles strained as she worked for an orgasm, her eyes squeezed tightly shut to savor every nuance of the pleasure flooding her body. His warm mouth continued to kiss and suck, gathering her juices, then she was flying, the rush of sensation making her cry out. She shuddered as he kept teasing more vibrations from her needy flesh.

Susan pushed weakly at his shoulders, her clitoris tender now that she'd climaxed.

Tyler understood her silent message and stood. Without taking his gaze from her, he unbuttoned his shirt and tossed it aside. He must have taken his shoes off earlier before she'd arrived, and now he peeled off his socks and shucked his trousers and underwear in one efficient move. Boxer-briefs. She beamed in approval.

With long strides, he reached his bag and crouched to

retrieve something from the side pocket. Condoms. He turned fully and she scored her first real visual. Broad chest, the perfect amount of dark hair to emphasize his masculinity. Narrow hips and the enticing ripple of muscles. Her mouth watered, and she couldn't wait to explore. Then there was his cock—thick and in full bloom, the head ruddy and swollen. A little shimmy worked through her and settled low at the thought of Tyler filling her.

When he reached the bed, he ripped open the packet and grabbed a condom. Seconds later, he rose over her. She welcomed his solid weight and the freedom to touch him. No surplus flesh on his body. The man was gorgeous, his chest still tan from long days of working shirtless in the sun. Or at least that was what she presumed.

"Okay?"

She smiled. "If I felt any better, my heart wouldn't handle the strain."

He guided his cock to her entrance and impaled her with the broad head. "God, that feels good."

From her end too. She closed her eyes and gripped his shoulders, canting her hips and silently encouraging him to fully slide into her wet, needy depths. She wanted to feel him stretching her inner muscles, to hear his grunts as he strove for pleasure.

He pulled back and glided into her again, going deeper. "God, Susan." His large frame shuddered as he withdrew.

"I can't go slow." Even as he said the words, he shoved into her with one hard thrust, pushing her into the mattress. He groaned and shafted her with several rapid strokes before freezing in place, face contorted in a mask of pleasure. His orgasm seemed to thunder through him, and his cock jerked with explosive contractions.

Susan held him through his climax, receiving a dose of pleasure even though she hadn't come again. The way he'd grabbed for every sensation and his muscles bunched then heaved in a convulsive manner made her feel special, needed.

"I guess I've just proved I'm alive." Tyler levered up and away and smiled ruefully. "I'm sorry about that."

She brushed his cheek and smiled up at him. "We have the rest of the night. Simultaneous orgasms are a myth anyway."

"I beg to differ. We'll have to make you a believer." He disposed of the condom. Uncaring of his nakedness, Tyler ambled over to the room service tray, lifted a silver dome and gave a grunt of approval. Susan studied the long lines of his body, the curve of his butt and wished he was close enough for her to take a bite. A shiver slid over her and she grabbed the nearest article of clothing—Tyler's gray shirt.

"I like looking at you."

Tyler turned, his teeth a flash of white as he opened a bottle of champagne. "Yeah?"

Her heart did a little change up in speed. "It would be

better if you came closer. I wanna touch, take a bite or two."

"Someone told me we have all night." He filled two glasses with champagne and handed one to her.

Susan accepted the glass and took a sip. "Nice. I'll need food as well if I'm going to drink this."

"Got that covered." He set down his glass and wandered over to grab a plate of sandwiches. "We have ham sandwiches and strawberries and chocolate sauce for dessert."

"Yum." Susan propped two pillows against the headboard and nibbled on a ham sandwich. She hadn't eaten much of her dinner, nerves doing a number on her stomach. "Strawberries, huh?" Ideas fired in her, naughty suggestions of things she could do with strawberries. She cast him a considering glance. "What do you think about body painting?"

"Could be fun." He settled on the bed beside her and offered her another sandwich. "I'm glad I came up to see you." Honesty shone from his eyes and echoed with his satisfied grin and relaxed posture.

"You just came for a booty call," she scoffed.

"No." The reply came instantly, an explosion of objection. "If you'd said no, I would've taken your rejection like a gentleman. I wanted to meet you in person. I didn't come with expectations." He had the grace to shrug when her brows rose. "Okay, so a guy can hope."

"What do you want to do tomorrow morning?"

"I'd like to sleep in, get a room service breakfast so I can ogle you for longer and if we have time, I'd like to visit an art store to stock up on my supplies. By then it will be time to head for the rugby game."

"Are you really going to play?"

"I said I would. Besides, Connor is big and protective of you. I need to get on his good side."

Susan sipped more champagne, happiness making her giddy and bubbly, not unlike the effect of the drink.

"Time for dessert," Tyler said and bounded off the bed. He returned with the bowl of fresh strawberries and another bowl of thick and glossy chocolate sauce. "Want one?"

"I could force myself."

He picked up a berry and swirled it through the chocolate before holding it to her lips. A dollop of the sauce fell and plopped into her cleavage. "No, let me," he said when she went to swipe it away with her finger. He unbuttoned the top two buttons of his shirt and peeled the material back to frame her breasts. Meanwhile, Susan squirmed at the tickly slide of the chocolate down her breastbone.

"Are you ticklish?"

"No." Her hasty reply gave away the truth and his evil chuckle informed her he'd take advantage of her vulnerability.

His work-roughened hands grasped her shoulders, holding her as he lowered his head. His mouth skimmed the upper curves of her creamy flesh.

"There's no chocolate there."

"Haven't you ever done anything because it feels good?" The naughty boy twinkle in his eyes made her grin.

She sniffed. "You want to make me suffer."

"No," he said, all signs of humor falling away. "What you'll get from me is the straight up truth every time. My dawdling is giving me time to tease you and to lead you into temptation."

"Don't you need an apple for that?"

"Chocolate is the modern version. Don't you know chocolate cures everything?" Before she could reply, his tongue followed the path of the sauce, shooting the air from her lungs with a whoosh. The stroke across her breast didn't make her want to giggle. No, instead the intimacy made her want to offer herself for a taste test.

The corners of his eyes crinkled, and he winked. "It's time for the shirt to go." He drew the garment off her and studied her chest with avid attention. "We need more chocolate." He plucked up another strawberry, drowned it in chocolate and used the fruit like a paint brush, dipping it again and again and spreading a Māori tribal design over her chest.

"You're good," she said, impressed by the design.

"I'll enjoy cleaning it off even more. Want a top up?" He

gestured at the bottle.

"Sure." She did a flirty eyelash flutter. "What are you going to do with me?"

He tapped the side of his nose, his lips curving into a charming grin that warmed her insides and tightened that coil of lust again. So, maybe she'd wait and let things unfold at his pace. The man had skills—that was for sure. With their champagne topped up, she nibbled on another strawberry, letting the juices drizzle across her tongue. "This was a great idea."

Tyler took her glass and rearranged her on the mattress. He sat back and cocked his head to the side. "Hmm. The line of your body isn't quite right." He paused. "Try this. Hands above your head and hold onto the headboard."

Desire roared through her at his words. The certainty in his tone told her he expected her to obey. Slowly she raised her hands and curled her fingers around the long bar on the head of the bed. His gaze stroked her body from head to breasts to the tips of her red toe nails.

"Perfect," he said, a touch of reverence in his voice. He backed away from the bed and crouched by his bag. An instant later, he returned with a sketch pad and a pencil.

Susan stared, felt her mouth drop open. This wasn't about sex? Then she saw the glow in his eyes, the excitement in his face and she decided to wait before she told him he was crazy and wasting good sexy times.

He grabbed the upright chair, dragging it from the desk

over to the bed and plonked his naked butt on it. Then he looked at her again and slowly smiled. "Perfect."

Susan's chest tightened with a blast of hope. She'd decided to meet Tyler because she'd liked the tone of his emails. Meeting him in person had been better than her expectations. He was sexy, funny and intense too. Sleeping with him was no hardship and breaking the dry spell—excellent.

This was something else. She frowned a little. The tipping point, maybe? The moment in time when a relationship tipped from casual into serious?

"Why are you frowning? Are your arms hurting?"

"What?" Susan came back to the present. "No, I'm fine." She consciously smoothed her expression. "How would you like me to look?" The question emerged in a purr and was immediately trailed by a spike of heat in her cheeks. *Jeepers!* She was way too old to blush.

"Like that," he said. "Flushed and heavy-eyed as if you'd just had a bout of hot sex."

"And that would be the truth," she murmured.

His head lifted from his drawing and grinned. "Glad to hear it."

She pursed her lips and blew him a kiss. "I'm hoping we can do it again. Soon."

"Flirt." His pencil flashed across the page.

"Only with you." She wished she could see his drawing. "Are you any good?"

He made a few more deft strokes, scanned her body with his gaze and did another strong line. This time he held his pencil in a different way. Every time he looked up, her body tingled under his intense focus. The dried chocolate on her chest itched, but she held her pose because he'd asked—no, ordered—her into position. His gaze jerked from his page to concentrate on her breasts. Her nipples reacted to the visual stimulation and trails of pleasure reached out to frisk other points on her body. She squeezed her thighs together in an effort to hold the sensation.

"Don't move," he ordered. "I won't be much longer."

His stern timbre sent a rush of moisture to her pussy. A quake of urgent need flailed her brain and sent lustful messages skipping the length of her torso. A moan built deep in her chest, fought for release.

"Done." He stood abruptly and grabbed a condom. Seconds later, he approached the bed. "You can let go now." He uncurled her fingers and gently rubbed her shoulders. "Okay?"

"Yes," she whispered, touched by his concern and care. This man might be younger, but he was streets ahead with his charm and mature nature.

"Good, because I'm so damn randy I could hammer nails with this big boy."

A chuckle burst from her, a laugh of joy and relief, and she parted her legs in invitation. "Thank goodness."

He surged into her with one hard stroke, rubbing her

swollen clit with his well-placed thrust. The moan slipped free as she gripped his shoulders and raised her pelvis to silently urge him onward. He set a rapid pace, hammering into her with hard plunges. Susan gripped his shoulders and went with the ride.

Tyler cursed, muttered something else she couldn't interpret and slipped his hand between their bodies. His fingertip pressed against her clitoris and pleasure twisted her belly. He rubbed back and forth, keeping the massage gentle. The wave of pleasure was almost agonizing with its sharpness and it dragged her under, tossing her into a tempest of bliss. Her channel pulsed around Tyler's hard cock.

A masculine shout rang out, resounding. Tyler thrust a couple more times and stilled, his heart hammering against her breasts. After a long moment, he pulled out of her and discarded the condom. He gathered her in his arms and kissed her softly, none of his previous urgency evident in the seductive press of his lips. His mouth trailed down her neck, and he licked a spot on her collarbone.

"Yum, chocolate," he said.

Susan glanced down at her chest. The pretty design was splotchy now with some of the chocolate transferred to Tyler's pectoral muscles. Her fingers coasted over the light dusting of dark hair on his chest and stopped to rub at a chocolate spot. She lifted her finger to her mouth and sucked. "Yum."

His eyes crinkled at the corners and amusement twitched his mouth. He drew back and studied her with heavy-lidded eyes. "Let me clean up some of this chocolate."

Before she could answer, his head dipped and his tongue ran a crooked path across the curve of one breast. "Tastes good."

"Let me." She licked solid muscles and finished with a flick of tongue over his nipple.

He jumped and grinned at her. "That zapped straight to my cock." A yawn punctuated the words.

Susan saw beyond his smile to the fatigue settling on his shoulders. "Connor is gonna kill me if you're too tired to play rugby tomorrow." She sighed. "Guess it's a guy thing, pride or something. Maybe we should shower and get some sleep."

"Probably a good plan. We can resume this in the morning." He paused to check his watch. "In about four hours."

"It's a deal," she said and slid off the bed, holding out her hand.

"Go start the shower," he said. "I'll be there in a sec."

Susan hovered for long seconds before turning away, feeling as if he'd rejected her. Stupid, really. The bathroom was tiled—a luxurious wet room with a spa bath in the corner, the requisite toilet nearby. Susan padded across the cool tiles. Nice. She twisted the control and jumped when warm water came at her from several directions.

"Great shower," Tyler said as he strode into the room.

Susan pushed aside her earlier pique and watched him approach. Pretty. So pretty. Her hands moved to his shoulders and slid around his neck before her brain issued the instruction. He wrapped his arms around her, resting them in the small of her back.

"This beats my lonely bed at home." His lips nibbled then his teeth closed on the lobe of her ear. The bite of teeth reverberated and awoke her slumbering passions.

"If you carry on like that, I'll jump you. Connor will get pissed at me and I'll have to take it out on your sexy hide."

Tyler chuckled, a full sound of delight that made her want to laugh in return. "Part of me is tempted to continue because I'd like to see if your prediction comes true."

"Wretch," she said, turning in his arms to face him.

His amusement faded away, replaced by another more elusive emotion. He lifted a hand and smoothed his finger over her cheek. "You're even better in the flesh."

She rose on tiptoes and pressed her lips to his. "So are you."

Tyler reached around her to fill his hands with liquid soap. "Don't distract me," he said sternly. "My willpower is teetering and I need my beauty sleep."

Susan snorted, the need to tease swelling inside her like one of the orgasms she'd experienced tonight. She filled her hands with soap and rubbed them over his chest. "Nice muscles."

"I'm hoping you'll give me a rub-down after the game tomorrow."

"An excuse to run my hands all over you," she said. "I don't want to miss that opportunity."

While she'd turned on the shower, he'd straightened the room, turned back the covers and placed a pink rose on one pillow. The romantic gesture brought tears to her eyes. It was a long time since a man had cared enough to spoil her with treats. Her heart was full and she felt like bursting into song as they slid into bed. Tyler spooned against her back, warming her with his larger frame. She fell asleep with a smile on her face.

"I DON'T KNOW WHY it never occurred to me," Susan said, her distasteful gaze on her wrinkled blue dress. "I'll have to do a walk of shame through the foyer. What happens if someone recognizes me?" *Stupid*. Why hadn't she thought of this before?

Instead, she'd let her hormones do the talking. Tyler hadn't needed to talk her into sin. She'd walked through the door on her own two feet.

"Could you ring one of your friends and ask them to bring you a change of clothes?"

"Yes." Susan whirled around to plant a kiss square on

his lips. "Not only sexy but a brain box too. That's a great idea."

"I'm going to need to find some rugby boots before I can play this afternoon. Would Connor be able to help me with that?"

"Probably. Ring him."

Someone tapped on the door. "Room service."

"Would you mind getting it? I'd prefer if they didn't see me," Susan said with a frown.

"You're ashamed of me."

"Not true. I don't want everyone to think I'm a total slut." Even if it was true when it came to Tyler.

"No one will think that," Tyler said.

Room service knocked again, and Susan scuttled to the bathroom and closed the door. Bother, if she'd been smart she would have grabbed her cell phone to ring Christina. Now she'd have to wait for room service to leave.

Susan paced back and forth in front of the mirror. When she noticed a bruise on the curve of her breast, she pulled the robe around her tighter to cover the mark. She waited another few minutes and pressed her ear to the door. Nope, she couldn't hear a thing.

She opened the door and stepped out coming face-to-face, with the room attendant. And he recognized her. His quick up-and-down gaze filled her with irritation, his smirk the added insult as he left the room.

CHAPTER SEVEN

"WHAT DID YOU DO after I dropped your clothes off this morning?" Christina asked with nosy interest.

Susan checked the expressions of the nearby people and decided she was safe. "We went shopping. Tyler wanted to buy art supplies and a present for his daughter. By the time we had a late breakfast, there wasn't that much time before the game."

"Tyler is an artist?"

"Yeah." Susan recalled the drawing he'd done of her, the one currently tucked inside her handbag. "He's good."

"How do you know?"

"How do you know what?" Maggie asked as she joined them on the sideline. She wore a green beanie and her breath emerged with a puff of steam. "Julia and Ryan had a last minute appointment to view a house. They'll be here in about half an hour."

"I hope this one suits," Christina said. "They've been looking for ages."

"I've got a good feeling about this house," Susan said. "My spidey senses tell me so."

Christina snorted. "We'll see." She grinned at Maggie. "Susan needs to spill some details about her date."

"We had a very nice time," Susan said in a prim voice. "The game's starting." She scanned the faces and bodies, finally recognizing Tyler. He ran up and down the field, doing warm-up drills with the rest of Connor's team. A spurt of anxiety filled her for a moment until she saw how competent he was with the football in hand.

"At least it's not pouring with rain," Maggie said. "Connor said I didn't have to come, but I know how much he likes me to watch his games. After the last one, I was soaked by the end of the first half. I got a spanking for not using my common sense."

Susan grinned while Christina said, "I don't want to hear about your love life. You and Julia have hunky men to hold you in the middle of the night. Now Susan has a sexy farmer. There's no justice in this world."

Maggie giggled, a joyful and intoxicating sound that pulled an answering grin from Susan.

"Your birthday is coming up soon. Maggie, Julia and I can chip in and buy you a new battery operated boyfriend," Susan said.

Christina let out a huff. "I knew you got some last

night."

"Never said I didn't."

"Quiet," Maggie said. "The game has started."

Usually Susan attended the games to keep Maggie company and to support Connor since they'd been friends for a long time. *The Tight Five ruled again.* She thought of her circle of friends and the nickname for their group, the name of Tight Five taken from a rugby term where five players bound in a tight formation to face the opposition team. They were like that. Four women and one man—friends—who used to work together at the accountancy firm and who maintained the friendship away from the job. Although at the rate they were adding husbands and friends, they'd soon manage an entire rugby team.

"Tyler knows what he's doing," Maggie said.

"He certainly does," Susan said.

Maggie and Christina turned to smirk at her.

"Glad to hear it," Christina said. "Are you going to spend tonight with him?"

Julia and Ryan hurried up to their group, followed by Caleb.

"Have we missed much of the game?" Julia's blonde hair flowed around her shoulders and healthy color filled her face. She'd bloomed since Ryan's return.

"About ten minutes," Christina said. "How did the house hunting go?"

Julia beamed. "It's perfect. Five bedrooms, open plan with a few acres of land and some outbuildings we can renovate for Ryan's music."

"What about you, Ryan?" Susan asked. "Did you like it?"

"The property is just what we were looking for," Ryan said with a wink at his wife. "Plenty of room for kids and a nanny and for the guys to crash if we end up working late."

"Wait—kids?" Maggie asked with a rush of excitement. "Are you...?" She trailed off and Susan knew she didn't want to upset Julia.

"We're pregnant," Julia said, her wide smile putting them all at ease.

"That's great!" Susan said.

"Congratulations," Christina added.

"I'm so pleased for you," Maggie said.

"The doctor said she's healthy as a horse," Ryan said.

Susan glanced at Caleb and noticed his grin. "You knew," she said, her tone slightly accusing.

"Julia let Ryan tell me because he was bursting with excitement," Caleb said.

"It's perfect timing because we're home for a while to work on some more songs," Ryan said.

The whistle blew and the people standing on the other side of the field jumped up and down.

"*Oops*," Maggie said. "We've missed a try. Who scored? Please tell me it wasn't Connor."

"Matthews scores a try for the Panthers," the announcer said over the loud speaker. A blast from a classic rock tune about champions rose above the clapping and sideline celebrations.

"You're safe," Susan said. "So am I. We'd never hear the end of it if we missed a try."

"Excuse me," someone said from behind them.

They turned to face a group of teenage girls.

"It is. It's Susan from *Farmer Seeks a Wife*," a spotty-faced brunette squeaked. "Could we have your autograph?"

"Go on," Ryan said with a broad grin. "Sign for the girls."

Susan found paper and pen thrust at her. "What's your name?"

"Carol," the girl said.

Ryan bent close to whisper in her ear, and Susan nodded. She wrote, *Life is an adventure* and signed her name. More pieces of paper were handed over and she was so busy with autographs she missed the next try too.

"Thanks, girls. I'd better watch the rest of the game now."

"Well done," Caleb said. "You have to be firm or they walk all over you."

"It was fun. I didn't realize the show would be so popular," she said.

Caleb pulled a face. "It gets old fast. I don't mind if the

fans are genuine, but some people think because you're a public figure they own you."

"I don't aspire to those heights," Susan said.

"If you go further with the show, you might not have an option," he warned, speaking softly so no one would overhear.

"Nolan isn't interested in me. At least I don't get that vibe. If he showed any interest, I wouldn't have agreed to meet Tyler. I doubt I'll go much further."

"MY THREE CHOSEN DATES are Lucy, Jasmine and Susan," Nolan told Hailee.

Famous last words.

Susan stared at Nolan, shock striking her with the force of a misdirected rugby ball. An ache dug into her chest, rippled down into her belly, and she realized she needed to breathe. She sucked in once, twice, but panic jellified her knees.

Cherry, the woman standing beside Susan, nudged her none too gently in the ribs. "It's you," she gritted out.

Susan forced her legs to function and joined Lucy and Jasmine who stood beside a beaming Nolan.

"Congratulations, ladies," Hailee said. "You'll join Nolan at his farm in Clare for two weeks. This will give Nolan a chance to get to know you better while you'll receive a taste of life on the farm."

SUSAN LIFTED A HAND to massage away the ache at her temple and wandered into the kitchen to grab tablets for her headache. Thank goodness Christina was out, running one of her makeup and clothing evenings for teenage girls. Susan needed this time alone to tamp down her apprehension.

For the life of her, she didn't understand why Nolan had chosen her in the final three. After the filming, Jennifer's assistant had given her an envelope detailing travel arrangements and the filming format during her farm visit.

She needed to tell Tyler, to warn him before the show aired. Yes, maybe he'd have a suggestion or two because it was him she thought of when she was alone in bed at night. Nolan was like the annoying brother who kept niggling at her to get a rise, which was why she didn't understand his selection. Lucy and Jasmine—yes—but her? One of these things was not like the others.

Her.

Still unsettled, she picked up her cell phone and dialed.

"Hello," a feminine voice said. "This is Tyler's phone."

"Oh, can I speak to Tyler please?" Susan asked.

"He's putting Katey to bed. Are you Tyler's friend from

Auckland? His mystery lady?"

"Maybe," she said with caution shading her tone.

"I'm Josie, his mother-in-law. Tyler has been very close-mouthed about you. I think he's worried about hurting our feelings."

"Oh?"

"Yes, he's a good boy, and he deserves happiness after— Ah, here comes Tyler now. It was nice to chat to you, Mystery Lady."

Susan smiled. Tyler had told her about his in-laws and how much they'd done for him and his daughter. The sentiment was obviously returned since love and caring filled Josie's voice.

She heard Tyler's husky laugh before he spoke into the phone. "Did Josie grill you?"

"You didn't take long enough. I think she was winding up to nosy questions."

"Just a sec," he said.

The snick of a door sounded and the background noise cut off abruptly.

"I've missed you," he said. "How did today go?"

Frustration filled her at the enforced distance. She wished she could see his face. Maybe she should've used the computer, but she'd been impatient to speak with him. "Your brother picked me again, but every time we meet, he goes out of his way to embarrass me. This week he visited *Maxwell's* and he dared me to do a pole dance."

"Damn," Tyler said. "I would have liked to see that."

"No doubt you will because Jennifer told me I'm good for ratings. My quick and dirty dance will be on the show for sure."

"Maybe that's why Nolan is picking you," Tyler said.

"I don't think so," Susan said. "There's some other reason."

"What happens next?"

"I come down to the farm with the other girls to give Nolan an opportunity to get to know us better, then he decides on his favorite two candidates. For the final show, Nolan turns up at his chosen woman's house. That's if he picks a woman. He can pick no one if he wants."

"You're coming to Clare," Tyler said.

"Yes, but I don't know if I'll have an opportunity to see you."

"We'll work out something. I'd like you to meet my daughter and my in-laws."

"I have to be careful."

"Don't worry. We'll swing something. I'm not missing an opportunity to get my hands on you again. My bed has felt very lonely since I left Auckland. Sexting, emails and phone calls are a poor substitute."

"Okay." Susan closed her eyes and, for about the hundredth time, wished she knew what Nolan was up to. "I miss you too."

NOLAN SAT AT THE dinner table, impatience simmering in his gut. He checked his watch. An hour before the show aired. *Ring, damn it.*

Almost at his silent demand, the phone rang.

"I'll get it," he said, springing to his feet.

His mother sniffed with disapproval. "I don't know who rings at this time of night. We haven't finished eating. You tell them we're in the middle of dinner and to ring back in an hour."

Nolan ignored his mother and strode to the kitchen to answer the phone. He wished the timing had been better and his grandparents weren't off cruising the world. They would have helped rein in their daughter and acted as a buffer. Yeah, too bad. He missed chatting with them every day. He'd have to make do with the materials at hand.

"Hey, man, it's me," his friend Scott said. "How was my timing?"

Nolan grinned. "Perfect. I'll head out now. Are you already at the pub?"

"Not yet. I'll be there in ten minutes," Scott said.

Nolan hung up and returned to the dinner table. He didn't sit down again. "I'm going to the pub to meet Scott."

His mother's gaze narrowed while his father continued

eating his beef casserole.

"Aren't you going to tell us about the show?" his mother demanded, impatience a red tide of color in her lined cheeks. She set her knife and fork on her plate in a soldier-straight line.

"No. I've signed a contract stating I won't divulge the results before each show is aired."

"But we're your parents." The same shade of brown eyes he saw in the mirror each day glared at him.

"I didn't want to do this show," Nolan reminded her. "I'm an adult and I don't have to take your advice." The blunt speech was long due. His mother had gone behind his back and submitted his name for the reality show because she disapproved of the woman he was seeing. Simple as that.

"You work on the farm your father and I own," she retorted.

"Don't make threats," his father said in a harsh voice. "You've already run off one of my sons. I won't stand for you alienating Nolan too. This farm will belong to him one day."

Hell, when had it come to this? His parents lived in the same house and barely spoke a civil word. Nolan wasn't sure of the reasons for their hostility, but the ongoing battle had raged as long as he could remember.

God, one look at his parents' marriage was enough to keep a sane man single. He didn't know why his parents remained locked in their loveless union when they were both so unhappy.

"Thanks for dinner," Nolan said into the strained silence. "Dad, I'll see you tomorrow morning. I'll get the ewes in first thing, so we can draft them for the sale."

"I'll be there." His father stood. "I'm going into town for a few hours."

His mother's mouth firmed to a hard line, and Nolan decided to retreat before the war flared into violence. Both he and his mother knew exactly where his father was going—to spend a few hours with his friends at the pub. Thank god he lived in a farm hand's cottage as a haven from the ongoing battle.

Half an hour later, Nolan walked into the pub. *The Fox and Hounds* was busy for a Thursday night, the feminine shrieks and hilarity coming from the function room indicating a hen's night was in progress.

Scott sat at the end of the bar and hailed him with a wave. "Want a beer?"

Nolan nodded. "Is anyone using the pool table?"

"There's a tournament." Scott slid him a sly glance. "Guess you'll have to shoot the shit with me instead."

Nolan rolled his eyes. "God, not you too."

Scott signaled for the barmaid and placed his order. "Give me a hint. Did you pick the sexy dancer?"

Nolan grinned. "I might have."

"You did. Damn. Have you seen her dance?"

Nolan's grin widened to a full-on smirk. "Yeah."

"Man, do we get to see her dance on the show? I want to see her legs. Imagine her naked with all that long hair flowing over bare skin." Scott jerked his head in the direction of an empty booth. "Let's grab that. I want to grill you in private."

Nolan had already seen the eager eavesdroppers and didn't argue. He slid into the booth and grimaced at Scott's eager curiosity. "You need to get laid."

"Nope," Scott said. "Been there, done that."

"You have to swear you won't discuss what I tell you with anyone," Nolan said.

"Scout's honor."

"You and I both know you were never a scout," Nolan said.

"I won't tell anyone," Scott said, his face settling into earnest lines.

Nolan gave a nod. Fair enough. He'd trust his best friend with his life. "I picked Susan, Jasmine and Lucy."

"What about Yvonne?"

Guilt slapped Nolan. "I've talked to Yvonne. She understands about the show."

"There aren't many women who would understand."

"Yeah." Nolan hoped this show didn't screw up what they had together. Tyler might be disowned, but Nolan bet his younger brother's life ran more smoothly.

When Nolan returned home—after watching the show at the pub—he powered up his laptop and logged onto his blog.

The worst part of this entire process is choosing which women to move on to the next stage of the show. All of the women I've met are brilliant. Most of them live in the city, and I reckon the men who live there are blind.

The current dating system is broken if men and women need to resort to a reality show to find their life partners.

Nolan paused and reread his words. He started to delete them before he reconsidered. Jennifer's assistant had told them to write from the heart and not censor. An evil grin spread across his face. His mother read his blog. He knew because she'd made a couple of comments about his grammar. Why not give her something to worry about?

During my last visit to Auckland, I visited all my ladies at their place of work. There is a real variety of jobs and I stopped at a dentist's office, a veterinary clinic, a high school, an office, the museum and at Maxwell's, the night club on K'Road.

I had fun at each place, picked up a stray pup at the vets and ended up bringing him home. I'll load up a photo of Charlie at the end of this post. He's part Border Collie, and I think he'll make a good farm dog.

To my surprise, I had the most fun at the night club. I watched Susan and the other girls learn a new dance routine. I had no idea what to expect—well, not true. I thought I knew what to expect. Lots of naked girls and a seedy atmosphere. They surprised me. Firstly, if any of you have been curious enough to visit Maxwell's, you'll know it's a class joint. Both men and women frequent the place, and I'm told groups of women go on their own because it's the kind of atmosphere where they feel comfortable. The club holds both hen and bachelor parties, and the place is high class all the way.

Back to the dancers. Those girls are fit. Julia, who runs the club, asked me if I'd like to join the training session. Since it was a new dance and none of them knew what they were doing, I figured, why not? We'd make mistakes together. They left me in the dust and had the dance moves down after one run through. They're super flexible and seem to bend themselves into shapes that even fencing wire wouldn't take. I came away from the club awed at the focus and dedication of the employees.

While the industry has a bad name and collects innuendo, I can see Maxwell's *is run as a family business with an emphasis on customers having a good time in a safe environment. If you haven't visited* Maxwell's *already, you're missing a great night out. Grab a bunch of friends and go with an open mind. I think you'll be pleasantly surprised.*

Nolan read his post and nodded with satisfaction. That would give his judgmental mother something to gnaw on tomorrow.

CHAPTER EIGHT

WITH CHRISTINA'S HELP, SUSAN had taken a range of sexy pictures with her cell phone. While she was waiting at the domestic air terminal for the flight to Napier, the nearest city to Clare, she picked one at random—a shot of her legs clad in black stockings—added a text message and sent it to Tyler.

Her phone beeped almost immediately.

U expt me 2 concentr8 on cattle when my thoughts r on yr sexy legs?

Quick texter. She grinned as their flight was announced. She switched off her phone and followed Jasmine, Lucy and the other passengers onto the plane.

Almost an hour later, nerves danced like marionettes in the pit of her belly, and the anxiety had nothing to do with the plane landing. She wanted to see Tyler so badly, feel his arms wrap around her, but with a cameraman trailing her, arranging a meeting would be tricky.

"I'm so nervous." Jasmine's oval face was pale, her blusher standing out in a curving sweep across her cheekbones. Her honey blonde hair lay in casual curls, framing and highlighting her neat features.

Jasmine's insecurities spread like rumors, and the beginnings of panic stirred in Susan. When she realized her stupidity, she almost laughed aloud. No need for her to worry. She didn't want Nolan. It was his younger brother she wanted to impress. "You'll be fine. Think of this as a holiday. Even if things don't work out with Nolan, this is a change from routine. An adventure, right?"

"I don't understand you," Lucy said. "You don't seem to care. You say the most outrageous things in front of the camera and everyone loves you."

Susan bit her bottom lip. She didn't mean to release the brake on her tongue. There was something about Nolan that pushed her buttons and led her into freefall. Luckily, Tyler thought she was funny. He said his in-laws loved her, and the public seemed to like her too. Her blog and forum were popular. Even Jennifer had sent her an email of congratulations and approval. It seemed her notoriety was doing good things for the ratings.

"How about if we tell Nolan to share the naughty questions around?" Susan asked. "I'd be happy. Blushing and freckles is not a good combination."

Lucy muttered something under her breath. The seat

belt sign went out, and Lucy stood abruptly, her blonde ponytail swishing at the surge of motion as she jerked her hand luggage from the overhead locker.

"I really am sorry," Susan said to Jasmine. "I don't mean to hog the limelight."

"Don't be silly," Jasmine said. "This is a competition and only one of us can win. I intend to grab every advantage and you should too. Every woman for herself."

Susan grinned, but traces of guilt crept into her mind. Little did Jasmine know, but it was a two-woman race. Even if things didn't work out with Tyler, she couldn't see herself settling with Nolan. They were too different, and Nolan was right. Now that she'd discovered dancing, she couldn't imagine herself leaving the city. She snorted inwardly. It had taken a reality show to make her see she belonged in the city.

Susan collected her bag with the others. Before she'd left, she'd gone to the art store and purchased the box of pastels she'd seen Tyler drool over plus a selection of water color paints, charcoal and a couple of small sketchpads. She figured he'd use the supplies eventually and it was something he'd really enjoy. She'd also included a soft toy—an owl that Julia said her son loved.

"There's Nolan," Lucy said and was off like a show horse, her blonde ponytail waving behind like a flag.

"What did I say?" Jasmine asked.

"Every woman for herself," Susan said with a grin.

They watched Lucy throw her arms around Nolan and give him a big kiss. The cameraman followed Lucy, filming her exuberant hello.

Susan trailed Jasmine and gave Nolan a quick hug. No kissing for her, thank you very much.

"Nolan, we don't have much time," a woman said from behind them.

Nolan nodded. "This is my mother." He introduced each of the girls by name and they received a chilly nod from his mother. Susan found amusement bubbling to the surface and flashed a grin at the woman. Tyler had told her about his mother and her sternness, the way she'd rejected him when his girlfriend had become pregnant. Even after they'd married, she remained distant. Tyler said he didn't see her and that his father would pop by to see Katey occasionally, but he never took his daughter to visit the house where he'd grown up. Suddenly Susan was glad she'd received a wakeup call after Maggie and Connor started dating. She never wanted to turn into this woman with her tight held emotions, her mask of disapproval permanently etched into her face.

"Hello," Susan said, and the woman's harsh features didn't budge. "I'm pleased to meet you."

Nolan cleared his throat, attracting Susan's attention. "The local school is having a gala day. I'm helping out with the pony rides. Mum has organized you all to help out on stalls."

"Sounds like fun," Susan said.

Jasmine and Lucy added their agreement, and they left the airport terminal. "I can only fit two in my truck," Nolan said, after surveying the luggage.

"One of you will travel with me," Nolan's mother said.

"I'll go with you," Susan said. "I'd love to hear more about the gala day and the town of Clare."

Nolan sent her a grateful look, and as she'd suspected, the other two girls didn't offer an argument.

Susan lifted her bright red bag into the rear and climbed into the passenger seat of a compact orange car.

Mrs. Penrith pulled out of the parking area and turned onto the main road. "I'm not going to let Nolan marry the likes of you," she said in a frosty voice.

"Isn't that up to Nolan?" Susan asked, chilled by the malice in the other woman. "Besides, you don't know me. It's a bit early to assassinate my character."

"You work in a night club. You dance and disrobe in front of men."

"But I don't sleep with them," Susan said. "Look, I was surprised when Nolan picked me. Lucy and Jasmine are beautiful and they're nice girls. I doubt you have a thing to worry about."

"We'll see," Mrs. Penrith said.

Cold silence filled the vehicle. Susan thought about packing the void with bright chatter before deciding to study the scenery instead. It was a gorgeous winter day with a warm sun and a vivid blue sky. There was still a nip in the air from the frost the previous evening, and Susan noticed the patches of white on the grass in places where the sun hadn't yet reached.

"How big is the school?" Susan asked finally. She might as well learn something about the area.

"We have almost two hundred pupils," Mrs. Penrith said.

"And is the gala day to raise funds for a particular project?"

"We want to buy more computers and uniforms for our sports teams. We have a hockey team, several netball and rugby teams."

"Does Nolan play rugby?"

"He used to," Mrs. Penrith said, noticeably thawing when Susan mentioned her son. "The farm keeps him busy these days. He loves the land."

Susan nodded. "Which stall will I work on today?" She made a mental note to take her camera. Tyler hadn't mentioned the gala, although they'd both been busy during the last couple of days and hadn't managed more than a quick phone call and a few texts.

"You're on the white elephant stall," Mrs. Penrith said. "They sell a bit of everything."

"We had a white elephant stall at the hospice charity," Susan said. "They're usually very popular. You never know what treasures you'll find."

"Do you...do you do charity work?" Mrs. Penrith seemed to force the question out.

Susan ignored the awkwardness and smiled. "I used to do a lot more than I do now. I work in a soup kitchen once a month and help out with the hospice. We've done door-to-door collecting and organized several gala days and sausage sizzles. It's hard to get people to part with their money, and we've tried to get creative with our fundraising. In two months we're organizing a rubber duck race."

"Oh? How does that work?" Mrs. Penrith was interested despite herself.

"We have five hundred rubber ducks, which are all numbered. People pay twenty dollars to buy one duck. Then they're all dropped into a fast-running stream. The first duck across the finish line wins a holiday donated by the local travel agency."

"I wonder if we could do something like that here," Mrs. Penrith mused. "The local volunteer fire brigade needs more funding."

"If there are lots of single men in the area, you could ask the single women to make picnic baskets and people can bid for them. The winning bid would secure the picnic basket plus the company of the young lady who made the basket. It's an old-fashioned idea, but if you hold it at a town picnic, something like that is lots of fun."

"That's a good idea," Mrs. Penrith said. "Our

fund-raising efforts haven't been very successful recently. I think it's because we're using the same old ideas. We need fresh ideas to encourage people to donate their money and time."

"Egg throwing contests are always fun," Susan said. "Especially on a gorgeous day like this. Are you having one of those?"

"No, we didn't think of it. We have the usual stalls plus some friendly games between the different sports teams."

"If you'd like to try an egg-throwing competition today, it's easy enough to organize. I could do it for you if you like. All we'd need is lots of eggs and an open field."

Mrs. Penrith turned to her and actually smiled. "We'll detour via the farm," she said. "My chooks are laying very well this year. How much should we charge?"

"Since the eggs are donated and we don't need to pay for them, how about two-dollars per person. That's not too expensive and everyone, regardless of age, would be able to afford to play. All we'll need is a prize."

"Would you volunteer your time? Maybe an outing with one of the gentlemen?" Mrs. Penrith asked.

"As long as Nolan approves, that will be fine," Susan said, understanding Mrs. Penrith's subtle maneuvering away from Nolan. Susan wondered what the woman would say if she discovered Susan preferred her younger son. Mrs. Penrith needed to worry about Tyler, not Nolan.

They arrived at the school to find Nolan pacing back and

forth in the car park.

"Mum, where have you been? Did you have a puncture?"

"No, Susan and I had to stop by the farm to get some eggs. Susan volunteered to arrange an egg-throwing competition."

Nolan turned his gaze on Susan, approval shining above his initial hint of surprise. "That's a great idea."

"I'll speak to the principal and draft you some helpers to set up a table and anything else you need." Mrs. Penrith climbed out of the car, plucked her brown handbag off the rear seat and bustled away.

Nolan's features blazed with curiosity. "What did you and my mother talk about on the drive over?"

"Nothing much." Susan climbed out of the car. "We discussed the school gala and ideas for fundraising. She seemed surprised I had experience in the area. I think she believes my morals reside in the gutter."

Nolan squeezed her shoulder briefly. "My mother sets high standards of behavior for herself and doesn't take it well when others fall short. Don't let her frosty manner get to you. She's like that with everyone."

"She seemed to approve of your other chosen dates." No wonder Tyler clashed with his mother. A pregnancy out of wedlock wouldn't have gone down well, even if Tyler had married his girlfriend.

Nolan laughed. "I have no intention of choosing a wife

to suit my mother. Don't worry. She'll find fault with Lucy and Jasmine too. It's her way, and I've learned to ignore her and get on with my own life."

"What about your father?"

"My father checked out of their marriage a long time ago," Nolan said. "My mother doesn't believe in divorce."

"I see." And she did. She saw a path she'd never go down. Yes, it was true she wanted children, a family, but she didn't intend to marry for the sake of tradition. If she loved the man—that was different. Julia and Maggie had great marriages with men who were their best friend as well as their lover, and she refused to settle for less.

Nolan's mother appeared with two reluctant teenagers. "These young girls will help you carry the eggs. Susan, the principal said you can use the far rugby field and he's going to organize an adult to help. Nolan, you're due to help at the nail driving competition before the pony rides start. Off you go."

Susan bit back the urge to salute. She lifted out two boxes of eggs and handed one to each of the teenage girls. She picked up the last one and smiled at the girls. "You'd better show me the way."

She followed the teenagers and grimaced at the mud splattering her boots. Up ahead a man carried a table, his butt displayed in a pair of black jeans. *Nice.* Evidently the girls thought so too because one whispered to the other and they giggled.

The man set the table down on the try line, pressing on the wooden surface to make sure it was stable.

"Tyler," one of the girls called.

He turned and grinned at them before turning his attention to Susan. "Thanks, Marie. Karen. Mr. Black said he was going to sort out a sign and find a tape measure in case we need to measure the length of the throws. Can you go and collect them for us?"

"Sure, Tyler."

The girls set their boxes of eggs down and wandered away, leaving them alone.

"God, I've missed you," he said. "I want to kiss you in the worst way."

Susan grinned, the frisson of lust that frisked her a familiar one. "All your late night naughty texts have cost me a fortune in batteries." Her hands shook and she hastily placed her box of eggs on the tabletop.

Tyler let out a whoosh of air and came half a step closer. His hands fisted at his sides, as if he didn't quite trust himself not to touch her. "My hand doesn't do the job as good as you."

This time she was the one who fought for control. "Can we work out some way to meet?"

"Count on it, sweetheart." He took a deep breath. "You could always withdraw from the show."

"I've tried that already. I rang Jennifer and spoke to her in person, said I'd met someone else and that it was serious.

She pleaded with me to stick the course. Evidently, every time I'm on a show, the website hits go off the charts. I said to her that it wasn't fair on Nolan and the other girls, but she was adamant. Then she said that the funding for her next project depended on the success of this show. She guilted me into staying. I gave her my word I'd stay the course."

"As long as they don't expect you to kiss Nolan," he muttered. "I won't like that."

"I have no desire to kiss your brother."

"Good thing," he said with a sly wink. The two girls returned, and he stepped away from her. "Thanks, girls. What do we do next, boss?" he said to Susan.

Susan scanned the handwritten sign. Perfect. Mrs. Penrith had done well with her organization. "We need to mark the places for the people throwing the eggs to stand. One for the person throwing the egg and one for the person catching. The first one should be easy, and we'll do about four different levels, getting progressively harder."

Once they'd marked the egg-throwing course to her satisfaction, Susan organized the two teenagers to spread the word and let people know they were in business.

"Are you really the prize?" one of them asked.

"Yes, Mrs. Penrith asked if I'd donate my time for the winning team. I can bake a cake, do some housework or teach dancing."

"A date?" Tyler asked.

"Yes." Susan shot him a frown. "Can you tell people that?" she asked the girls.

Tyler waited until the girls were out of earshot. "Are there any rules against me entering?"

Susan shrugged. "You'll need a partner and the entrance fee."

"I think I can manage that. Will you be okay on your own while I round up my partner?"

"Sure. Oh, look. My first two victims." Susan grinned at two teenage boys. "Would you like to try? Can you throw the egg without it breaking?"

"Are the eggs boiled?" one of the boys asked.

"No." Susan smiled and offered a dare. "Do you think you can do it? Since you're my first interested customers, why don't I give you a go for free?"

"Okay," one of the boys said. "You throw," he said to his mate. "I'm a better catch."

"It wasn't my fault I dropped the ball," the other boy snapped. "If you'd thrown a better pass I might have caught it."

"You guys play rugby?" Susan asked.

"Yeah," the first guy said. "We're in the first fifteen."

"Perfect. Here's an egg. We've marked out the different stages. If you can toss your egg and catch it without breaking it, you can move up to the next level. Think you can do that?"

"No sweat. You can take us out to the new movie that's

starting in Napier next week."

A laugh rippled from her, part surprise and part entertainment at his attitude. "I like your confidence. Show me what you've got." She gave one of them an egg and carefully observed to make sure they stood on the lines.

Tyler arrived with an older woman in tow just as the two boys were going to throw. "Here's my partner," he said. "Josie, meet Susan. We're going to win a date with her."

"Hi, Josie." She'd heard a lot about his mother-in-law and instantly liked the bright, smiling woman. "Ready?" she shouted at her first two victims. "They think this is easy," she said to Josie and Tyler.

"Catch!" the guy throwing yelled.

The egg flew through the air.

"Aw!" The other teenager caught the egg, but it went *splat* in his hands.

"You want to try that again?" Susan shouted.

"Yeah. I'm throwing this time."

"And you're also paying this time," Susan said.

"I'll take the money for you, dear," Josie said.

Tyler slipped his arm around Susan and steered her to the start line. He glanced at the boys then pinched her bottom.

Susan jumped and let out an *eep* of surprise.

"I'll take care of handing out the eggs for you," he said, moving to stand by the table before Susan had a chance to object. He grinned as she trotted away to direct the egg-throwers into position.

"Tyler Penrith, I saw that," Josie said in a low voice. "You pinched that girl's bottom."

"Did I?" He aimed for innocent and failed. Badly.

Josie scanned his face while Tyler pretended to watch the boys throw their next egg. "Do you know her?"

"No comment."

"We'll take one egg please." The elderly woman leaned forward and whispered loudly, "I'm going to throw the egg. I might aim for my husband's head."

Tyler chuckled and handed over an egg. "Maybe I should warn Stan his wife is gunning for him."

"I'm more interested in learning about Susan," Josie said.

"I want to win that date," Tyler said.

Josie sent him a quizzical glance. "I see."

"We could never pull anything over on you," Tyler said.

For ten minutes, they were busy taking money and handing out eggs while Susan kept everyone honest.

Stan and his wife managed to get to the second marker before the egg broke in his hands.

"Old fool made the mistake of saying he had a thing for dancers. That will teach him," Mabel said as she watched Stan rub at the egg yolk decorating his white shirt.

"I think a few people are interested in dancers," Josie said with a knowing glance in Tyler's direction.

Tyler grinned widely, his gaze going to Susan. She was good with people and already they'd collected a crowd of participants. Each waited impatiently to have their turn. When the crowd started to tail off, Tyler whispered to Josie, "You ready to have a go at winning a date?"

"Is this important to you?" Josie asked, her gaze on Susan.

"Yes."

"Well, then," Josie said. "I'll bring my A game."

"AND THE WINNER OF the egg throwing competition is Josie Murdoch and Tyler Penrith," the principal announced an hour later. "Sam Gibbs is the winner of the nail driving contest and Rita James wins the prize for guessing the correct weight of the porker. Come and collect your prizes."

Everyone cheered, and Tyler clutched his daughter's hand while Eric shooed Josie up to the makeshift stage to claim their prize.

"Nolan, you'll have to share one of your girls," someone shouted.

"Hell, he's got three of them. Maybe I could have one too," a male voice shouted from the rear.

"If you wanted a wife, you should have applied to appear in the reality show," Nolan said.

"Daddy, you're hurting my hand," Katey objected.

Tyler loosened his grip. "Sorry, sweetie."

"Can I do a lucky dip?" she asked.

"Soon," Tyler promised.

He and Katey clapped hard when Josie received a certificate.

"Now that I've distributed the prizes and still have you gathered," the principal said, "we're going to do some quick fire raffles. Dig deep folks. The first prize is a meat pack donated by Judson Butchers."

"Daddy? I want to win a bracelet."

Tyler laughed at her determination. "Let's go." He maneuvered his daughter through the crowd. He saw his mother speaking to two blonde women. He recognized them as Nolan's other dates, and he steered his daughter in a slightly different direction. His mother ignored Katey, and he preferred to minimize their meetings. "What color bracelet would you like?"

"Purple," she said.

"What happens if you get the wrong color?" he teased. "What if you get green?"

"If that happens," a feminine voice said, "we could make a purple one."

Tyler's heart skipped a beat and happiness grabbed him by the throat. "Katey, this is Miss Webb."

"Susan," Susan said with a smile.

"Hello." His daughter cocked her head and surveyed

Susan without shyness. "Can you make a bracelet?"

"I can," Susan said.

Tyler led Katey and Susan over to the lucky dip stall. Two large tubs of sawdust sat in front of a desk, one labeled boys and the other girls. He handed over two dollars and turned to his daughter. "I've paid the money, now it's up to you, sweetie."

"No pressure," Susan murmured into his ear. She stood so close he could feel the warmth coming off her skin and smell her scent. More than anything, he wanted to reach for her hand and show everyone she belonged with him. Instead, he acted the friendly stranger and when no one else was looking, he spoke to her with his eyes.

"The sawdust is tickling my nose," Katey said.

He grinned at the intense concentration on his daughter's face, his heart swelling with pride. "Can you feel a parcel?" He and Susan hadn't spoken about children, except in general terms.

"Yes." Katey frowned. "It's not a bracelet shape."

"It might be something better than a bracelet," the girl on the stall said—one of the Gibson clan, judging by the carrot red hair and freckles. "If it's a big parcel it might be a necklace."

"Can you make those?" Katey asked.

"No," Tyler said. "I'm a boy."

"No," Katey said. "You're a daddy."

"And a very fine daddy you are," Susan whispered, her

words having nothing to do with his parenting skills.

"There you are," Nolan said from behind them. "We're going to head back to the farm now. Tyler."

He gave his normal stiff welcome. Tyler sighed, wondering why his family was so fucked up that they couldn't even talk to each other. "Susan and I were discussing our upcoming date."

"We can do that later," Susan said. "I'll give you my cell phone number." She opened her handbag and pulled out a business card. "It was nice to meet you and Katey."

Nolan gave him a curt nod and escorted Susan over to where his mother stood.

Something twisted inside Tyler on seeing her leave with his brother. He liked Susan a lot. She was fun and made him laugh. She'd been good with Katey and he thought Josie had liked her too.

"I've picked a parcel, Daddy."

"Okay, pull it out of the sawdust, and we'll see what you've got."

His daughter pulled out a parcel and eagerly ripped it open where they stood. The excitement in her face faded. "It's not a bracelet."

He shot a quick glance at the girl in charge of the stall. "Let's see what you've picked out."

"*Ooh*, a tiara," the teenager said. "Lots of girls picked bracelets but there were only a few tiaras. You'll be a princess. Would you like me to put it on for you?"

"Thanks," Tyler said. After watching many Disney movies, he was up with crowns but he figured the teenager would sell the sparkly tiara to his disappointed daughter far better than he could.

"You put it on like this," the teenager said, crouching beside his daughter. She placed the tiara on Katey's head and rose to admire the effect. "The blue stones are pretty with your hair."

"Tyler, are you and Katey ready to leave?" Josie called. "Oh, Katey. You look pretty, just like a princess."

Katey pulled a face. "Wanted a bracelet."

Tyler shared a rueful glance with his mother-in-law. Their little princess was tired and about to have a tantrum. "Thanks," he said to the teenager.

"Eric is going to stay and help with the cleanup," Josie said.

Tyler nodded and scooped up his daughter. Five minutes later, they were on their way home, Katey almost asleep in her car seat.

"I think the principal was pleased with the takings," Josie said. "Everyone was impressed with Nolan's women. The three of them pitched in to help."

"They did." Tyler's thoughts jumped to Susan. Not unusual since the track in his mind was well-trodden.

"I liked Susan."

Tyler slowed to avoid a cow and calf on the road. The animals ambled over the seal to an unopened gate. "That's one of Jim's. Grab my phone and let him know."

"I'll run and open the gate," Josie said. "It won't take a minute."

Tyler nodded and picked up his phone to ring their neighbor about his AWOL stock. With the call made, his mind drifted yet again. How was he going to swing some privacy with Susan? The cameraman kept appearing to film for the show, which made spontaneity tricky. He had their date up his sleeve, but that would need to be at a public place and there was no way he'd keep her for a sleepover.

"Stupid animal," Josie muttered when she climbed back into the car, a whiff of cow manure coming with her. "My good boots. They'll never be the same."

"You volunteered."

"Next time remind me," Josie snapped. "When did you meet Susan?"

Tyler's hands clenched on the wheel. "Today." He forced himself to glance at Josie.

"Don't try to pull the wool over my eyes, Tyler Penrith. I saw you pinch that girl's bottom, and since she grinned instead of smacking you, I figured you'd met before because despite what some people might say, Susan is a nice girl. She didn't flirt with any of the other men who tried to chat her up. Besides, you practically blackmailed me into the egg-throwing contest. I wondered why you were so adamant."

"I might have met her before," Tyler said, turning his attention back to the country road.

"She's your mystery woman," Josie said.

"No," he said quickly. Too quickly. He cursed under his breath. There was no question in her statement. Somehow, his mother-in-law had worked out everything after seeing them together once.

"She's a lovely girl."

"Yes," he said.

"Yes, you're admitting the truth or yes, you're agreeing she's attractive?"

"Yes to both," he said, giving in to the inevitable.

"How did you manage to meet her?"

Tyler checked on Katey, but she was sound asleep, her tiara still sparkling on top of her head. "I emailed her after the show. We clicked and I asked if she wanted to meet in person."

"Did you share a room?"

"Josie," Tyler said.

She clapped her hands together. "Oh, that's good. She likes you."

Tyler pulled up in front of the farmhouse. "I like her too."

"You don't do things the easy way. What are you going to do if your brother picks her?"

"Susan doesn't think he'll pick her again. You've seen the show. Nolan goes out of his way to embarrass her."

"Does Nolan know?"

"No one knows apart from Susan's friends and now you. We were careful."

"We have a date each," Josie said. "We'll manage some time alone for you."

"You approve?"

"I liked Susan very much, and it's been good to see you happy, to see the spark of fun you used to have as a youngster," Josie said.

Tyler unbuckled Katey and carried her into the house. In her bedroom, he pulled off her shoes, her tiara and her jacket before putting her in bed for a nap. She was asleep before he'd tiptoed from the room.

"That sounds like Eric," Josie said. "Do you want a cup of tea before you go out to shift the sheep?"

"Looks as if the rain will hold off for a bit longer," Tyler said.

Eric bustled indoors carrying a pink and white cyclamen in a brass pot. "Look what I won for you, Josie. Another plant for you to kill off."

"Thanks, I think." Josie wrinkled her nose at her husband. "At least I can plant this one in the garden and it will survive despite my lack of skill."

Tyler grabbed the biscuit tin from the cupboard, listening to their familiar bickering with a slight smile.

"I know the identity of Tyler's mystery woman."

"Josie," Tyler protested, although he'd known she'd tell

Eric.

"How? Who?" Eric demanded.

A teasing smile played over Josie's lips as she glanced from him to Eric. "I'm accepting bribes. Whoever offers the highest bribe wins."

"I'm not playing," Tyler said. "Go ahead. Tell him."

"Pooh, you're no fun."

"Josie," Eric said. "We still need to shift the sheep."

"I can handle it on my own," Tyler said.

Eric shot him a frown. "Are you sure?"

Tyler accepted the cup of tea Josie handed him and took a quick sip. "Positive. The sheep practically move themselves." Tyler could do with some time alone to formulate a plan. "Besides, it will give the pair of you plenty of time to gossip about me."

"We do not associate with that man," Mrs. Penrith lectured as they drove down country roads, passed paddocks full of cows and sheep, a few horses.

"What man?" Susan asked. *Ooh, alpacas. Cute.* "I met a lot of people today, and everyone was friendly and welcoming. You have a lovely town."

The compliment didn't soften the brackets outlining the woman's mouth, didn't put a dent in her set expression, didn't promote a sliver of personal satisfaction. The woman continued driving like an emotionless machine. "If I'd known he was helping you with the egg-throwing, I would've fixed the problem. Immediately."

"Tyler? He seemed like a great guy." Susan forced a friendly smile when she wanted to snarl an accusation. What was wrong with the woman? Why did she dislike her son so much she couldn't even say his name?

"He has a bad reputation and we do not associate with him."

"Oh. Okay." Susan bit her tongue. *Don't respond. Don't react to her pettiness*. Listening to this judgmental woman was like an unhealthy blast from her past. Once she'd been guilty of the same behavior—a black and white kind of woman. Once she'd judged others by her own rigid standards. Once she'd been an uncompromising bitch. Luckily, she'd wised up and fought the battle to correct the nasty flaw in her character.

"You have enough strikes against you as it is," Mrs. Penrith said. "You don't need to add more by exhibiting a lack of commonsense."

"Yes, Mrs. Penrith." *Witch*. Both Nolan and Tyler struck her as decent men. How they'd managed it with a mother like Elizabeth Penrith, Susan didn't know. Good grief, how much longer would this car ride take? "I enjoyed the gala. Do you know if they raised the amount of money they needed for the computer equipment?"

"Yes, the gala was a big success. Of course, we gambled with the weather. It often rains at this time of the year."

"What is the next fundraising event? I met the minister of the local church. He said you help raise a lot of money for the various charities and to meet the needs of the community."

"We're trying to start an afternoon group for the children to keep them out of trouble. With the school holidays coming up soon, we're organizing a pilot program of different activities."

"That's a great idea," Susan said. "The school holidays start next week, don't they? I'd be happy to teach a dance class, if you think some of the kids would be interested."

Mrs. Penrith gasped, took her eyes off the road. "I hardly think that would be appropriate."

Chilly silence bloomed, coating the interior of the vehicle with permafrost. Thankfully, five minutes later, Mrs. Penrith jerked the car to a halt in front of a white bungalow.

Nolan opened Susan's door and waited for her to climb from the car. He took one look at her tight expression and squeezed her hand. "I'm sorry."

"It doesn't matter," Susan said.

"Susan's bag is in the back," Mrs. Penrith said. "Nolan, I still don't think that it's appropriate for the girls to stay in the house with you alone."

"Mum, we're hardly alone. The cameraman will spend

a lot of time at the house, and I believe Jennifer's assistant will be dropping in for a visit."

"It doesn't look right."

"Thank you for giving Susan a lift," Nolan said.

Mrs. Penrith scowled and looked as if she was winding herself up for a tirade.

"Thank you." Susan almost choked observing the polite niceties.

"I'll show you to your room."

Susan followed him through a wooden gate, past a bed of pink flowers and up a curved path to the three steps leading to the entrance. A verandah wrapped around most of the bungalow—the perfect place to while away lazy afternoons or late summer evenings and savor the views into the valley and beyond, the township of Clare.

"What a gorgeous view," she said. "Looks as if a storm is coming fast."

"The forecast predicted rain. You should see the view from my parents' house. It's even better."

Susan bet the frigid atmosphere didn't extend to this house. It raised curiosity about Tyler's father. What sort of man ignored one of his sons?

"I'm afraid your room is small. Jasmine and Lucy are sharing the larger room."

"No problem," Susan said. "As long as the bed is comfortable." She peeked through the doorway he indicated. "Oh, you weren't kidding."

"Jasmine and Lucy are in the lounge."

"Sure. I'll join them once I freshen up. Which way is the bathroom?"

Susan walked into the lounge fifteen minutes later, her hair tied back in a braid. She'd donned a clean T-shirt—pink—and a pair of black leggings, figuring comfort was the way to go. Her phone beeped, and she plucked it from the pocket of the vest she'd pulled on over the long sleeve tee.

I wish you were here.

She'd enjoy a sanctuary with Tyler too.

Not gonna happen. Instead, she did the next best thing. She sent a return text and attached a photo of her in a showgirl costume. This one focused on the beaded bra top, her cleavage. A casual observer wouldn't recognize her in the photo. Tyler would know since the single freckle on the upper curve of her right breast would give away her identity. He liked to kiss and lick that freckle. A hot swell of lust blasted a path to her pussy and she inhaled sharply.

"Something wrong?" Nolan asked, coming up behind her.

Susan hit send and dropped her phone into the depths of her pocket. "No. Everything's fine."

"What are you cooking us for dinner, Nolan?" Lucy asked.

"Beef stew, mashed potatoes and Brussels sprouts. Apple crumble and yogurt for dessert."

Lucy wrinkled her nose. Jasmine's expression duplicated Lucy's.

"Sounds great," Susan said. "Let me know if you need a hand."

The cameraman entered the lounge, his camera on his shoulder. "I need to record the girl's initial impressions of their day and the farm."

"I'll be in the kitchen," Nolan said.

Susan followed the scent of beef stew and sauntered into the large kitchen, scanning it with interest. Nothing fancy, the scarred counters bore evidence of hard use, but the place appeared clean. Her estimation of Nolan rose. Not the stereotypical bachelor.

"You might as well set me to work," she said. "I can set the table or peel potatoes." She rounded the wooden dining table at the far end of the kitchen and halted at the island counter where Nolan stood.

"Feel up to peeling apples?"

"I can go one better and make the entire crumble if you want. I don't peel my apples. It's much quicker my way."

Outside, rain spilled from the sky, the splatter amplified by the iron roof. Susan peered out the kitchen window and shivered. "They were lucky with the gala."

"Yeah. Can I leave you to do that? I'd better light the fire in here and the lounge before it gets too cold. That way we'll have plenty of hot water."

Susan nodded, and Nolan left his pile of potatoes and

apples on the counter. Susan got to work and started on the apples, quartering and coring them before hunting through the cupboard for a grater. In the pantry, she located spices, flour and oats to make her crumble topping and quickly assembled the dessert ready to go into the oven.

Her phone beeped again. A text from Christina asking about her day. Susan fired off a quick reply, promising to email soon.

Nolan wasn't back yet, so she started peeling the potatoes. She peeled a dozen, figuring if they didn't eat all the mash, they could make something with the leftovers.

Nolan stomped back into the kitchen, his arms laden with kindling and small logs. A gust of icy air followed him through the rear door. A crash of thunder made Susan jump, and she glanced out the window in time to see a flicker of lightning. Another thunderous crash boomed almost immediately.

A whimper sounded at the open door. Nolan cursed softly, shot her a swift glance. "Sorry. I'll take the dog back to his kennel."

"He's terrified," Susan said. "Is that the one you adopted?"

"Yeah. I've been letting him sleep inside."

"Set up his bed where he can see us, and maybe he'll calm down."

"Thanks, but hasn't learned his manners. Once he

settles, he'll want to play."

"He's a puppy. You need to cut him some slack."

Nolan grinned, a wide, honest smile that showed hints of Tyler, and disappeared outside. They hadn't inherited that smile from their mother.

"Susan." The cameraman appeared in the kitchen. "Oh good. I'll film you here for a change of scenery. Can you cook?"

"Yes, my mother taught me and my sisters when we were young. I enjoy cooking, but I don't get much time these days."

"What do you think of Nolan's house and Clare? Could you live here?"

"I'm not sure," Susan said, going for honesty. "I've spent most of my life in Auckland. I enjoyed the gala day, and what I've seen of the farm and the surrounding countryside is beautiful. I guess, what I'm saying is I'll need more time before I come to a decision. It is a big change." And she wasn't sure she wanted to deal with the wicked witch of Clare on a daily basis. "When I applied to be on the show, I didn't have any doubts. Things have changed."

"What sort of things?"

"I've found my niche. I like who I am and where I am in my life." She paused, shrugged, trying to marshal her thoughts. "I'm happy," she said finally.

"What about a man? Wasn't that the whole point of the reality show?" the cameraman asked.

Susan hesitated and finally, she went with a partial truth. "Everyone wants and deserves love, but settling for something that doesn't fit is a mistake. I'm not going to force a relationship because my family or society says it's time."

"It takes a strong woman to go against tradition," the cameraman said.

An indelicate snort escaped. "Are you trying to tell me I'm not a traditional girl?"

"You're interesting," the cameraman said.

"I have a great set of friends and through them, my horizons have broadened. Maybe I've stepped outside conventional lines, but life would be boring if we all trod the same path. As long as I'm true to myself, that's the important thing."

"Thank you," the cameraman said, lowering his camera and switching off the power. "I'll head back to the motel and sort out this footage to send to Jennifer. Tell Nolan, will ya?"

"Sure." Susan peeled the last potato and tidied the counter.

Nolan returned with a blanket and his puppy. He commanded the black-and-white dog to sit. "Thanks for the suggestion, although my father would say that's not the right behavior for a farm dog."

"You don't talk about your father much," Susan said.

"He's slowed down after a fall from his horse. He spends

more time in his workshop making furniture these days."

"Is that a problem?"

"No, I enjoy taking charge and doing things my way. It's my ideal life, and I can't imagine doing anything else."

Susan nodded, her thoughts drifting to Tyler. She couldn't imagine leaving the city now. A long-distance romance? That hadn't worked for Julia, and if Susan were honest, it wouldn't work for her either.

CHAPTER NINE

TYLER MADE A POT of tea and poured mugs for Josie and Eric. After delivering them, he settled in front of the television with his own tea, frustration stalking his mind.

Susan was here in Clare, but he hadn't managed to glimpse her since the gala day. Three days of snatched chats and texts. A couple of emails. Now it was time for another episode of the reality show and he thought he might explode if he couldn't see her, touch her. Kiss her.

"What is wrong with you?" Eric asked. "You got ants in your pants?"

"He's been like that for days." Josie's eyes gleamed with secrets and Tyler was glad she wasn't sharing her opinion, at least not to his face. "Maybe you need a change of routine? When are you going to go on your date with Susan?"

What he needed was a good hard fuck, and only one

woman would solve his problem. But how did he get his hands on Susan?

He could hardly bring her here to the farm, and he couldn't take her to a motel room without causing speculation. The downside of country town life—eyes everywhere.

His cell phone buzzed and he straightened, pulling it from his pocket. *Phone sex at ten. Are you up for it?* Lust ran a path directly to his dick and he shifted, careful to make his move casual.

The opening credits for *Farmer Seeks a Wife* ran across the screen, and Tyler took a moment to reply. *Hell, yeah! It's a date.*

"You look happier," Josie said.

Tyler lifted his head to discover Eric and Josie staring, their expressions a hairsbreadth from nosiness.

"Shush, the show is starting," Tyler said.

"Katey keeps mentioning a bracelet and Susan in the same sentence. I thought I'd ask Susan if we could buy supplies and make bracelets at Katey's birthday party. Maybe she could teach the girls a dance or two as well. I'm sure that would stack up well against pony rides," Josie said.

"Sounds good. Did you still want me to do face painting?"

"Yes, I think so. It's good to plan indoor activities at this time of the year. If the weather is fine, we can move outside.

We'll play it by ear."

"I'll ask Susan," he said, his attention on the television screen.

"Give me her number," Josie said. "I'll ask her."

And there went his only viable excuse for contacting Susan. On screen, Nolan was teasing the two blondes—Jasmine and Lucy. There was lots of flirting and eyelash fluttering before the scene shifted to a shared dinner.

"Who is Nolan going to choose?" Eric asked when the show went to a commercial break.

"Not Susan if your mother has anything to do with it," Josie said. "The most awful rumors are circulating in the supermarket. I know they're false because I spent time with Susan at the gala." Her innocent gaze swung to Tyler. "I liked her very much. What do you say, Tyler?"

Tyler shot Josie a narrow-eyed stare. She was yanking his tail and doing an excellent job of ramping up his angst. "I think she's sexy, a lot of fun and Nolan should watch out or some other local will snatch her from under his nose."

"Well," said Josie. "Are you interested in Susan? I thought you had a special friend up in Auckland."

"You know it's Susan. Shush, the show is starting again." Tyler fastened his attention on the screen, his breath catching on seeing her. She spoke candidly, not shying from hard, soul-searching questions.

"She's gutsy," Eric said. "I like what I've seen of her too."

"I like the fact she doesn't resort to girlie tricks with Nolan," Josie said. "She's straight and true to herself. She doesn't deserve the slurs your mother is casting on her character."

Tyler remained silent, digesting her words of country life. A potential problem. He'd talk her round. His mind moved on to his mother and her dirty tactics. As a kid, he'd tried to be good, yet his attempts had never been enough. His mistake in getting a girl pregnant had given his parent a reason to toss him from the family home, and his father and brother hadn't offered support.

"*Ooh*, look!" Josie cried. "We're on the telly."

The camera had caught him laughing with Susan while Josie grinned like a woman in a toothpaste ad in the rear of the shot. His stomach bottomed out. Everything he felt for Susan shone on his face. He was certain Josie would recognize his open emotion, since she knew him well. Hopefully, everyone else would miss his reaction.

He tensed, waiting for his in-laws to tease. The ribbing didn't come, and his breath eased out in silent relief. Maybe his feelings for Susan weren't as transparent as he suspected.

Onscreen, the camera cut to Hailee. "Next week, our farmers will choose their favorite two girls. Tune in on Thursday to watch the farm antics and learn if your favorite girl reaches the next stage of the competition."

Tyler yawned as the closing credits ran across the screen.

"I might have an early night. I'll check on Katey and head to bed."

"Goodnight, son," Eric said.

"Night, Tyler."

Tyler wandered from the room while his brain demanded he break into a sprint. He had a bout of phone sex coming up. No time to waste.

SUSAN JUMPED WHEN HER phone buzzed. She checked the screen. Tyler. About time.

"I might have an early night," she said, her gaze going to Nolan, then Jasmine and Lucy. "It's been a long day." Even longer since her clever idea to make a date for phone sex. Never had a show seemed so lengthy.

A chorus of half-hearted goodnights came from the girls.

Nolan smiled. "See you in the morning. Thanks again for cooking dinner."

"No problem." Without her normal busy routine, the days were dragging, despite the new situation and the number of new people she found popping into her schedule.

Before she could reply to Tyler's text, her phone rang.

"Hello, Susan. It's Josie. I'm ringing to ask about our date."

Susan listened while Josie ran through her list of requirements and the date of Katey's birthday. "I'd love to help. Let me run it past Nolan and the cameraman first. Jennifer, our producer, has given them a strict schedule to keep in order to complete the show by deadline. I think that should be all right, but I'll double check tomorrow and confirm with you after I've spoken to them."

Once she'd finished the call, she sent a quick text to Tyler telling him to get naked and wait for her call.

In her bedroom, she closed the door, then turned the lock to prevent anyone from entering without permission.

She stripped and placed her clothes over the top of a straight-backed chair, the only other piece of furniture in her tiny bedroom. The last thing she did before she climbed into bed was apply some perfume, dabbing it on her pulse points. Breathless, she wiped damp palms on the green cotton duvet and reached for her phone.

"Susan. What took you so long?"

"Josie rang to organize our date. I'm coming to Katey's birthday party, as long as I can get time off from the show."

"I look forward to seeing you in my territory." His husky voice slipped across her senses like the smoothest whisky slid down a throat.

"I wish..." She swallowed and started again. "I wish I was there now."

"How would you feel about dinner and a movie for our date? We can have dinner at the pub and go to the drive-in movie on McDierment's farm. How does that sound?"

"That sounds great," Susan said. He hadn't returned her sentiment and she found her confidence taking a dive. "I'm switching to speaker phone."

"Already done. I'd like it if we could share a bed every night."

"Me too." Except she didn't see how that would ever happen with her in Auckland and Tyler in Clare with his daughter.

"What are you wearing?"

"Nothing except perfume."

"Describe the scent for me."

"It's spicy like cinnamon with a touch of citrus. Lime, I think. It reminds me of a Christmas cake. I put some behind my ears and on the crook of my elbow. And just a dab between my breasts."

"Nice," he said. "I'm not wearing anything either and all my blood is jammed in my cock."

She laughed, picturing him with the blunt end of his cock red and swollen, his eyes glittering with need while his taut muscles strained beneath her fingertips.

"Did you bring your vibrator with you?"

"I did as it happens. Let me get Mr. Blue."

"Your vibrator has a name?"

"He deserves one since he gives so much pleasure."

Tyler gave an audible swallow. "Good point." He cleared his throat. "Switch on your vibrator and tease your breasts.

I want you to describe everything you feel, the things I'd see if I was in the bed with you."

"Okay. Mr. Blue is shaped like a penis and he's bright blue. *Ooh*," Susan said as she slid the vibrator over the curve of one breast and nudged her nipple. "I've set Mr. Blue on a low speed, but I can feel the pulse against my skin. My nipple has pulled tight. My pussy feels wet already and—"

"If I touched you, would I see the glint of your juices on my fingers?"

"Let me see," she whispered, a delicious sensation pulling tight in her lower belly. "I'm reaching down my body." Her fingers drifted downward in a teasing caress. "I'm stroking, touching, imagining your fingers on me." Yeah, the rougher texture of Tyler's fingers, sliding over her belly, maybe dallying to dip into her navel. "Now I'm parting my legs. I can feel the chill of the air prickling across my hot flesh." Her fingers grazed her slit. "But my skin feels hot. Wet." The warmth of her pussy almost seared her fingertips. One of her fingers dipped into her entrance and it came away damp. A groan escaped.

"Don't keep me waiting," he ordered. "Tell me what you see."

"My finger is shiny." She placed her fingertip into her mouth and licked it clean. "I taste musky, a little tart."

"I'm frightened to touch my cock." Tyler's voice was strained. "It won't take much for me to explode."

"Imagine my mouth on you," she said, letting the

vibrator drift down her body. She teased it down her cleft and closed her eyes while she verbally seduced Tyler. "I lick around the crown then delicately probe your slit to gather the drops of pre-come. You taste good, so good and all I can think of is taking you deeper into my mouth and giving you pleasure." *He'd like this*. She'd tell him everything she couldn't normally say out loud because of a cock-filled mouth. "I want to make you feel good, so I tease you with the flat of my tongue."

Tyler's sharp intake of breath tugged like a kite string, firing need, desire. Susan swallowed and continued. "I want to drive you crazy, push you like you push pleasure through me with every touch."

"Tell me what you do next."

"I'm eager to taste you and take the tip of your cock into my mouth. I suck, take you deeper, let the underside of your shaft slide along my tongue. How does it feel?"

"Fuckin' great. God, I wish you were here in my bed."

Yes. Susan ran the vibrator over her clit and sighed at the sensual jolt. "I'm going to fuck myself with the vibrator now. You're not the only one in a hurry."

"Wait. Have you got any other toys?"

She paused, his question flinging her back into the past. She'd left her other toys with her ex after he'd abandoned her for her best friend. Funny, it didn't hurt as much now. "I used to own more in another life."

"I'd enjoy shopping with you. We'll buy some together,"

he said.

She pushed Mr. Blue into her channel, the silicon sliding easily into her aroused flesh. Turning the vibrator so the slight bend vibrated against her G-spot, she switched the setting up a notch. "Mr. Blue is inside me now, and he's doing his normal good work."

"Glad to hear you have a reliable male."

Susan spluttered a laugh, sent a guilty glance at her closed door. "I'm taking you deep now, pulling your shaft into my mouth. Your knob bumps against my throat. I'm breathing carefully through my nose and concentrating on giving you the best blow job you've ever received."

"Hell, yeah," he muttered.

"I can taste your pre-come. It's coming more quickly now, and your breathing is rapid. You're starting to burble and promise me all sorts of things—"

"Hell, yeah. I'd give you the moon if I could."

"You say that now."

"I mean it," Tyler said.

Susan stirred, pressure building in her pussy. "I go a little faster, bobbing up and down, pulling a loud moan from you." On beat, Tyler's soft moan came from the speakerphone and the pressure inside her increased. "Your cock swells and your balls are tight when I massage them. On the next down stroke, your cock nudges the back of my throat and I swallow against the thickness."

"Fuck," he said then hissed.

"Your eyes are closed and color surges into your face. You're trembling, so close it's as if you're balancing on a tight wire. I lift my head, go back down and you're coming, shooting into my mouth, spurting down my throat. This time I let you move, let you take what you want, what you need."

The words pulled her pussy tight, and she clenched her legs together. Her orgasm whipped through her, streaking tendrils of pleasure up her torso and down her limbs until the splendor of it roared like a storm. Like a tasty chocolate treat, she reveled in the deliciousness, greedily guzzling up every frisson until she floated back to the cupboard-size bedroom and reality.

For an instant, guilt colored the decadence—that she should do this with Tyler when she'd signed up to make nice with another.

"Suzy," Tyler's hoarse voice dragged her back, the aching sweetness of his tone. "Suzy, don't leave me hanging."

"I'd never do that," Susan whispered. "But it's not my fault you didn't keep with my program."

"I wanted to hear you." His words made her heart twist and ache.

Warmth filled her, a shifting in her chest made her aware of her breathlessness. She'd experienced these tumultuous emotions before and wondered if she should worry, if she should step back so she didn't stumble into the chasm of pain that marched along with handing over her heart.

He's not like that. But she didn't know for sure—not yet. The only way she'd know was to take a chance and let her traitorous spirit have the reins. She'd applied to the reality show because she wanted to find love...

Susan removed Mr. Blue and started speaking. "Take your cock in your hand and stroke it. Not the hard strokes you'd usually use. Instead, run your fingers along your shaft with the softer pressure a woman would use." Her inner self snarled at the idea. "Like I'd do it," she amended. "If I were teasing you. Run your fingers up and down again, brushing the tip."

"You're killing me here."

"You're lucky I'm not with you. I might torture you in person. Restrain your hands or blindfold you, so you won't know exactly what I'm gonna do next."

"We could try that some time. I'm happy as long as I get to try my ideas too."

A laugh bubbled from her. He was thinking of the future, their future. "Do you want to come or not?"

"My balls are turning blue, and that's only a good thing if you're a male baboon."

"You keep interrupting."

"I like talking with you."

And she liked him way too much, considering the obstacles. "I want you to grip your cock hard now and pretend you're buried deep inside me. You can feel the heat of my channel, even through the condom. You pull out and plunge back inside. The slick walls tease your cock. Can you feel how close you are? The tight pressure in your sac? How you feel as if you might explode in the next stroke?"

"Yes," he hissed.

"You pull back to take the final stroke, part of you wanting to go slow while the rest of you wants to pound into me. Which is it going to be?"

"Hard," he whispered.

"Feel my body quivering, ready to take you. I lift my hips, changing the angle for you to make the final stroke. Just perfect," she whispered. "Pound into me. Take what you need, Tyler. Take me."

Tyler's hard groan filled her bedroom, so loud Susan's gaze zapped to the door. Then there was silence. "Tyler?"

"I'm here," he said. "But for a moment I thought this was a near-death experience."

"I wish I was there."

"I wish you were too." Regret laced his voice. "If you feel up to a walk, there's a dam on the boundary. We could meet."

"Okay." Meeting was a bad idea, but she had to see him or she'd go crazy. "When will we go for dinner?"

"I'll ring you tomorrow. Are you filming tomorrow?"

"Yes, we're going into Clare with your mother. Something about volunteer work and how Nolan's wife needs to take an active part in the community."

"You don't like helping?"

"I've done a lot of charity work in the past. No, that doesn't bother me, but meeting your mother again—that's the part that makes me nervous."

"I don't blame you," Tyler said. "Josie says I should face off with her, but honestly, it's more peaceful and less stressful for all concerned if I turn my back and pretend she's not there."

"It can't be easy having your parents write you off because of a youthful mistake."

"I have Josie and Eric in my corner. The way I see it, they're my parents."

She nodded even though he couldn't see her sympathy. "My mother and sisters are supportive of everything I do. Even though they thought I was crazy for telling my fiancé to take a hike, they stood at my side."

"What did he do?"

"Slept with my best friend. They got married and divorced about a year after their wedding."

"Sounds as if you were well rid of him."

"Yeah. What about your wife?"

Tyler's voice drifted in and out, as if he were resettling his pillows. "Rebecca didn't like living in Clare. She wanted to move back to Auckland after Katey was born but didn't handle the responsibilities of having a baby well. She cried a lot and left me and Josie to deal with Katey. I knew it was best to stay here even though it wasn't our original plan.

Our marriage..."

"We don't have to talk about it," Susan said. *She wanted to live in Auckland too.*

"No, Suzy. I want you to know."

"Suzy?" She laughed at the nickname. No one had ever given her one before.

"Suzy is the part of you who is brave and funny and strives for what she wants."

"Thanks." His words sent pleasure swirling, made her realize how far she'd come in the last year. Heck, she actually liked herself.

"You're welcome. Our marriage didn't have a chance after Katey came along. We argued about leaving Clare. Katey mightn't have been planned but I fell in love with her pretty quickly. For her sake, we needed to stay with Eric and Josie. We needed their support."

"What happened?"

"Rebecca stayed. We argued a lot and were both miserable. Rebecca seemed to be depressed and lost a lot of weight. Josie and I finally persuaded her to see a doctor. They did a heap of tests and diagnosed cancer."

"I'm sorry."

"Me too," he said. "She was so young."

And so was he to go through a tragedy like that. His words also cemented his bond with Josie and Eric in her mind, the painful path of her thoughts stripping away some of her good mood. "It's getting late."

"Yeah, I have an early start tomorrow. Will you meet me by the dam?"

"I'll text you once I know if I can get away."

"I look forward to it," he said. "Goodnight, sweetheart."

"Goodnight." Susan forced herself to cut the connection and switch off the light. If only it were that easy to stop her mind and heart from conjuring a bright, shiny future with the wrong man.

CHAPTER TEN

SUSAN STACKED THE BREAKFAST dishes into the dishwasher, trying not to let resentment dampen her mood.

Jasmine and Lucy sat at the table with Nolan and the cameraman, enjoying a second cup of coffee and discussing the upcoming day. A persistent drizzle clattered against the iron roof, the gray sky and dull landscape paralleling her worsening disposition. If this rain continued, there was no way she'd manage a clandestine meeting with Tyler.

A black truck rolled to a stop outside the kitchen door, its mud-splattered appearance typical of the farm vehicles she'd seen since her arrival in Clare. A man climbed out of the driver's side and walked around to open the passenger door.

"You have visitors," Susan said and reached for the

empty coffee carafe to put on another pot.

The kitchen door burst open and Nolan's mother stalked inside, a newspaper clutched in her right hand. She scanned the kitchen until her gaze settled on Susan.

"You! How could you betray Nolan in such a public manner?"

The coffeepot wavered in Susan's hand. She turned away and poured cold water into the coffeemaker.

"Don't turn your back on me! I want you to pack your bags and leave."

Susan glared at the cameraman. "Turn that thing off."

"Nope." His smug smile showed beneath the camera. "You signed away your rights and gave me permission to film anything."

"Nothing to stop me leaving." Susan turned to escape the nasty gleam in Mrs. Penrith's eyes.

"Not so fast." Mrs. Penrith caught Susan's arm and tugged her to an abrupt halt. The woman was stronger than she looked, her fingers digging into Susan's biceps.

"Let me go," Susan demanded.

"Mum, what are you doing? Let her go."

"I knew someone with her morals—a stripper—would tow bad gossip to our family. This town. She's tarnished our good name with her presence, and now she's sleeping with Tyler."

"What are you talking about?" Susan demanded.

At the table, Jasmine and Lucy started whispering to

each other.

"Mum," Nolan said. "Susan doesn't know Tyler."

"According to this paper, she does." Satisfaction oozed from Mrs. Penrith's voice. "She spent the weekend with him up in Auckland. Look, it gives all the details here in this article and they say the internet is buzzing with the news this morning."

Someone spilled the beans. It wouldn't be one of her friends—they'd never do that. She rifled through memory files, frantically wondering what to do or say, how to react.

Deny.

Yes. Deny, deny, *deny*.

"I have no idea what you're talking about." Susan rubbed her arm and did her best woman-done-wrong expression.

"Read the newspaper and judge for yourself," Mrs. Penrith snapped, almost flinging the paper at her son.

"I don't have to do anything." Nolan stood. "Dad, did you want to help me check the sheep?"

"Yes, son."

Nolan's father stood inside the door like a timid mouse. Susan hadn't noticed him in all the drama. He turned and left as quietly as he'd entered.

"You tell my son the truth." Mrs. Penrith approached, her gaze stabbing into Susan like pointy daggers.

Time for a strategic retreat. "I'm going for a walk," Susan said.

"But it's raining," the cameraman said.

"You can't run away from the truth," Mrs. Penrith spat.

"The fresh air would be a welcome change," Susan said, swift steps taking her from the kitchen to the privacy of her bedroom.

Inside, she shut the door and leaned against the hard wood while marshaling her thoughts. Someone had blabbed. She sighed and pushed away from the door. Not that it mattered when she'd changed her mind about country living.

A quick glance out the window showed her it was still raining. Too bad. She had a coat and the fresh air might clear her head. She plucked her coat from the wardrobe, and a few minutes later, she was hurrying outside. The second she breathed in cool air, the weight on her shoulders lightened. She turned her face to the sky, letting the drops of rain splatter across her skin, the cool water waking her from her stupor, washing away some of her guilt.

Mrs. Penrith disliked her and intended to lob torpedoes at her head. Maybe she should go home, despite Jennifer's objections and arguments. Gravel crunched underneath her feet with each long-legged stomp.

Unsure of which way to go when she reached the end of the drive, she hesitated then turned right.

Her phone buzzed and she pulled it out of her pocket, trying to shield the screen from the rain. She read the message and some of her irritation faded.

Instead of texting back, she rang Tyler. "Did you know that we're in the newspaper today?"

"Me? Why?"

"Someone saw us together in Auckland. They added two and two and like all mathematicians came up with a creditable answer. They implied I was seeing another man. They said I was cheating on Nolan."

Tyler was silent for a moment. "You are having an affair with me."

"I know, and right now I don't feel good about myself. I stomped out of the house in righteous indignation and now I've no idea where I'm going."

"Which way did you turn coming out of the drive?"

"Right."

"Good choice," he said. "I'll see you in a few."

"Wait—" She muttered a rude word under her breath when Tyler hung up. Sighing, she wiped the screen of her phone and tucked it away in her pocket. Too late to tell Tyler she didn't think it was a good idea for them to hang out—not until the reality show ended.

Susan continued to stomp in her chosen direction, keeping to the shoulder of the road. About five minutes later, a wave caught her attention.

"Over here," Tyler said. "You'll have to climb the fence."

Susan squeezed her body through two sagging wires and stood to right her appearance.

"You're gorgeous." Tyler stepped closer until the distance between them was gone. He stared down at her upturned face and brushed his fingers across her cheek. "I've missed you."

"We shouldn't be doing this, meeting secretly. It's not right." An understatement for sure.

Tyler pulled her against his chest, his comforting touch easing her scattered emotions, her anxiety. "Do you want me to tell Nolan? I can't walk away from you, Susan." His grip on her back tightened to a point shy of pain.

"No, if anyone tells Nolan, it should be me. I keep thinking he won't choose me. Logic tells me that." She pulled back to stare up at him. "I don't understand your brother."

Tyler laughed, the sharp bark full of tension, confusion. "Hell, I don't understand my brother, and we grew up together."

"Doesn't he talk to you either?"

"In a social situation—sure. We'll say hello if we see each other in the street or the pub, but we don't go out of our way to promote contact."

"I'm sorry. I don't want to cause trouble between the two of you. I suppose I could tell Nolan I'm homesick and want to leave."

"No!" Tyler stepped back, breaking the contact between their bodies. "Are you homesick?"

"I miss my friends, my job."

"Would you miss me?"

Yes. "We haven't known each other for long."

"Susan."

"Yes, I'd miss you."

"Thank you. Stay," he said, grasping her hand. "You only have another week."

BRACED FOR FALLOUT ON her return, it took hours for Susan to relax. She interrupted Jasmine and Lucy in a huddle a couple of times, and finally retreated to the kitchen to make dinner.

"I want to interview you on camera about Mrs. Penrith's allegations," the cameraman said on entering the kitchen.

Susan stirred her pan of onions. "No."

"Mrs. Penrith is correct. The forum is full of gossip."

"Leave her alone," Nolan said.

Susan flinched. Bother, she hadn't heard him enter the kitchen.

The cameraman lifted his camera and zoomed in on Nolan. "Don't you want to know if the gossip is true?"

"Susan has said it isn't true, and that's enough for me."

The camera shifted to her, and Susan grasped for innocent-woman-done-wrong. *Please let her pull this off.* Admitting the truth now would mean she'd have to leave. Was it so wrong to want a few more days with Tyler?

"Do you have any comments, Susan?"

Susan lifted her chin and stared into the camera. "No."

And wouldn't that just stir the gossip pot, she thought. Another gross understatement.

THE NEXT FEW DAYS were free of Mrs. Penrith, free of nosy questions, free of drama. While Jasmine and Lucy lazed in bed or visited the local hair salon during the afternoons, Susan took long walks. Apart from helping out with Katey's birthday party—a huge success thanks to Christina's help via Skype—and taking part in the reality show activities, she kept to herself and her thoughts.

Tyler.

She couldn't resist the man. Their snatched meetings, hurried kisses...

Today, the sun fought the cloud cover, piercing the sullen gray to cast bright patches of light on the mud landscape—a decided improvement from the last days of intermittent rain. Susan splashed through a puddle in her new red gumboots—her recent purchase after becoming tired of cold, wet feet and muddy runners.

Laughing, she jumped into the next puddle. The rumble of an approaching vehicle had her scurrying behind a nearby bush. She grasped a branch and let out a yelp when stupid prickles bit into her palm, but maintained her secretive crouch.

"Lucky escape." Her gaze narrowed on the rear bumper of the vehicle. Mrs. Penrith was about to inflict herself on Jasmine and Lucy. No problem for them, since the woman adored both girls, and they liked her back. Stupid rose-tinted glasses.

The growl of the vehicle faded, and Susan rose. A nearby sheep let out a *baa* and Susan's world righted. She might miss the city and her friends, her daily bowl of latte and the local library, but the country had its charms.

Sexy red gumboots.

Cute animals.

Hunky men.

She turned off the road onto the narrow sheep trail that led down the hill to the dam. A fantail flitted around her, snatching up the tiny bugs she disturbed with each step.

Susan spied Tyler first. "Hey."

Nice ass. Very sexy farmers in the country.

He turned, and his welcoming grin pushed her pulse rate up a gear. "I missed you." With two giant steps, he reached her and hauled her into his arms. She clung, glorying in the instant lust, the urgency in his kiss. Passion rolled over her like a wave, dragging her under until every thought, every concern melted away. When Tyler lifted his head, they were both breathing hard. "You're later than usual."

"Your mother decided to visit today. I had to hide behind a bush." She offered her hand palm up. "It bit me with its prickles."

"What bush? There aren't any trees on the road..." He trailed off with a blinding grin. "Did this bush have yellow flowers?"

"Yes."

"That's a gorse bush. The earlier settlers introduced the plants and used them as fencing. Dad likes to keep the old fence, but in most places they're a noxious weed." He examined her hand, grinned again and brushed his lips on the delicate skin of her wrist.

A shiver blasted through her at the touch of his lips, the sensation cavorting at lots of hot spots on the way. "I need to get a sexy outfit that comes with gloves." Who knew hands were erogenous zones?

"Liked that, did you?"

"I like everything you do to me."

"The feeling is mutual." Tyler swung her off the ground. "Like the gumboots."

"Cool, huh? I've no idea what I'll do with them when I go back to Auckland."

"Shush, too much talking." He settled her on her feet next to a blanket. The spot he'd chosen was in the sun, yet protected by trees on three sides. They'd have plenty of warning if someone decided to interrupt their tryst. "Let me see those pretty breasts of yours. I want to watch your nipples pull tight when the winter air hits them."

"Perv."

"When it comes to you—guilty."

Susan kicked off her boots and wriggled out of her clothes. The minute she saw him, her doubts, her insecurities, her guilt sped away on angel's wings. Her blood thickened and pulsed through her veins while his kisses were plain intoxicating. She didn't think when she spent time with Tyler. She just felt.

His cool hands cupped her breasts, his callused fingers following the curve of her bra cup.

"Your hands are cold."

"When I get my mouth on you, you won't feel a thing."

"Promises, promises." Heady desire surged through her, prompting the siren out to play.

"I wish I had time to draw you like this." His gaze lingered on her limbs, the curve of her hips, her breasts. "I'll give it a go from memory."

"I hope no one sees these drawings of yours."

"My eyes only."

Susan dropped onto the blanket, the waterproof undercoating crinkling as she settled her weight. "Undress slow. Do a strip for me." She started humming appropriate strip music.

Tyler's wide grin did things to her insides, heated her sex with a sensual ache. Tiny lines fanned the outer edges of his eyes as his hands worked the buttons on his heavy denim shirt. Slowly, he removed the garment and swiveled his hips in a slow circle.

"Nice."

His shirt landed beside her, and his fingers went to his belt buckle.

She paused her humming. "Unless you're wearing special jeans, you're gonna want to remove your boots first."

"Did I mention we're running against the clock here?"

"No." Disappointment stripped away her smile and brought a halt to her playful hum.

"I'm sorry."

"No, it's not your fault."

Tyler rapidly removed his boots and shucked his jeans and boxer-briefs in one swift move. He grabbed a condom from a pocket and donned it before turning to her. "God, you're so beautiful. I can't believe you're here with me." His kiss grazed her lips, as if he were uncertain and intended to give her time for a rejection.

Their meeting was wrong on so many levels, yet...no, she couldn't turn him away. She couldn't. Her arms wrapped around his neck, drawing their bodies together. Her legs splayed in silent invitation. No foreplay necessary, not when she craved him, thought about him whenever they were apart.

Tyler reached between them and guided his cock into place. She sighed, the pleasure of his initial stroke always so special. Magical. Perfect.

He set up a slow rhythm, pushing into her heat and

retreating while kissing her lips, her throat and pausing occasionally to tease her nipples. Her climax built layer upon layer with each brush of his penis against her clit. Susan lifted her hips into his surges, silently demanding more, but he kept the steady pace, his knowledge of her body guiding his lovemaking.

Finally, the swell of her climax burst over her and she cried out, clinging to Tyler's broad shoulders. *So, so good*.

He powered into her now, each thrust sending another tiny jolt through her vagina. She held him as he shuddered, his groans of pleasure smothered against her neck. Beneath her stroking hand, he trembled.

The elimination would take place tomorrow. Nolan would send her home this time for sure. Mrs. Penrith hated her and made this clear to anyone who asked her opinion.

Susan fought her urge to cry. Tyler...she'd miss him, yet she couldn't stay here either because she'd end up making both of them miserable.

A FEMININE CRY RANG out, jerking Nolan to a surprised halt. Not the normal call he'd hear in the dam paddock. The sultry sob repeated, and this time he caught a flash of movement down by the dam—a pale backside.

"Fuck," he whispered.

He blinked and looked again. No mistake this time.

Nolan sank down and watched. Suspicions flashed through his mind, but he wanted to make sure. His hands clasped his knees, the knuckles bleeding of color.

The couple kissed, the kiss of long-familiar lovers, and his eyes narrowed. The sun scooted behind a cloud, bleaching the day of its warmth.

Fitting.

The man stood and reached out to help up the woman. Soft laughter floated over the gunmetal gray of the dam water. Dark clouds skittered over the sky and the rain started again. Below, the couple scrambled into their clothes and donned coats against the weather.

With one quick embrace, they parted, the woman taking the trail leading to the road while the man, a cheerful whistle floating in his wake, strutted along the path leading to the Murdoch farm.

Tyler and Susan.

His baby brother.

Nolan peeled his cramped hands from his knee, let the blood flow back into his fingers and stood before silently walking down to the dam to open the gate for the cattle.

"You're a depraved woman," Mrs. Penrith snapped.

Same old, same old. Susan ignored the woman's wrath and hung up her coat to dry. During the walk home, she'd tripped on a concealed stick. Her hip ached, mud soaked her clothes. Her mood hovered a hairsbreadth from depression.

Behind Mrs. Penrith, Jasmine and Lucy covered their mouths, their eyes dancing with mirth—a warning of a storm set to land at her expense.

Susan's shoulders slumped. "I'm going to have a bath."

"What have you to say for yourself?"

"Nothing," Susan said, too miserable to whip up her temper.

The cameraman appeared behind Jasmine and Lucy, the smirk beneath the camera casing alerting Susan that Mrs. Penrith wasn't talking general depravity. Something specific had rattled the woman's cage.

Too bad she didn't care.

Susan turned away, ignoring Elizabeth Penrith's rising squawks. Susan grabbed her robe from behind her bedroom door and headed for the bathroom.

Mrs. Penrith followed her. "I should have known you'd be one of *those* girls."

Susan shut the bathroom door in her face and shot the lock.

"I'm not finished."

Too bad. Susan ran a hot bath and stripped off her clothes, prodding at her hip. Sore, but she'd live. She had a tub of arnica rub. Susan sank into the bathwater, letting the heat soak into her aches and drive away her encompassing chill.

Half an hour later, she limped into the kitchen and started to make a pot of peppermint tea.

"What's wrong with you?" the cameraman asked.

Susan eyed his camera with foreboding. "It's slippery out there. I tripped and took a fall."

"You okay?"

"Bruised hip and battered pride," she said. "Want a cup of tea?"

"I don't want any of that herbal shit."

"There are some English Breakfast teabags."

"Thanks," the cameraman said. "Milk and—"

"Two sugars," Susan finished. The murmur of feminine voices came from the lounge and Susan glanced in that direction. "Care to give me a heads-up on what's jabbing Mrs. Penrith in the arse?"

"Nope." The instant smirk sparked humor in the cameraman's brown eyes.

"Joy," Susan said, her tone dry enough for him to bark out a laugh.

"It would be better if you got the full impact." This time he sniggered.

"There you are, you hussy," Mrs. Penrith shrieked.

The outer door opened and shut. A coat rustled, and Nolan entered the kitchen.

"Nolan, she has to go home," Mrs. Penrith ordered. "She lacks moral fortitude."

Susan made another mug of tea and handed it to Nolan. "Thanks."

"Nolan!"

Nolan glared at his mother. "I heard you the first time. I'd also like to point out this is my home. If you want to rant and rave, you can do it at your place. I moved here to escape arguments and screaming matches."

"There's no need to air our private affairs." Mrs. Penrith sent an uneasy glance at the camera.

Nolan snorted. "I'm sure every family owns dirty laundry."

"But, Nolan, you don't know what she's like," Mrs. Penrith said, her glance at Susan full of spite.

"Oh, I have a pretty good idea."

Something in his tone dragged Susan's focus to him. It wasn't what he said, but the slight inflection. Her stomach hollowed out, and she felt the need to sit. Instead, she picked up her cup of tea and leaned against the kitchen counter.

"I've done everything asked of me," Susan said.

Mrs. Penrith snorted. "You grab attention from the other girls with your unguarded tongue and your controversial blog entries. You don't give the other girls a chance to shine. But that's not all."

Susan tensed at the malice in the older woman. She worked hard to be a better person, and while she didn't always succeed, at least she tried. This woman did her best to make people miserable.

"Spit it out, Mum," Nolan said in a tired voice. "We're not going to get any peace until you've accused Susan to her face."

Fear swelled in Susan as she glanced at Nolan. Her attention shifted to the cameraman who was recording the entire scene. Did Mrs. Penrith know about her and Tyler in truth? It wouldn't be the end of the world, but she might land in trouble with Jennifer.

"Look at this." Mrs. Penrith produced a sealed plastic bag and held it up like a courtroom specimen.

Susan stared.

Everyone else stared.

A blush sneaked up Susan's neck, crashing over cheeks and heating her face. She was not going to apologize. *She would not*. "It's a vibrator. Mr. Blue," she added. "Is there any reason in particular why you felt the need to search my personal belongings?"

"Don't try to shift the conversation, you hussy! A proper girl wouldn't consider bringing one of these into Nolan's house."

"That's enough," Nolan snapped. "Give it back to Susan."

"But...but..." Mrs. Penrith stuttered. She recovered quickly, drawing herself up. "What sort of girl has...has...things like that?"

"Enough." Susan held out her hand. "I'm not going

to apologize for packing my vibrator. Jasmine and Lucy probably have one too, but they weren't clever enough to bring theirs with them." Susan drew a breath, beating down the urge to say more.

"Despicable," Mrs. Penrith said.

Susan failed, words spitting from her like machine-gun bullets. "Doctors invented vibrators to cure hysteria. Maybe you should have a treatment. It might cure your viperous tongue." She snatched the plastic bag from Mrs. Penrith and marched from the kitchen, escaping the heavy, pulsing silence.

In her bedroom, she chucked Mr. Blue at the wall in lieu of howling. Her hands shook as she cradled her mug of tea, the peppermint fumes doing nothing to aid her state of mind.

Well, no doubt about who would head home after the filming tonight. But surely they wouldn't show this segment on public television? A groan escaped. Of course they would. Once the show ran, viewers would fall over themselves to discuss Mr. Blue.

THE LOCAL PUB WAS packed when Susan followed Nolan, Lucy and Jasmine inside. A rock band from nearby Napier belted out cover songs and sang about hungry hearts. How long would it take for the latest juicy rumor to spread? No doubt it would grow in absurdity, taking off like Chinese whispers as it ranged from person to person.

"Would you like to dance?" Nolan asked.

Surprise struck Susan at the same time it hit Jasmine and Lucy. "Sure."

She refused to apologize for a healthy sex drive. Surely that was a good thing. Certainly better than jumping from bed to bed in order to cure an itch. "I'm sorry if I've created friction between you and your mother." *Dang it*. She hadn't meant to do that. Hadn't meant to apologize when she wasn't the one at fault.

But she was guilty. Her inner self lashed out with a brutal kick to remind her of her culpability.

"It's all right," Nolan said. "Mum had no business poking around in your room. She won't be coming to the house again, not without my direct invitation."

Susan nodded. Too little, too late. Nolan should have stood up to his mother years ago and then she wouldn't be shoving her nose into his personal life. Not that it was any of her business. It wasn't as if she'd have to deal with Mrs. Penrith again.

The music came to a halt.

"I'd better go and grab one of the other girls to dance," Nolan said.

"I'll see you later in the private function room."

This time he nodded, a curt jerk of his head before he strode away. Susan frowned after him. A hum of chatter rose and swelled over to her right.

Mrs. Penrith.

Susan stomped rapidly in the other direction, glad she'd donned a simple pair of black trousers and a tunic top rather than her good dress that would have restricted her freedom and consigned her to high heels. Instead she wore a pair of boots, which aided her quick getaway.

A glass of wine. That would steady her nerves, make her forget the X painted on her back. And it would give her something to do with her hands.

She made for the bar.

"Squeeze in beside me," a blonde woman said.

"Thanks." Susan waited for judgment.

It didn't come.

Instead, the woman smiled. "I hear you've had quite a day."

Susan wrinkled her nose. "Which is why I'm desperate for a drink. I'm Susan, in case you didn't already know. Are you a local or are you one of the many press who've suddenly decided I'm fatally interesting?"

The woman shook her head, and her blonde curls swayed with the movement. She held out her hand while Susan waited for bar service. "I'm Yvonne, and I've lived here for a few months now. My aunt owns the local bookstore—the one with the café—and I help her out."

Susan noticed Yvonne's almost empty wine glass. "What are you drinking? Sav Blanc or Chardonnay?"

"The house Sav," Yvonne said. "It comes from one of the local vineyards."

"I might as well buy a bottle. *Ooh*, look! There's a table. Grab it and we can sit together—that's if you're willing to risk it. I am a fallen woman. The jury is out, but I hear it might be catchy."

Yvonne barked out a laugh and slid off her bar stool. "I'm divorced with children. I believe I hit the floor before you."

"Ah, thanks for breaking my landing. Since we have so much in common, would you like to share my bottle of wine?"

A strange expression flickered across Yvonne's face, but after a brief hesitation, she smiled—a friendly one without barbs. "That would be lovely. If I sit alone, the local men think they need to keep me company. In return, they expect fringe benefits."

"*Ugh*. Be there to save you in a moment," Susan said.

A few locals whispered behind their hands when Susan joined Yvonne. Susan ignored their rudeness.

"I think I walked past your aunt's store the other day when I came to town to buy a pair of gumboots. There was a queue out the door, so I figured you must serve good coffee."

"You should have come inside. My aunt makes really good blueberry muffins and delicious cheese scones. She loves to bake, but hates serving customers. This works for both of us, because after spending a lot of time with my kids, I need adult conversation."

"That's what my friend Julia says. You need a balance, otherwise it's easy to drift into crazy."

Susan poured wine for Yvonne and sloshed some into her own glass. "Are people staring?"

"A little. The people who live in Clare are mostly nice and supportive. They're only gossiping because Mrs. Penrith is stirring them up with a big, ole wooden spoon."

The nuances in Yvonne's tone snapped up Susan's head. She eyed the woman closely. "You've had a run-in with her too."

Yvonne pulled a quick face. "I went out with Nolan a couple of times. She didn't think I was a suitable girlfriend candidate."

"Nolan needs to grow a spine."

"Not my problem," Yvonne said.

Susan sipped her wine, taking in the other woman's body language—her careless shrug and the contrasting tremor of her hand. The giveaway signs were subtle and most people wouldn't notice.

"Ladies," a masculine voice said.

Susan tipped back her head and smiled. Probably a bad move, but she couldn't resist the naughty twinkle in Tyler's eyes. "Is Josie babysitting tonight?"

"She volunteered. Hi, Yvonne. How are you?" He brushed a friendly kiss on the other woman's cheek and a sliver of jealousy pierced Susan.

The touch of envy was still throbbing through her when Tyler pulled up a seat. "I hope you don't mind me joining you."

"Of course not," Yvonne said. "David and Michael had a lovely time at Katey's birthday party. Did you do the face painting?"

"Yes, I had as much fun as the kids."

The two discussed their children and the party, and Susan started to feel left out, even though she'd attended. A local man asked her to dance, and she stood with alacrity. Yvonne was a nice woman—the type of woman Tyler should hook up with. Someone who had interests in common. Children. Roots in a community.

When she returned from the second dance, Nolan sat with Tyler and Yvonne.

"Ah, there you are," Nolan said. "I wondered where you'd disappeared. I was just telling Tyler and Yvonne about Mr. Blue." His lips quivered while he fought his amusement.

"Did you have to?"

"I can't believe she went through your stuff," Tyler said, indignant on Susan's behalf.

"You're lucky Mum didn't decide to follow Susan on her walks," Nolan said. "Yvonne, would you like to dance?" He held out his hand when she hesitated while Susan stared at him in horror.

Had Nolan seen them together?

Susan waited until Nolan and Yvonne were safely on the dance floor before leaning toward Tyler. "What did he mean? Do you think he knows something?"

"He would have said," Tyler said.

"I keep telling you he's not interested in me. He displayed more interest in Yvonne than he shows to me."

"They dated a couple of times."

"So she said." But maybe Nolan was playing games with everyone. She turned on her seat to search out Nolan on the dance floor. "Those two are more than friends."

"They're not even touching each other."

"Tyler, we don't touch each other when we're together in a public place. It's what they're not doing that tells the story." And the way Nolan looked at the blonde woman when he didn't think anyone was watching. She recognized the quick glance for what it was because that was how she studied Tyler.

"Maybe." He stood. "Dance with me." He leaned closer under the pretext of not having to shout against the music. "Give me a reason to touch you."

"You're always touching me."

"Not enough for my liking," he whispered and drew her to the crowded dance floor.

At first she struggled to keep a respectable distance from Tyler. Impossible with the force of the bodies, all seeking to squeeze into the limited space. Finally, she gave up, plastered a friendly grin on her lips and rested against him.

Like most people around them, they swayed on the spot.

"Stop copping a feel."

His hands whisked over her butt again, drawing their lower bodies together. "But it's so much fun." His warm breath tickled her ear, transmitting hot, lustful messages where they had no business traveling—especially in a public place.

When the song ended, she pulled away and fought fluster. "Thank you for the dance." If all else failed, she'd resort to the polite niceties drummed into her by her mother.

"My pleasure." A wicked light shone in his eyes, the curve of his mouth lifting in an uptick of amusement. "Any time."

"Susan, it's time to head to the function room." Nolan stood with Yvonne at his side, both studiously ignoring the other.

"It was lovely to meet you, Yvonne," Susan said.

"Drop by the bookstore. I'll buy you a coffee," Yvonne said.

Susan didn't think she'd still be here to visit Yvonne. Despite her doubt, she smiled and nodded. "I'd like that."

Nolan trailed Susan as she wove through the crowd to the function room.

"Good luck, Susan," one of the guys from the Clare rugby team shouted.

"Yeah!" another man called.

Nolan caught his mother's glare and grinned inwardly. She'd rung him earlier. He'd taken great pleasure in hanging up on her. Then he'd left the phone off the hook and switched off his cell.

Ignoring his mother had felt really good.

He spotted his father standing with his friends and stopped to say hello. "Hey, Dad."

"Son." His father leaned close. "You should choose the girl with the vibrator."

"Mum told you about that, did she?"

"Oh yeah. I got an earful during the ride here." His father grinned. "I like a girl with a spine. Makes me want to be a better man."

Nolan nodded because he understood what his father meant. "See you in the morning."

"Son?"

"Yeah, Dad?"

"I'm going to move out of the house. Your mother refuses to give me a divorce, but I don't have to live with her in misery."

Nolan blinked. His father had gone and got some balls. "Is there someone else?"

"No. There was a long time ago, when you were ten. I wasn't brave enough to walk away from my marriage. I need to talk to Tyler. Do you know where he is?"

"Over there with Yvonne." Nolan's stomach sank at the

admission.

"We'll talk tomorrow. Good luck with the filming, son."

Nolan gave his father a curt nod and sauntered to the function room. He smiled at everyone who thought he needed advice, but he knew exactly what he had to do.

CHAPTER ELEVEN

"ARE YOU GOING HOME?" Tyler paced the confines of his bedroom, his phone glued to his ear. The idea of Suzy leaving had him dragging his hand through his hair. Damn, his bloody hand was shaking.

"I'm not meant to tell you."

"Please, put me out of my misery." Tyler strode from his bed to the door and back, his nerves not allowing him to stand in one spot.

"Jasmine is going home."

Elation soared then plummeted to the bottom of his gut. "Nolan picked you."

"Yeah, I'm still in shock. So is Jasmine. She accused me of trading sex for my place on the show."

"You're having sex with me." The possessive nature of the words flooded him with satisfaction. Huh, he was doing a caveman act—doing everything except beating his chest.

"Last night I thought Nolan suspected something." Suzy paused. "I guess I was wrong."

"You think Nolan is serious about you?" *Over his dead body.*

"I don't know what to think."

"Can you meet me tomorrow?"

"I'm sorry. If it's fine tomorrow, we're filming outside. The cameraman wants some farm scenes."

"We haven't had our date yet," Tyler said. "Are you free tomorrow night?"

"The drive-thru isn't on until the weekend."

"No, wait. The show is tomorrow. I want to watch it. Friday night," he said. "I'll ring Nolan and ask him myself."

THE NEXT DAY

"Do you know who Nolan picked?" Josie settled on the couch beside Tyler.

"Yes." Tyler drummed his fingers on his thigh and waited for the reality show to start.

"Is it the same girl you're meeting most days down by the dam?" Eric said.

Tyler's fingers stilled. "I don't know what you're talking about."

"*Ooh*, he's good," Josie said to her husband. "Just the right edge of innocence and surprise. If I didn't know him well, I'd think we were way off beam with our assumptions."

"Katey likes her. So do we," Eric said.

"Nolan likes her too," Tyler snapped.

"But you're the one she visits in secret," Josie said.

"I don't want to sneak around. I don't like it."

"So you are serious about the girl," Eric said with a healthy slice of satisfaction.

"The show is starting," Tyler said. "From what Suzy says, we don't want to miss a thing." Eric and Josie exchanged a knowing glance, and even the fact they knew the truth didn't settle the angst riding his gut. He needed to see, to hear what Nolan said on the show, how he worded his picks.

"Welcome to the knockout show," Hailee cooed. "It's been a very tense week down on the farm for our contestants and farmers. First, we'll go to Graham in the far south and see which girls he's picked to stay at the farm."

Tyler's fingers started into motion again, impatience fueling his need for movement.

"We like Susan," Josie said.

"So you've said." Tyler's tart reply echoed in the lounge. He sucked in a deep breath. "I'm sorry. That was rude." He plucked his small notebook and pencil from his pocket and started drawing. Instantly, his nerves flowed out of him and a picture of Susan appeared on the page. "I like her too. Very much."

"What are you going to do about it?" Josie demanded. "You can't sit back and let Nolan steal her from under your nose."

"I'm taking her out on Friday night. I called in the date I won."

"Good plan." Eric nodded with approval. "Where are you taking her?"

"I haven't got that far yet. I rang Nolan and asked him if I could take Susan out," Tyler said.

Josie and Eric gaped at him.

"You look like a pair of fish," Tyler said.

"What did Nolan say?" Eric asked.

"Nothing. What could he say? I won the date fair and square."

"Take the entire day," Josie suggested. "Pick her up in the morning and go to Napier. Show her the art deco buildings and go to a vineyard for lunch. Go for a walk on the beach after your meal."

"Stay the night somewhere in Napier," Eric said. "Make it a real event."

Tyler felt his mouth drop open.

"What?" Eric said. "You like the girl. You're sleeping with her, aren't you?"

Josie let out a girlish giggle and winked at her husband.

"Good plan. We'll babysit."

Tyler let their teasing wash over him this time. They weren't going to leave it alone. "I'm not sure Suzy will agree to staying out for the entire night."

"Ask her," Eric said. "She can only say no."

"Shush, Nolan's segment has started," Josie said.

"Life is never boring with Nolan's women," Hailee said. "We never know what to expect and this week was no exception. At the end of the show, we're going to place a special poll on the website to learn about popular opinion on a certain subject, so make sure you visit and have your say."

"That sounds intriguing," Josie said.

The show cut to an interview with Nolan. His big brother appeared at ease in front of the camera, his mouth quirked into a tiny smile.

"What is your ideal woman like?" the cameraman asked.

"I want someone who loves the land and the countryside as much as I do," Nolan said. "I can't imagine not living here in Clare."

"And what about physical characteristics?"

"Someone who looks after themselves. They don't have to be ultra skinny, but someone who is fit. A woman who is adaptable and possesses a sense of humor."

"You're determined to give a PC answer," the cameraman said. "All right. What color hair do you prefer?"

"Dark," Nolan said.

"Height?"

"A few inches shorter than me. I don't like to get a sore neck."

Tyler's pencil skidded to a halt on the page.

"He's describing Susan," Josie whispered.

"He didn't hesitate saying yes when I asked if I could take Suzy out on our date." Tyler stared at the screen. What the fuck game was his brother playing? "Susan likes Clare, but I think she's missing Auckland and her friends." Which was a problem for him. He couldn't leave Clare, not after Eric and Josie had done so much for him. Eric needed his help on the farm and Katey would start school in a few months.

No, his roots were here in Clare.

Somehow, he'd have to persuade Suzy that life in Clare was an attractive proposition.

The scene changed on the television screen. Eric let out a guffaw.

Tyler found himself grinning. So that was Mr. Blue.

"Oh my," Josie said, her voice emerging in a weird squeak.

On screen, Suzy lifted her chin and squared her shoulders. "Doctors invented vibrators to cure hysteria. Maybe you should have a treatment. It might help your viperous tongue." In the startled silence that followed, she snatched up Mr. Blue and stomped from the room.

"Oh my." Josie flapped her hand in front of her face. "I do like that girl."

The next segment was an interview with Suzy. Tyler stared at her familiar face, his heart aching. Damn, this was one battle he had no intention of losing. His parents might have deserted him, Rebecca hadn't believed in him enough to fight for their marriage, but he didn't intend to fail a third time.

"What happened after you stomped out of the kitchen?" the cameraman asked.

"I had a tantrum and threw Mr. Blue at the wall. He made a dent."

"Damn, I wish I could have filmed that."

"I broke Mr. Blue. If you'd been present, I might have aimed my wrath elsewhere." Suzy stared right into the camera, and Tyler found himself smirking when she didn't blink. "Now I'll have to find a replacement."

"Nolan seems to prefer women with dark hair," the cameraman said, his slyness coming through in his tone as he shifted topic. "You might have the real thing soon."

"Mr. Blue didn't try to boss me around," Suzy snapped, her cheeks full of color and her eyes flashing. "He did exactly what I wanted."

Tyler couldn't help but stare because she was beautiful in her anger. He made a mental note to go shopping online for more sex toys. He'd had a couple of things delivered already. A vibrator would make a great addition. His lips curled as he fought a smirk. He was man enough to cope with a faux penis.

"You go, Suzy," Josie said in approval.

"Hey," Eric said, but he was grinning.

The camera flashed back to Nolan, who was now with Suzy and the other two women.

"I had a big problem narrowing my choice down to two women," Nolan said. "Jasmine, Lucy and Susan are wonderful and they all possess qualities I admire in a woman. Jasmine has a sense of humor and loves family. She enjoys the country and likes animals. Lucy also has a great sense of humor. She gets on well with my family and friends and enjoys living in the countryside. Susan is funny and makes me laugh. She's also a great cook and is always helping others." Nolan patted his tummy. "She's a really good cook."

"We'll have Nolan's results after a word from our sponsors," Hailee said in her bubbly voice-over from the studio.

"I can't stand the suspense," Josie said. "Does he pick Suzy?"

Tyler gave a curt nod, heartsick at the acknowledgment.

"Damn." Eric sent Tyler a sympathetic look, his brow furrowed. "If that's the case, then why did Nolan agree to let you go on a date with her?"

"I didn't give him an option," Tyler said. "I told him if he didn't permit our date I'd create a ruckus like he hadn't seen since our mother kicked me out of home."

"Go you," Josie said, her eyes containing pride and approval.

The show started again.

"Please tell us your two choices," the cameraman said to Nolan.

"As I said this was a difficult task, but after weighing the pros and cons, I decided to pick Lucy and Susan."

The camera moved to Jasmine and caught her flash of disappointment, the slap of rejection. Tyler's stomach flip-flopped in sympathy. He knew exactly how she felt.

EACH SHOW I THINK my embarrassment levels can't get any higher. Big time mistake! I don't think I'll be able to look anyone in the face again. Actually, I'm surprised Nolan picked me after the dramatics I've brought to his life. Not that I'm going to apologize for being myself.

If anything, this latest debacle with Nolan's mother has made me take a good hard look at myself.

I have a great circle of friends, but not so long ago, I almost destroyed that friendship by judging a friend and finding her guilty of breaking a stupid rule. A part of it was jealousy.

I wanted what she'd found—a happy relationship.

My love life prior to this show wasn't inspiring. Try learning that your bridesmaid is having an affair with your fiancé. That was only one blip. I started dating another man months later. The relationship was serious on my side and I was ready to take the next step. Then I discovered he was married, and I was his patsy—an innocent bit on the side for his amusement. Those two relationships warped my thinking, and I held myself and others to high standards. I became judge and jury.

Anyone seeing a theme here?

Mrs. Penrith doesn't approve of me. That's fine with me. It would be a boring world if people came with one character setting. But where I have a problem is when she tries to hold me to the standard of behavior that she perceives is correct.

If I've learned anything in the last couple of years, it's that you should treat others as you would have them treat you. The saying about what goes around comes around is a cliché for a reason.

When my high and mighty attitude almost ruined my friendships, I took a good, hard look at myself. I didn't like what I saw, and I've since made a conscious effort to become a better person. Some people might say that my friend let me off lightly. Heck, she did. She accepted my apology and we moved on. I think we're all closer now because of it, and I know better than to judge anyone.

Individuals are responsible for their own behavior. For all the Farmer Seeks a Wife *fans out there who are reading this blog, put yourself in others' shoes before you react in a manner that might damage a close friendship, a marriage. We all make mistakes. It's a human trait. It's how we make amends or try to improve that makes us special.*

Love Susan

P.S. Interesting poll results on Mr. Blue. I'm glad you guys are on my side!

This blog entry might come across as preachy, and to some, it might feel as if she was making a dig at Mrs. Penrith. Newsflash. Of course she was, but she was also sincere in what she said. If she hadn't done a swift turnaround in her attitude, she wouldn't have the great friendships she had now. She'd acted like a sanctimonious twit back then, and Maggie had been so nice, accepting her apology when Susan had acted the bitch, kicking Maggie in the teeth when she'd been at a low point in her life.

No longer.

She'd changed and no way would she let herself slide into another pair of judgmental shoes. And she wouldn't put up with people like Mrs. Penrith telling her what to do or how to act.

Someone knocked on her door. "Susan."

It was Nolan. "Come in."

"Tyler asked if it were okay for him to take you out tomorrow." A flicker in his expression snagged her attention, made her look closer. He leaned his weight against the door jamb.

"You don't want me to go?"

"No, it's okay. He won a date with you." He hesitated. "I wanted to make sure it was okay with you. He said he hadn't asked you yet."

Susan frowned. "Why wouldn't it be okay?"

"No reason." His shoulders lifted in a kind of a half shrug. "I...um...wanted to apologize for my mother. Her behavior toward you has been disrespectful. I should have put a stop to it earlier instead of letting her trample your feelings."

"Don't forget the pawing through my belongings part and her bad-mouthing me all over town."

His brows drew together, his cheeks turning ruddy. "Yes, that too. It's unforgivable."

"Why do you let her carry on that way? She walks over everyone, bossing them around and telling them what to do. She's horrible to your father."

"She might try to tell me what to do, but I don't always listen," Nolan said. "My dad said he's moving out. Their marriage has been over for years—for as long as I can remember. I didn't think he'd ever have the balls to leave." The last was said with a sense of puzzlement. "He wants to talk to me and to Tyler. He never says more than a few words to Tyler."

Susan cocked her head, curious despite herself. "Do you know what he wants to talk about?"

"No idea. I guess we'll find out." Nolan pushed off the jamb. "Do you like my brother?"

Susan blinked and felt heat steal into her cheeks. "He seems very nice." *Ooh, very prim and proper.*

"I haven't been the brother I should be. I aim to change that." He left abruptly, disappearing down the passage.

Susan stared at the gap where Nolan had stood, confusion settling on her shoulders like a heavy bale of hay. All the subtext, the hidden messages. Maybe Tyler would understand because she didn't know what was going on with Nolan. One minute she thought he knew about her and Tyler and the next she didn't know what she thought.

The phone rang in the kitchen.

"Susan, the phone is for you," Lucy called. "Some guy."

"It's probably Tyler," Nolan said when Susan entered the kitchen. "I wonder if Dad caught up with him."

Susan picked up the phone. "Tyler?"

"Hey, Suzy. Are you free tomorrow? I'd like to take you

out. I thought we could go wine tasting and maybe do a little sightseeing in Napier."

"I'd love to."

"Good, can you be ready around eleven? I'll pick you up."

"Sure, I look forward to it."

Nolan signaled that he wanted to talk to Tyler and she handed over the phone. She heard Nolan mention their father before she went to her room.

Tyler arrived on time the next day, and with a cheery goodbye to Nolan and Lucy, she slipped outside.

"Did you catch up with your father?" she asked when she jumped into the passenger seat.

"He rang just as I was leaving. I told him I'd visit him tomorrow."

"You don't see him often."

"No, usually only when I go into town or attend a sale. Ask Nolan. The atmosphere at home was always like Antarctica and university was like a warm haven. No more talking about the past." He sent her a quick smile. "I don't want to spoil our day."

"Did Nolan act strange when you spoke to him?"

Tyler scowled. "He told me to make sure I didn't hurt you, which made no bloody sense. My entire family is acting weird. Eric told me I should keep you out overnight. He practically ordered me to have a sleepover. Not that I dislike the idea..." He trailed off, his dark brows waggling.

She gasped. "They know?"

"I didn't tell them. They guessed we're seeing each other." He shrugged. "No problem. Today, I thought we'll do the sightseeing part first and have a late lunch. I know a great picnic spot where we can relax if the weather stays fine."

"Are they going to tell anyone?"

Tyler shot her a surprised glance. "Of course not. They'd never do anything to hurt me and by extension you." He reached over and placed a hand on her knee. "Don't worry. Please, just enjoy the day. We have the entire afternoon to have fun, and for once we don't have to sneak around."

Tyler was right. Slogging down to the dam, through the mud and rain to meet with him got old, and the worry about someone catching them kept her awake. Score one for a guilty conscience.

Tyler was also right about enjoying the day. "Tell me about the art deco buildings."

"You know about the earthquake we had down here in 1931. Most of Napier was destroyed in the quake and the resulting fire afterward. When the townsfolk wanted to rebuild, they chose the art deco style because it was cheaper and the buildings were strong. The buildings are cool. I've sketched quite a few of them. I'll show them to you when we get back to Clare."

Half an hour later, Tyler parked the car. They purchased a local guidebook and started doing a self-guided walk around the blocklike buildings. Susan kept busy with her camera, snapping photos of the art deco designs on the facades, the straight lines of the buildings and some of Tyler, handsome in his light blue shirt and jeans, his black vest cutting the cool air of the winter day.

"This is great. I'll post some pictures on my blog tomorrow." The instant she mentioned her blog, Tyler's smile faded and she silently cursed—she who seldom uttered a naughty word. Instead of driving her to drink, the Penrith family was responsible for coloring her language blue. She reached out, placed her hand on Tyler's forearm and gave a reassuring squeeze. "I'm sorry. What say we make a deal—no more talking about anything related to the reality show for the rest of the day?"

She needed to tell him Jennifer had decided to change the filming schedule. Both she and Lucy were going home in a few days. On Tuesday, to be precise. She opened her mouth to tell Tyler but changed her mind. She didn't want to spoil their day. She'd tell him when he dropped her back at Nolan's.

"Deal," he said. "Would you like to have a coffee?"

"Hot chocolate," she said. "With chili, if possible. I like it hot."

His gaze went straight to her lips. "Me too."

Laughing, she tucked her arm in his, and they entered the nearby café, coming face-to-face with Yvonne.

"Susan," Yvonne said, her smile pleasant and welcoming

until she spotted Tyler. "Tyler." Her voice flattened with disapproval when she spied their linked arms.

Susan thought about jumping into explanations, even opened her mouth to blurt out one before she relaxed. She had nothing to be guilty about.

"I'll order our drinks," Tyler said and left the two women together, an awkward silence between them.

"Well, I'd better get moving. My aunt is taking care of the store on her own while I complete errands. She's likely to bark at the customers and drive them off." Yvonne half turned away.

"I'll make sure I stop by before the final filming. I'd love to see you before I go home."

Yvonne turned back to her. "You're going home?"

Bother, she hadn't meant to blurt the info out. "Early next week. This morning they decided to film a final show at home since both Lucy and I are from Auckland. Nolan will fly up and visit his chosen woman."

Yvonne wavered on her feet, her face leaching of color.

"Are you all right?"

"I...I'm fine," Yvonne whispered. "I...I'd better go." She fled the café and Susan watched her race around the corner and out of sight.

"I thought you said Nolan and Yvonne only dated casually," she said when Tyler joined her at a table by the window.

"They did, as far as I know. They're just friends."

"I think there's more. They both acted a bit weird the other night at the pub and now, Yvonne practically ran away when I mentioned Nolan."

"I don't want to talk about my brother."

An elderly lady carried over their hot chocolates and set them on the table.

"Thanks," Susan said.

"You're Susan from the television," the woman said. Her gaze darted to Tyler and her eyes narrowed. "This isn't your farmer."

"No," Susan said. "This is my friend." She wasn't about to explain to a stranger. She met the woman's accusing gaze without faltering and finally the woman muttered something under her breath and stomped away. The minute she rounded the counter, she started whispering to her fellow server. "I'm starting to understand Ryan and Caleb a bit more."

"What?"

"Nothing," Susan said and she picked up her mug. The rich scent of chocolate filled her nostrils and she closed her eyes to indulge her senses. Her first sip had her giving an appreciative sigh. "That is delicious. Do you like it?" Her eyes popped open when Tyler didn't reply.

His pencil raced across the page of a battered notebook—the one he carried with him everywhere.

"Are you drawing me again?" Faint exasperation rippled through the air. "I'm starting to get a complex."

"You're my inspiration." He leaned closer. "I'd love to paint you. I'd paint you sprawled against satin sheets, your hair loose and messy and your lips swollen from a night of passion."

"Shush, someone will hear you." Susan glanced at the cash register and intercepted a scowl from the elderly woman. "I should have brought a hat and sunglasses." The reality show wouldn't leave her alone.

"We can buy you a hat," Tyler said.

"Done deal. That can be our next stop."

With her new hat firmly in place, Susan followed Tyler around the rest of the buildings, taking more photos to remember the day.

"Are you ready to taste our local wines?"

"Lead the way." *His local wines,* Susan thought. Leaving the town of Clare and Tyler was going to be hard. Really hard.

"I know the owners of this vineyard since I went to school with them in Clare. I thought I'd ask them to pack us a picnic lunch, and we'll stay away from people."

"Good idea." No wonder Ryan and Caleb's band had decided to use stage makeup. People intruding and butting into personal moments made her edgy.

While Tyler rounded up a picnic lunch, Susan started tasting wines, working her way from white to the reds.

"This is our Pinot Noir," the woman dispensing wines said. "It tastes of plums and summer sunshine. There are also layers of rich chocolate. Do you taste them?"

"Nice," Susan said, after taking a sip. "I need to take one of everything."

The woman laughed. "Good, my job is done."

"Do you ship to Auckland?"

"We ship worldwide."

"Great. I'll take six bottles of the Pinot Noir and six bottles of your Sauvignon Blanc, please." She handed over her credit card. "Oh, I'll take a bottle of the Sav now. No, make that two."

"No problem," the woman said. "I'll need you to complete this form with your name and delivery address."

"I'm sorry I took so long," Tyler said, curving his arm around her waist. "Marissa wanted to catch up on the news." He lifted the picnic basket in his other hand. "We're all set."

"Your friend has a great vineyard. The wines are excellent."

"You should receive your wine next week," the woman said.

"Perfect. Thanks for guiding me through the wine list," Susan said. "It was fun."

"You're welcome," the woman said.

Susan turned to Tyler and caught his frown. *Uh-oh*. "What's for lunch and where are we going?"

His frown smoothed away and Susan's panic subsided. Crisis averted. For now. He grasped her hand and led her to the right of the car park.

"Marissa said we can have a picnic on their property. There won't be any interruptions. She said we'll have total privacy."

"Did she ask why you wanted privacy with a woman who's meant to be with another man?"

Tyler grinned at the memory of Marissa's pointed—nah—nosy questions. "She was nosy. She interrogated me, much in the way your friends grilled me when we first met."

Suzy gave a theatrical shudder. "I'm glad I went wine tasting instead."

"Don't worry. She won't spread any vicious rumors."

"Someone is bound to start talking soon," Susan said. "Jennifer said a few papers had contacted her wanting interviews."

Tyler ignored the stab of pain near his heart, shoved aside thoughts of the show, his suspicions that Suzy intended to leave soon. Somehow, he needed to change her mind.

Today, he'd woo her—charm her with his teasing and conversation, feed her soul with delicious food and wine and when she was weak, he'd fuck her so good she'd never consider leaving him again.

Failure was not an option.

Tyler turned down a narrow gravel path and led Suzy to a clearing by a stream. While it was too cold to swim, the clearing was sheltered, and he intended to get Susan naked.

His fingers itched to sketch her with the sunlight and the contrast of shade dappling her body while his cock ached to plunge into her silky depths and pour himself into her until he didn't know where she ended and he began.

As they veered off the path, the traffic noises receded, replaced by the song of a thrush and the occasional guttural gurgle of a native tui.

"Do you know where you're going?"

Tyler glanced over his shoulder. "I think I should be insulted."

"Just checking. I didn't bring my gumboots. If I'd known we were going bush, I would have chucked them in the car."

"It's not much farther." Tyler started walking again, lengthening his stride in eager anticipation. Once the show ended and the publicity died, they'd be able to walk through town without attracting attention.

He burst into the clearing, satisfaction filling him because his memory hadn't played him false. This was the perfect place for seduction.

After turning in a slow circle, he decided on a sunny spot near the water where the ground was fairly dry, despite the recent rain.

"It's lovely," Susan said. "Is that a kauri tree?"

Tyler glanced at the tall, straight trunk of the tree to their right. It seemed to dwarf the other trees in the vicinity and he had to crick his neck in order to glimpse the leaves of the lower branches. "Marissa's grandfather decided to keep some of the native bush instead of clearing the land."

"Wise man."

"Come here." Tyler didn't want to talk about wise men. Already his dick pressed insistently against his fly. "Are you hungry?"

"Not really."

"Great." Tyler opened his wicker basket and pulled out a rug. He spread it on the ground then sat on a corner to pull off his boots. His vest hit the ground near his boots.

Susan let out a croak and he found her staring. Time to up the stakes. His fingers worked the buttons of his denim shirt. He shrugged it off his shoulders and started on his jeans. They slid down his legs with a rasp of fabric while his cock took the opportunity of the extra freedom. By the time, he tugged his boxer-briefs down his legs, he had a fully blown erection.

"What are you waiting for?" His voice was a husky interruption to the silence in the clearing.

Suzy cleared her throat. "Just appreciating the show."

He grasped his dick with his right hand and slowly stroked up and down, teasing himself while watching Suzy closely. The color that flooded her cheeks and screened her freckles told him she wasn't unaffected.

"Strip," he ordered. "I want to bury my cock inside you. Hard and fast until I explode."

Her body jerked at his explicit words.

"I want to hammer into you and take you like a greedy boy having his first experience. I want to suck on those pretty tits of yours and mark you with my mouth." Tyler was the one who shuddered this time. He sought her gaze, her wide eyes. "I want to fuck you, Suzy."

A noticeable tremble shook her hand when she started to remove her clothes and footwear.

"And I want to taste you. I want to fill my mouth with your salty-sweet flavor and tease your clit until you think you're gonna explode." Tyler tugged on his balls to the point of pain, scaring away his impending climax. Not gonna happen. He craved the tight fit of her cushioning his dick. His gaze traveled her naked breasts and followed her jeans as she pulled them down her legs. Tiny black panties were all that remained, guarding her feminine secrets. "I never tire of watching you."

"Likewise."

Tyler grinned. "And speaking of sex, I ordered some toys this week. I thought about bringing them today, but I want a bedroom, guaranteed privacy before I use them."

"What sort of toys?"

He tapped his nose. "That's for me to know and you to wait until I show you."

"Tease."

"Off with the panties, Suzy. I want to see all of you. Good. That's good." He stared at her pussy and gave his balls another scolding tug. "Lie in the middle of the blanket and part your legs for me."

Susan followed his instructions and slowly parted her legs until he could see her slit, the swollen folds of her labia and the glistening honey that told of her arousal.

"Tyler." She held up her arms in invitation, her smile sultry with a solid edge of teasing.

His woman.

Tyler reached for his jeans and pulled out condoms. The way he was feeling right now, he wasn't sure these three would suffice. He crouched between Suzy's parted legs, his gaze stroking her jaw, down her neck and settling on her breasts. The faint chill in the air had already pulled them to tight peaks. He continued his visual journey, taking in her narrow rib cage and the sensual flare of her hips, memorizing every part of her so he could sketch her later while in the privacy of his bedroom.

Unable to resist, he ran a finger down her slit, grazing her hot flesh, then swirling his finger through her arousal. His finger glistened when he lifted it and he held her gaze while he licked her juices away.

"You're teasing me."

"A little. I don't want to hurt you."

"You won't hurt me. I ache here." She cupped her mound.

"Touch yourself while I put on the condom. I want proof that you're ready for me. Suzy, I'm serious. I don't have much willpower right now. I will take you hard."

While he ripped open the foil packet, he watched her finger circle her clit, the way her eyes flickered. Then, as if she'd lost a battle, her eyes closed and she chewed on her bottom lip. She inserted one finger inside while her thumb rode her clit. A rose-colored flush started in her breasts and crept up her neck.

Tyler sucked in a hoarse breath. "Enough." When she was slow to react, he grabbed her hands with his and lifted them to imprison them above her head. Her spicy scent filled every breath, underscored by the earthy smell of the ground and the piquancy of the surrounding trees and plants. Because he could, he kissed her, wild and fast, sliding his tongue against hers and enjoying the hell out of her eager response.

Not wanting to stop, but needing air, he separated their mouths. "I've got to get inside you."

"Tyler."

"God, Suzy. I love it when you say my name like that." He pushed inside her, just his tip and the warmth of her made him gasp. There really was no chance of going slow. He pushed inexorably into her and paused, balls-deep and enveloped in her heat, his chest almost bursting with happiness. This woman—she really did it for him, made him feel whole again after Rebecca.

He pulled back, the muscles of his stomach flexing as she ran her hands over his back and pushed at his fragile control. With every stroke, blood crowded his cock, the sting of her nails drawing a raw groan from deep in his chest.

"Suzy. *Suzy*."

She clutched his shoulders and buried her face at his throat. The warm suction at his neck was like an erotic caress, and he hummed a note of pleasure, not even caring she'd leave an obvious mark that would draw curiosity.

He pulled back, shuddered at the drag along her inner walls and lost hold of his fragile control. He hammered into her, desperate for the rip-roaring climax that only she could provide. Satisfaction swelled inside, his dick throbbing unbearably.

Pleasure. Pain.

The sensations combined until he thought his heart might fail him, then his orgasm stormed him, body and mind. All he could do was hold tight and ride out the passion storm.

Her hands pushing at his chest dragged him from stupor. "Hell, sorry." He pulled out of her and yanked off the condom.

She attracted his attention by yanking on his ears.

"*Ow*, woman. What are you doing?"

"I know the blood hasn't redistributed properly yet, so you're not thinking right." She tugged on his hair this time. "I haven't come. If you don't get me off, an essential part of me might drop off. That would make me grumpy because I like sex, and I love orgasms." She closed her legs in a prim manner.

Tyler stared at her in the seconds it took his brain to function. Humor notched into place next and curled his lips upward. "Can't have that. I wouldn't like any of your bits to drop off." He shoved her legs apart, offering his best pirate grin. "I have treasures to plunder."

Her snort made him chuckle, and the happiness dancing a jig inside him swelled until his chest ached. How was it possible for one man to hold so much joy?

Tyler slipped his hands under her butt and lifted her to his mouth. His inventive licking stopped her complaints dead. She moaned, the long, drawn out sound like heady music to his ears. His precision work on her clit drew another moan. Time to up the pace. He slipped two fingers inside her, stroking over her G-spot. A shudder pierced her tense muscles. *More,* he thought. His tongue circled. The swollen nub pulsed, and when he closed his lips around her clitoris and sucked, she shuddered violently and her vagina clenched around his fingers in rapid pulses.

"Tyler," she whispered.

His name from her lips was the sweetest music ever.

CHAPTER TWELVE

SUSAN STARED OUT THE car window at the rapidly darkening sky. She had to tell Tyler before gossip swept Clare and he learned from another source.

But it was so hard.

Tyler was the man she'd always searched for, possessed the qualities she wanted in a husband.

Yeah, right man. Wrong circumstances.

An ache clamped around her chest and communicated unhappiness to her stomach. Soon her gut churned and not even her hand pressed to her belly halted the inner turmoil. Honesty was best. She had to face the truth. Small town life wasn't for her—not for the rest of her life. She enjoyed the amenities of the city and dance—she couldn't give that up now that she'd found happiness.

"Would you like to come to my place for a drink?" Tyler asked.

"It's been a lovely day, but I'm tired and they say we have an early start tomorrow." She shot him a quick glance and died a little inside at his transparent contentment. "Tyler, I need to tell you something." Her heart beat a fraction faster, and her stupid stomach dipped and lurched like a boat in a storm. She curled her hands to fists and hid them in her lap.

"Sounds serious."

She sighed, the sound heavy, full of gloom.

"Should I pull over?"

Maybe that would be best. "Yes."

"Sounds really serious," he teased.

Tears welled in her eyes and she blinked hard. Once. Twice. Somehow, she managed to keep them from overflowing. Crying wouldn't help one single bit.

He pulled over on the outskirts of Clare and switched off the ignition. In the resulting silence, panic clawed at her, fought with the need for honesty. Above all, Tyler deserved her candor.

"Jennifer told us this morning she's changed her mind about the filming schedule. We're wrapping up this weekend. Tyler, I'm going home" She couldn't face him, so she spoke to the front window. "Nolan has to choose either me or Lucy. They'll film him as he arrives at one of our houses."

"But I thought—fuck," he muttered.

Susan didn't even wince.

"Marry me," he said. "Tell Nolan you're off the market and marry me."

The sting in her eyes became too much and the tears broke her mental barrier, flowing down her cheeks unchecked.

"Suzy." He reached for her hand and linked his fingers with her hot and sweaty ones. "I love you. Stay in Clare with me."

"I love you t-too," she said, her voice faltering. She tugged her hand away. "But I can't move to Clare."

"Why not? We love each other. We can have a good life here. Have more children. Do you want children?"

"Oh, Tyler. I want that more than anything, but I love my life in the city. My job. My friends. I like Clare too, but as a place to visit for a little while. I...I'd start to resent you if I had to move here permanently."

"But I can't leave." Tyler's words, his stark disappointment, knotted her throat.

She swallowed and swallowed and swallowed again, hating the pain she was inflicting, hating the situation, hating herself.

"I can't leave Eric to run the farm alone. Eric and Josie are my family. I can't leave them in the lurch."

Susan gulped. "Maybe if you asked them—"

"What would I do in the city? I don't have any qualifications. I have a daughter to think about," he said. "I thought you liked it here. I thought you loved me."

I do, she wanted to say, but she held her silence because nothing she could say would make this right.

Tyler rubbed his hands over his face. "Fuck," he said finally. He started up the car, and Susan stared at the blurry streets as they drove through the town.

They didn't speak until Tyler pulled up in front of Nolan's house.

"Are you sure?" Tyler asked.

"Yes." Susan turned away and fumbled for the car door. She grabbed her bag and scrambled out, slamming the door before she straightened her back and strode to the house. Tears ran freely down her face and a sob broke free. She'd known telling Tyler wouldn't be easy, but she hadn't expected the pain that would crash over her, wrenching her heart and making her want to crawl into a dark hole.

TYLER DROVE HOME ON autopilot. If he hadn't had responsibilities at home, he would have detoured to the pub and tied one on. He thought...he'd never considered...*fuck*!

Nolan's vehicle sat outside when he pulled up. Great. Just what he wanted. The only bloody good thing about this was that Susan wouldn't consider a relationship with Nolan either. For the same reasons she'd rejected him.

He pulled himself out of the car and headed inside.

Voices came from the lounge, but he ignored them to check on Katey. His daughter slept on her side, a multitude of dolls and soft toys tucked into the bed to keep her company. He studied her for a long minute, the ties of parental love making him ache. As much as he loved Suzy, he'd survive. They'd survive. He knew because he and Katey had done it before.

Silently, he stepped out of the bedroom and pulled the door closed. Facing the inevitable, he entered the lounge and came to an abrupt halt. He'd expected Nolan, but not his father.

"What's up?" he asked, in no mood for socializing.

"Tyler," Josie said in a chiding manner.

He straightened from his defensive hunch and tried for a welcoming grin. He suspected it was more grimace, but he'd made an attempt.

"Would you like a beer?" Josie asked.

Beer wouldn't do. Not tonight. "Do we have any of that whisky left?"

Her look was searching and followed by sympathy, which made his gut roil.

"We need to talk," his father said. "It's easier to talk to both of you at once."

"I'll leave you to it," Eric said, starting to stand.

"No," Tyler snapped. "You and Josie are my family. You can stay."

Eric sent an uncomfortable look at Tyler's father.

Samuel Penrith gave a curt nod. "I deserve that. It's okay. I'm sure I can count on your discretion."

Josie returned and handed out drinks. Tyler's hand curled around the tumbler of Scottish whisky. A healthy double. *Thank you, Josie.*

His father climbed to his feet. He took a few steps before halting behind an armchair. His big hands curled around the headrest, his knuckles turning white with the force of his grip. "I should have told you this a long time ago, but I promised your mother. Appearances are important to her." He shook his head. "Before we moved to Clare, we lived in Ashburton in the South Island. Elizabeth is a demanding woman. I loved her, but our marriage was up and down. Rocky." He sighed as he stared at his hands. "Full of drama. During one of those downs, I had an affair. I didn't love Rochelle, and it didn't take me long to realize I was a fool for jeopardizing my marriage. Elizabeth didn't know about the affair, and I didn't mention my slip. I'm ashamed to say I put my fling at the back of my mind and set it aside."

Tyler gulped more whisky. Why was he telling them this? His father's expression slunk into rueful and the foreboding slapped at Tyler, the urge to move striking him with hammer blows. Instead, he remained rooted to the spot like a mighty kauri. This was old history. Hell, he didn't even like to imagine his parents *doing* it. What kid did?

His father took a sip of his beer, his gulp loud in the edgy silence. He cleared his throat, his gaze fastening on the label of the beer bottle. "Things were going well between Elizabeth and me. We were happy. We had Nolan and we were trying for another baby. Then..." He seemed to drift for a moment before recalling where he was, his mission. "A year had passed since my affair. Rochelle and I hadn't had any contact since we parted. Out of the blue, a lawyer contacted me. Rochelle and her parents were in a car accident—killed at the scene. There was a baby—my baby. Tyler, that baby was you."

White noise roared through his brain. He stared at his father, watched his mouth move, didn't hear a thing. A hand settled on his shoulder, yanking him free of his stall.

"Tyler," Josie said, concern a furrow on her brow. "Are you all right?"

Tyler swallowed hard, turning to her. "Elizabeth isn't my mother." God, now so much made sense. The woman hated him, made no secret of the fact, except he'd never known why.

"Why did you take me?" he asked. His gaze slid to Nolan, and he could see his brother—half-brother—was as shocked as him.

"There was no one else. You were my blood. I couldn't walk away."

"What happened after the lawyer contacted you?" Tyler didn't want to know, yet he couldn't walk either.

"I had to tell Elizabeth the truth." His heavy sigh seemed to come from the depths of his belly. "She didn't take the news well. I told her I intended to raise you as my son."

And Elizabeth hadn't wanted anything to do with him. He stared at his father, wanting more explanations. Nolan remained silent and watchful.

"It was a standoff, both of us determined to get our way. In the end, Elizabeth laid down an ultimatum. She doesn't believe in divorce and told me she'd agree to have you in the house and raise you if we moved to a new town where no one knew our history. She didn't want neighbors looking at her sideways or gossiping behind her back."

Tyler closed his eyes and the roaring inside his head escalated. Elizabeth—he couldn't think of her as his mother—had acquiesced to his presence. Grudgingly, he'd bet, and she'd never treated him like a son, never comforted him when he'd fallen and skinned his knees. Instead, he'd received a perfunctory order to clean up and stop crying. From Elizabeth, he'd learned independence.

The memories, the demands to behave, to do as he was told...the punishments when he didn't conform to her standards. Every transgression commented on and the meting out of an appropriate punishment. After a while he'd given up trying to please her because nothing he'd done was good enough. Leaving for university had come as a relief, until Rebecca had become pregnant and his entire future crashed around his ears.

His eyes snapped opened, and he poured his fury into his glare at his father. "Why didn't you stick up for me? Why did you let her treat me the way she did?"

"Guilt. The entire situation was my fault. My lust for another woman created the problem."

"You didn't have to take me. You could have had me adopted." Pain underscored his words, and Josie's arm went around his waist, trying to take some of his anguish with her loving touch.

"You're my son," his father said, as if that explained everything. He glanced at Nolan. "You're both my sons."

"You've a funny way of showing kinship. You never stood up for me. You let her treat me like a stranger in your home. Seen and not heard."

"It was part of my agreement with Elizabeth," his father said, his haggard face full of regret. "It wasn't right, but it was the only way I could keep you close."

"What about my real mother?" A mother he didn't know. Right now he ached to fill the gaps in his memory, to learn about her.

His father gave a heavy sigh. "She was beautiful with long, dark hair and big, brown eyes. She was an art teacher at a high school in Christchurch, and she did portraits in the square, not far from the cathedral, on the weekends. That's how I met her. I stopped to watch her sketching a portrait and she talked me into sitting for one. Things went from there."

His artistic talent came from his mother. He'd always wondered since his father and Elizabeth couldn't draw a straight line. A tiny spark of warmth bloomed in contrast to the chill wrapped around his chest. "Do you have a photo?"

"No, I'm sorry." His father glanced around the room before he let his gaze settle on Tyler. "I should have told you this a long time ago. I should have stood up for you more while you were growing up. I know you'll probably never forgive me—hell, I don't think I'll come close to making up for my behavior." His chest rose and fell in another sigh. "If you want to talk, I'll be moving in with Nolan once he has a spare room. I have a room at the Blue Gum motel meantime."

Tyler gave a curt nod, physically unable to say a word of reply. The door slammed behind his father and Nolan.

"Tyler." Josie tugged him around and stared into his face. "Are you okay?"

He shook his head. Talk about a prick of a day. First Susan and now this. "It's late," he finally said. "I might go to bed."

"Tyler, before you go." Eric stopped him with gruff words and a hand on his shoulder. "Josie and I think of you as family. As far as we're concerned, you're our son and we love you."

"Eric is right," Josie said. "We might not tell you often, but without you we'd have lost the farm. We know

Rebecca wasn't easy, yet despite that you stuck with her and then us when we were at our lowest." She smiled at him, her face soft and eyes misty. "We love you, son."

"Thanks. The feeling is mutual." Tyler struggled for the right words, the right response. "I...ah...I'm knackered. It's been a long day."

"Night, Tyler," Eric said.

"See you in the morning," Josie said.

Their soft murmurs drifted after him as he sped down the passage, desperate for the sanctity of his room. He shut the door quietly when the urge to slam it had him trembling. Heaviness shoved against his ribs, and he clenched his jaw to hold back his shouts of frustration. Nothing had changed yet the ground shook beneath his foundations, shifting the balance of his life.

No point resenting Eric and Josie. The way he looked at it—they'd saved him and Katey. They'd made him and their granddaughter into a family, giving his little girl everything she needed. Love. Security.

Art and his dreams...

Well, he'd had to grow up and take responsibility for his daughter, his sick wife. It wasn't as if he couldn't paint in his spare time.

In the darkness, Tyler stripped out of his clothes and slid into bed.

He closed his eyes and Suzy's sad expression when she'd told him she'd be leaving Clare floated through his mind.

Fuck! As much as he hated to accept the truth, she was right. Forcing the issue would end up like his marriage all over again with two people who loved each other torn in two different directions.

No, he'd stay here in Clare. Life would go on and he'd survive.

SUSAN KEPT HOPING TYLER would drop by to say goodbye, although she understood she'd hurt him. Trust her—she was an abysmal failure when it came to love, relationships. Maybe she'd concentrate on work and find another couple of interests to fill in her loneliness. A heavy sigh emerged and she powered up her laptop to write her final Clare blog post.

Part of me is sad to leave Clare because I've met so many wonderful people. The residents of Clare, from age four to ninety, have made me and the rest of the girls welcome. They've embraced us and made us a part of the community. The other part of me is excited to get back to my normal routine, back to my friends and the job I've come to love.

I won't have to wear my red gumboots in the city, yet I can't bear to part with them because I purchased and wore them here in Clare.

I'd like to thank everyone in Clare who has taken the time to speak with us, give us an encouraging word and invited us to share in your community lives. You have a wonderful town and I can see why Nolan chooses to make his life here.

Susan bit down on her bottom lip. Hard. No tears. The decision to leave Tyler was the right one. *Head up and no regrets*. She sniffed and concluded her blog entry.

I'm not sure how the show will end—only Nolan knows the identity of the woman he'll choose—so don't try to wrangle the answer from me. I don't know. I swear!

Make sure you tune in for the final show on Thursday night.

Goodbye, Clare.

Susan

"You're back!" Julia cried, her voice echoing through the almost empty club. She switched off the music. "Take five, everyone."

Maggie and Christina turned, broad grins on their faces.

"We missed you," Maggie said.

"I missed you guys too." Tears welled at her eyes when she found herself in the middle of a group hug.

"Are you here to work?" Julia asked. "I thought you were going to stay in Clare for a few more days."

"Jennifer changed the show format and said we could go home."

"Who won?" Christina demanded. "Who did Nolan choose?" She glanced over her shoulder. "And what about Tyler?"

"I...I..." Susan paused to clear her throat and had to blink extra hard to keep her tears confined. "Nolan picks his winner this week." She had to force the words past the constriction in her throat. "Tyler..." She trailed off and bit her sorely abused lip. "I might go and grab my dance gear from my locker." She hurried away before her friends voiced the other questions brewing in their fertile minds.

Behind her silence reigned before Julia—at least she presumed it was Julia—clapped her hands and ordered everyone back to work.

In the changing room, she took long seconds to compose herself, blowing her nose and wiping her eyes. She tied back her hair in a tight ponytail and grabbed the clean set of dance gear from her locker. Hard, physical exercise would help her forget everything she'd given up for the greater good.

Dressed appropriately, she returned to her friends and threw her heart into learning a new routine and reacquainting herself with ones she hadn't danced for weeks.

"Want to go for a coffee and catch-up once we've showered?" Christina asked.

"No, I think I'll head back—" She broke off abruptly, her brain racing. Better to get this over now. Like pulling a tooth, discussing a breakup was best done quickly. Get out the details and her friends wouldn't ask more nosy questions. "Okay."

"Great," Maggie said. "I'll ring Connor and let him know I'm having coffee. He might be able to join us."

Susan opened her mouth to object and then sighed. Her friends were curious. In their position, she'd feel the same inquisitiveness.

"I suppose you're glad to get a decent cup of coffee again," Christina said.

Susan let out a laugh that was half snort. "Clare might be a country town, but they're not the smallest dot on the map. They have two cafés. One is in a bookshop and the other one is part of the bakery. Both places do delicious food and excellent coffee."

"My shout this afternoon." Christina gave her a swift hug. "I'm pleased you're back."

They settled at a window table, gradually adding more chairs as their group grew in size. When Ryan and Caleb turned up, everyone was present, even though it was a workday.

"What is this?" Susan demanded, sharing her grumpiness around. "An intervention?"

"You don't seem happy," Julia said. "We thought you'd be excited about the contest and making it to the final two."

"Tyler and I broke up."

"Aw, Susan," Maggie said. "We're sorry. We really liked him."

"Do we need to take a hit out on him?" Caleb asked.

"No." Susan picked up her latte and took a quick sip, trying to swallow her guilt with the coffee. She'd really liked Tyler too, and that was the problem. After Tyler, anyone else would fall short.

"What happened with the show?" Connor asked.

"I'm not sure yet. The final one airs on Thursday night. I won't know anything until Thursday afternoon either."

Talk drifted on to other topics—thankfully—and Susan tried to respond to her friends in her usual manner. Control and normal activities were the secret. Eventually each day would become easier.

She hoped.

The rest of the week crawled, although Susan tried to keep busy. She walked to the bank to grab the change for the coming night.

"Susan!"

Susan turned at the call of her name and frowned at a complete stranger. "Do I know you?"

"I'm Jonathon Harris, a reporter with the Auckland News. This is good timing since I was on my way to see you. Who did Nolan choose? Does he know about your affair with the other man?"

"What other man?"

"I have an eyewitness who puts you with this man after the start of the show, just as the rumors say. My witness swears the man looks like Nolan's younger brother. Can I have your comment on that?"

"I don't have a comment," Susan said.

"Shame," the reporter said. "The article is going to run in tomorrow's paper. I thought it would be good to include your side of the story."

"No comment." She increased her pace and plunged through the front doors of the bank. Thankfully, the reporter didn't follow to prod harder at her inner turmoil. A story to coincide with the final show. It couldn't be that bad, right?

CHRISTINA PICKED UP THE Wednesday morning paper and let out a gasp.

"A story about me?" Susan asked as she shunted a mug of coffee at her friend. She'd been too chicken to open the paper to see if the reporter had spoken the truth.

"Third page," Christina said. "A full page story with a

picture of you and Nolan and another of Tyler."

The phone rang and seconds later Susan's cell phone started ringing.

"Well, I guess everyone is awake," Susan said, picking up her cell while Christina snatched up the landline.

"Susan," Jennifer boomed down the line. "If I were in the same room with you I'd kiss your feet. This is the perfect promotion to get people watching the final show tomorrow night. Girl, I'm gonna buy you a bottle of champagne. Hell, I'll get you a crate. Public interest has been so high in this show, the network has signed for another season, plus they're willing to consider my pet project. Thank you. Thank you. Thank you."

Not the reaction Susan had expected. "Ah, I'll see you at the wrap-up filming."

"Excellent. I'll get that champagne on ice," Jennifer promised.

"Okay." Susan hung up and her phone rang almost immediately.

"Susan, are you all right?" Maggie asked. "I saw the article in the paper."

"I haven't read it yet." Susan's stomach curled with apprehension, and she discarded the idea of breakfast. "Is it bad?"

"Lots of innuendo. There's a statement from an anonymous hotel employee. It mentions chocolate, strawberries and champagne. Not much more than the last story."

"So it's nothing new." Relief almost made her dizzy.

"The room attendant positively identified Tyler as the man you stayed with overnight, and one of the wait staff has confirmed you were both present in the restaurant that night. They said you were dining with friends."

"*Oy,*" Susan muttered when really only the crisp, ripe tones of a good curse would do the job. Oh, how her mother would shake her head if she glimpsed the inner workings of her daughter's mind. The dancing had come as a shock, so maybe a cursing daughter wouldn't spring at her mother like a jack-in-a-box.

"Is it going to create problems with the show?" Maggie asked.

"No, my producer is talking about champagne. The only one who might suffer backlash is me. The public love Nolan. I'm not sure how they'll react to me and Tyler."

NOLAN'S PHONE STARTED RINGING not long after six. His father, always an early riser, must have answered. When it rang again, Nolan groaned and crawled out of bed. After rapidly dressing in jeans and a long-sleeved shirt, he padded along the passage. The cool tiles beneath his bare feet startled him even more awake, and he retreated to grab a pair of socks.

"Tea?" his father asked.

"Thanks. Who's ringing?"

His father jerked his head in the direction of the newspaper. It was spread open on top of the kitchen counter—something to do with the reality show, rather than a cattle problem. He accepted a mug of tea from his father, added milk and sugar and walked over to see what had everyone's fingers pushing buttons this morning.

"A love triangle," he scoffed. "People believe this crap?"

"They were seen together," his father said in a careful voice.

Nolan turned away from the paper and leaned his butt against the counter. It didn't matter. He'd made his decision and intended to follow through. "I thought I'd shift the heifers down to the creek paddock after breakfast. Do you want to help?"

"I'd like that, son." His father seemed to have aged in the last week, yet he stood tall with shoulders straight. Nolan could only imagine how the burden of that secret had felt over the years. "I thought I might ask Tyler to go to the pub for a drink."

"That's a good idea." Nolan paused, thought an instant. "Why don't we go out for a meal together at the pub? Go for Sunday lunch and ask Eric and Josie to come. If we go for lunch, then Katey could attend." The extra people would help the conversation flow and take some of the pressure off Tyler.

"We could do that?" His father sounded so grateful Nolan felt as if he were the parent.

"I'll give Tyler a call."

The sharp squeal of brakes outside the house made them turn toward the kitchen door. A loud thump sounded on the door an instant before it flew open and his mother swept inside.

"Elizabeth," his father said. "Would you like a cup of tea?"

"No, I wouldn't. I'm too angry to drink tea."

Nolan sighed. What was new? His mother stomped around angry at the world.

Her sharp eyes spied the open newspaper on the counter. "I see you already know. That tart. I knew she was bad news the moment she told everyone she was a dancer. She's been an embarrassment from the moment she bared her bottom on public television. And Tyler." Her cheeks grew crimson as she wound into full-out temper. "Like his mother. I bet this was a game to him. He's nothing more than a man-slut, going around getting women pregnant and stealing women who belong to other men."

"That's enough," Nolan said in a sharp voice, the instant his mother showed signs of slowing her tirade. "This is my house, and I don't want to listen to you insulting Tyler."

His mother rounded on him, a vein pulsing at her temple. "You'd stand up for him—after what he's done."

"This fight is between you and Dad. Tyler is innocent

in this mess. None of the problems in your marriage are his fault. He was a kid, and you treated him like crap." He held up his hand when his mother showed signs of another explosion. "I haven't been the brother I should have been to Tyler, and I intend to try to make amends. He's a good man, a responsible one, and he doesn't deserve your verbal and mental abuse. Stay away from Tyler or you won't like the consequences."

"But—"

"I mean it, Mum. If I hear any gossip going around Clare, I'll take steps. I'll tell everyone the truth if I have to."

Elizabeth gaped at him. "You'd stick up for Tyler?"

"He's my brother."

"He's made a laughing stock of you," Elizabeth snapped.

"Gossip won't kill me." Something his mother should take on board.

"You're taking your father's side in this," Elizabeth said in clear disbelief.

"I'm taking Tyler's side," Nolan said. "You're both old enough to take care of yourselves. Dad, do you want to eat before we go?"

"Yes," his father said.

"I need to make a phone call," Nolan said. "I'll do it in my room." Without waiting for an answer from his parents, he strode from the kitchen. In his bedroom, he picked up his phone and pushed speed dial. "Hey," he said.

Chapter Thirteen

"It's a full house," Julia said with satisfaction. "We have a line of customers outside the club, waiting to get inside. On a Wednesday night!"

Susan checked her watch and continued to enter figures into the computer. "Already?"

"Thanks to you."

The slow roll of trepidation through Susan left her feeling nauseous. "Is it safe to show my face out there?"

Julia cocked her head to the side and considered her closely. "Ryan said you should wear a mask all night. In fact, he suggested the employees all wear masks to throw off the reporters in the audience."

"Reporters?" Susan didn't like the idea of more harassment.

"They're demanding a statement."

"I've signed a contract. I can't give them statements.

They need to contact Jennifer or her assistant."

"Should I tell them that during my welcoming speech?"

"Yes, please."

Susan continued hiding in her office and mentally flip-flopped about wearing a mask. *Darn it!* She wasn't going to hide. If this publicity helped *Maxwell's* flourish, all the better. She finished adding the last few invoices to the cashbook, saved her work and closed down the computer.

When she walked into the dressing room to change into her costume, the dancers fell silent. "I can't comment on the story in the newspaper or the final show," she said in a crisp voice.

"I saw that guy Tyler here in the club. He was with you and the rest of your friends," one of the girls said with a smile.

"Teasing won't work," Susan said. "I know nothing."

"What about bribes?" someone said.

"Yeah, we'll whip around a hat. Where's my top hat?" another dancer said.

"No bribes either," Susan said.

"What about sex?" another dancer piped up. "Would you like to take a walk on the wild side?"

Susan chuckled. "Thanks for the offer, but I want a man."

"Yeah, but which man?"

"Give us a hint."

"We promise we won't tell."

"Good try," Susan said and made a buttoning motion at her lips.

Christina poked her head into the dressing room. "Ladies, you're on in five."

Susan let out a yelp and started tearing at her clothes. "Where's my mask?"

"I'm wearing a mask if you are," one of the other dancers said. "Let the reporters think I'm Susan. Give me my ten minutes of fame."

Five minutes later, mask in place, Susan took her position with the other dancers.

The lights came on, spotlighting each of the dancers. Instead of the normal cheers, the audience remained silent.

"Which one is Susan?" someone shouted from the rear.

"I'm Susan," one of the dancers called.

Susan's mouth dropped open momentarily before she snapped it shut. The blast of camera flashes made white light dance in front of her eyes.

Another dancer stepped forward. "I'm Susan."

Susan kept dancing until the next quiet point in the music. "I'm Susan."

This time the crowd roared and the photographers went crazy. By the time the dance ended, each one of the dancers had confessed they were Susan.

They ran off stage and into the privacy of the changing room, giggling like a group of schoolgirls.

Julia and Christina appeared and silence fell in the changing room.

"I'm going to call that routine *The Dance of the Susans* from now on." Julia grinned and everyone relaxed. "That was brilliant. I'm going to kick out the photographers now and let our genuine customers into the club. Great job, ladies."

"Let's wear our masks for the entire night," one of the dancers said. "I want to be Susan tonight."

"Yeah, during the audience mingle I'm going to tell everyone my name is Susan," another dancer said.

"Whatever floats your boat," Susan said. "Bear in mind, they'll kid you about flashing your ass on public television."

"Don't forget Mr. Blue," another dancer said with a giggle.

Will the real Susan step forward? Tyler grinned as he read the story headline in the paper on Thursday morning. Despite the underlying pain that bit like an electrical shock every time he thought about her—which was often—he couldn't help liking her friends for standing up to the press. No wonder she wanted to stay in the city. A sense of longing crept into his mind—the idea of continuing his studies in art. Even part time.

He sighed.

Not possible, so he shouldn't even think about the unattainable.

"You're up early," Josie said.

Tyler shrugged. "Couldn't sleep."

"Susan?"

"Yeah," he admitted finally.

Eric shambled into the kitchen, looking as if he needed another hour of sleep. "Why is everyone up so early? Is there tea?"

"You should go to Auckland," Josie said.

"I can't stay in Auckland," Tyler replied. "I have responsibilities here." And even though his conscience told him he wasn't being fair, a tiny voice in his head declared Susan didn't love him enough to give up her life in Auckland.

"Eric and I were talking," Josie said.

"Which is why I look like something the cat dragged in from down at the creek," Eric muttered. "Please, woman. Let me have some tea before we start this conversation."

"Have you changed your mind?" Josie asked, her sharp tone making Tyler stare.

"Not on your life," Eric said. "But I need caffeine in some form to make my brain cells fire."

Tyler walked to the cupboard and pulled out two clean mugs. He poured tea for both Eric and Josie and handed the mugs over after adding milk and sugar. Curiosity nudged aside his continuous loop of Susan memories.

"Ah," Eric said with a satisfied groan. "Good brew."

"Can we tell him now?" Josie demanded.

Tyler stared at his mother-in-law. Excitement tinged her cheeks, and she danced from foot to foot, looking as if she might have itching powder in her slippers.

"A lot of this depends on you, son," Eric said.

Tyler wasn't sure he liked where this conversation was going. He took a seat at the breakfast bar and eyed Eric. "Okay."

"Josie and I have talked about taking an overseas trip ever since we got married. The time was never right."

They wanted him to look after the farm. No prob. He'd done it before when they'd had weekends away with friends and other family members. "I can look after the farm."

"No, that's not what we mean," Josie said, taking over. "We've decided to sell the farm."

"What?" Tyler swallowed his shock and forced his mind to gallop ahead. He'd have to find somewhere to live, pay someone to look after Katey while he worked each day. Hell, he'd need another job.

"Josie was a city girl before she married me," Eric said. "Her parents left her a property in Remuera. You know that, right?"

"Yeah, Rebecca told me. Isn't it rented out?"

"The lease falls due at the end of next month," Josie said.

"We've decided not to renew the lease, but instead we'll move to Auckland. We'll live there for part of the year and travel as much as we can."

"That's great," Tyler said, forcing enthusiasm into his voice while panic threatened to overtake his control. It was gonna be a hell of an adjustment for him and Katey.

"We want you to come with us," Eric said.

"If that's what you'd like," Josie said. "The house is huge and there is a separate dwelling, which used to belong to the caretaker. It has two bedrooms."

"You could see Susan," Eric said.

Both of his in-laws stopped talking and observed him closely.

Tyler's mind had stuck in a rut, dug at the start of the conversation. "You want to sell the farm?"

"Eric's heart isn't in farming anymore," Josie said. "We didn't think it was what you wanted to do for the rest of your life either. You could go back to university, concentrate on your art."

His breath caught. The road on the other side of his mind-rut was a long, sloping hill. He sailed down that hill, mentally screaming with exhilaration. No. He wasn't going to get excited—not yet. He'd had his dreams ripped away before.

Tyler gazed from Eric to Josie. "Are you sure?"

"Yes," Eric said. "You're family."

A knock sounded at the door.

"Who the hell is that?" Eric grumbled. "It's sparrow's fart o'clock in the morning."

"I'll get it," Josie chirped.

In the distance, a male voice rumbled. Josie returned a few minutes later.

Tyler stared at his brother. "What are you doing here?"

"Tyler," Josie chided.

"No, I deserve that," Nolan said. "Dad and I wondered if you'd all join us for lunch at the pub on Sunday. Katey too."

Tyler stared at Nolan for a long time. "Did you see the paper?" he asked finally.

"Yep."

"And?"

"I can't talk about the show." Nolan checked his watch. "I'd better go. Got a plane to catch."

Nolan's manner left Tyler puzzled. His brother didn't seem angry. Susan had kept telling him she didn't have Nolan's interest. Tyler hadn't held the same conviction.

"We're selling the farm and moving to Auckland," Josie said. "Tyler and Katey are going with us. Are you interested in buying?"

Nolan shot another glance at Tyler and sat down. "Maybe I have ten minutes before I need to leave for the airport."

ALL MORNING, SUSAN CLEANED the apartment until every surface gleamed. Christina leaned against the kitchen counter, watching in bemusement while she scrubbed the grout with a toothbrush.

Christina straightened abruptly. "Enough already. What time did you say stuff was going to happen?"

"In about an hour, I might hear a knock on my door."

"Why are you so nervous? You don't want to marry the guy."

"No, but I've come to like him, even though he's a jerk at times. He loves the land and small town life, and when he stands up against his mother, he's decent."

"His mother sounds awful. She— Never mind. She's the original dragon. You need to get changed," Christina said, her bracelets jingling as she gestured at Susan. "Go and have a shower. What are you wearing? Never mind, I'll put together an outfit for you while you shower."

Susan jumped in the shower. Her skin crawled with imaginary bugs, and she couldn't seem to keep still or wash them off. *Calm down*. Christina was right. It wasn't as if she wanted to marry Nolan. She bent her head and let the water pour over her, forgetting in her misery that she didn't have time to deal with wet hair.

She missed Tyler.

Not talking to him, not exchanging emails and texts left a yawning hole in her day. In such a short time he'd become friend, confidant and the man she loved.

She heaved a sigh. She'd made the right decision, but her heart still ached like a sore tooth. Aware of the ticking clock, she turned off the water and toweled dry. Wrapped in a towel, she scurried to her bedroom, pulled on black lingerie and sat down to apply makeup. Something to hide her lack of sleep.

"Christina," she yelled.

"Here," her friend said. Maggie and Julia poured through the doorway behind Christina. "We bought you a new dress. I think it should fit."

"Thank you!" Tears sprang up and she blinked rapidly. "Don't make me cry. I don't have time to redo my makeup."

"No thanks necessary," Julia said. "The boys donated to the cause."

"Try it on," Maggie prompted, her face full of excitement. "We're going to hide in the other room."

With her friends' help, Susan dressed and dealt with her hair in record time.

"Have you seen the paper today?" Maggie asked.

"No."

"Just as well," Julia said. "Do a twirl."

The red dress swirled around her legs while the tight bodice clung to her curves. Julia had braided her hair and pinned it up and now she looked sophisticated and sexy.

"You need a necklace and dangly earrings," Christina said. "I have just the thing." She scooted away and returned minutes later with a black and gold necklace in bold circles and matching earrings. "Put them on. Perfect," she breathed, clasping her hands together.

"Thank you so much," Susan said. "You're such great friends." She glanced at her watch and saw it was after the appointed time. "He must have picked Lucy," she said. "That's good. She's nice, and they suit each other."

"Ryan and Caleb sent champagne since they couldn't be here. They had to fly out to the States this morning. Caleb said we could either celebrate or drown our sorrows, whichever suited us best," Julia said.

Susan smiled her thanks. "I love your hubby and his friend."

"I do too," Christina said. "It's such a pity there's zilch attraction."

"No," Susan agreed. "But he's pretty to look at and he gives good champagne."

Another few minutes passed.

"Looks like it's a commiseration party," Susan said. "Let's crack those bottles. I'll get glasses."

Julia started to rip the foil off one of the chilled bottles. "Are you disappointed, Susan? You entered this show because you were depressed with being single."

"The show has been fun. I'm not disappointed about Nolan, but I feel flat."

"Are you sure you can't live in Clare?" Maggie asked.

"I've asked myself that so many times." Susan started

to rub her face with her hands, remembered her makeup and began pacing instead. "It would feel like turning my back on who I am, just when I've discovered myself, if that makes sense."

"But you'd have Tyler," Julia said, expertly popping the cork on the champagne.

Susan accepted a glass of bubbles. "I know, but I wouldn't be one hundred percent happy. Enough of this emotional stuff. Let's have a toast." She lifted her glass. "To love and friendship."

"To love and friendship," her friends chorused.

A brisk knock on the apartment door made them freeze. They stared at each other.

"Get the door," Maggie whispered.

Susan stared at the door. "It's probably one of those church groups doing the rounds."

The knock came again, and Susan took a deep breath, uneasy with nerves quivering through her tense muscles. She set her glass on the counter. It wasn't as if she loved Nolan or wanted to marry him. She licked her lips, the taste of lipstick bringing the action to an abrupt halt. On trembling legs, she walked to the door. Her hand trembled as she grasped the knob and twisted.

She stared at the man in the doorway, the bunch of bright early spring flowers in his hands, the cameraman standing behind him.

"Are you going to invite me in?" Nolan asked.

Why couldn't it have been Tyler? The thought flashed her mind before polite manners took over. "Hi, Nolan." She stood on tiptoe and brushed a kiss on his cheek. "Come inside."

She waited while Nolan and the cameraman entered, then closed the door behind them.

"A party?" Nolan asked.

"Would you like a glass?" Julia asked and poured one before he answered.

"Nolan, what are you doing here?" Susan asked.

"You're the woman I pick," Nolan said, humor lighting his eyes.

Susan was aware of her friends, the cameraman with his smirk fixed in place. "I like you, Nolan. I applied for the show to find a prospective husband, but things have changed. I don't think we could be anything more than friends." She'd thought emerging the winner would feel great. Instead, depression settled on her shoulders, digging in its nasty claws. "I thought you realized that too and would pick Lucy."

Nolan grinned and lifted the glass of champagne Julia had given him. "To friendship."

"Here's your glass, Susan," Christina said.

"I don't understand," Susan whispered.

"The object of the show was to find a prospective wife," Nolan said. "I didn't find the one for me, but I did find two women who'll make great friends. I know you love Tyler," he said abruptly.

Susan jerked. "What?"

"I saw you and Tyler down by the dam."

"What?" Susan narrowed her eyes, wanting to knock the smartass grin off his mouth. In her mind, she rummaged through the various meetings with Tyler, their lovemaking and tried to make sense of Nolan's words. She shot a glance at the cameraman and his wide, wide smirk. Maybe she'd thump them both then kick them out of her apartment.

"I saw you and Tyler get naked down by the dam."

"Fuck," Susan blurted seconds before she clapped her hand over her mouth. Had she said that? "Sorry."

"Don't be sorry. You're good for my brother. Besides, I have someone else too."

"We need popcorn," Maggie said.

"And refills," Julia added.

"Beware of my stink eye," Susan warned, her mind whirling. Nolan had known about them the entire time, and he'd still picked her instead of Lucy.

The cameraman sniggered, and Susan shot him one of her best.

Someone knocked on the door.

"I'll get it," Nolan said, and the cameraman followed him out.

"He knew all the time," Susan said. "Why didn't he say something?"

"No idea," Julia said. "Men still confuse me."

Maggie and Christina nodded.

"No more popcorn remarks," Susan said. "I want quiet in the cheap seats."

The cameraman returned from following Nolan and sniggered at her words.

Susan whirled on him. "Enough from you too, Mr. Cameraman."

"Filming you and Nolan is the most fun I've had in years," he said. "Gossip, drama and sex. A winning combination."

"I'm glad we've kept you entertained," Nolan said, reappearing.

A roaring sound rushed through Susan's head. Her heart gave a vicious wrench, and she was pretty sure something broke as she stared at the man who walked into her lounge behind Nolan.

"Tyler." His name emerged as a croak. She trembled so much Julia took possession of her champagne glass.

"Susan," Tyler said, his gaze roaming her body before returning to her face. "You look beautiful."

"Thanks." What was he doing here? Why was he with Nolan? He looked nervous, his face paler than normal.

"I talked to Eric and Josie," he said, his focus solely on her. "It turns out they want to sell the farm and retire to their house in Auckland. They asked me and Katey to come with them."

His words made her heart twist in that painful way

again. "You're moving to Auckland?"

"Yes." His smile was uncertain. It flickered then died and his Adam's apple moved with his hard swallow. "I love you, Susan, and I've been miserable without you." He plucked a small ring-size box from his jacket, opened it and held it toward her. "Will you marry me?"

Susan gaped at the glittering sapphire and diamond ring, then lifted her gaze to stare at Tyler.

"Say something," Christina blurted.

Susan's heart stuttered with another blip, but this time the traitorous organ slotted into place and everything synced. Happiness was like a soft glow, spreading through her. Her smile came slow but it spread wide until her lips hurt.

"Yes. *Yes.*" She hurled herself at Tyler, the ring box went flying, but she didn't care when his arms wrapped around her and his lips settled on hers.

"And that's a wrap," the cameraman said.

Applause broke out.

Susan pulled back from Tyler, staring into his gorgeous face. "I love you."

"Here's your ring," Maggie said and handed over the box. "It's beautiful."

"Welcome to the family," Nolan said with a broad grin. "Sister-in-law is almost as good as friend."

Tyler slipped the ring on her finger and gave her another quick hug. "I was scared you'd say no."

"I've missed you so much. I kept thinking about you and Katey. Especially you," she added, part of her unable to believe he was really here.

"This calls for a toast," Nolan said.

"I've got the perfect one," Susan said once everyone had a full glass. "To love and friendship."

"I'll drink to that," Nolan said.

"To love," Tyler whispered.

"To our happy future," Susan said, and the last of emptiness she'd experienced since returning to Auckland faded, crowded out by shiny new happiness.

Susan waited in a small room with several of the other successful girlfriends. Tyler sat beside her, neither of them saying much or explaining his presence, despite the curious glances.

Jennifer poked her head through the door. "Chelsea, they're ready for you in front of the camera."

One by one, the women left until only Susan and Tyler remained.

"Alone at last," Tyler said, and he whisked her off her chair and onto his knee with surprising speed.

Laughing, she looped her arms around his neck.

"Happy?"

"Very," she said. "Any regrets about leaving Clare?"

"I won't miss chasing stock around in all weathers, the hard grind of farming."

"What about the locals?"

"Probably, but it's not as if Clare is miles away. We can visit Nolan." Tyler halted further questions by stealing a kiss.

"Enough of that," Jennifer said from the doorway. "Susan, they're ready for you now. Once Hailee finishes your interview, we'll make our surprise announcement and introduce Tyler to our viewers. Five minutes, Tyler."

Susan ran her fingers over Tyler's cheek, smiled and hopped off his knee. "Lipstick," she said, tapping her lip. "I don't think it's your color."

Music played as she entered the set. Nolan stood and his broad grin settled some of the nerves that jumped to the fore. The forum was already full of anti-Susan comments.

"Susan," Hailee said once they were all settled in seats. "The public has followed you and Nolan more closely than any of the other couples. The studio has been inundated with email and comments on the forum about the newspaper stories of Susan and another man. Obviously, Nolan isn't bothered about the rumors because he chose you as his prospective wife. Are the two of you serious about each other?" Hailee flashed a bright smile at Susan, one that invited her to share a confidence. "I've asked Nolan but he's been very reticent. What's the next step for you and Nolan?"

Nolan reached for her hand and gave her a slight nod of encouragement. Susan took a quick breath. "Nolan and I are good friends."

"The kind of friends who get married?" Hailee prompted. "That is an engagement ring I saw on your finger?"

"The kind of friends who become brother and sister-in-law," Susan said. "I'm engaged to Tyler, Nolan's younger brother."

Hailee's smile faltered a fraction before she turned it on full-beam again. "So the rumors are true?"

"Tyler and I fell in love," Susan said.

"But what about Nolan?"

"There's another woman who has grabbed my heart," Nolan said. "Susan, Lucy and the other girls are all great, but they're not my lady."

Hailee leaned a little closer. "Are you going to tell us the identity of your mystery woman?"

"No, I'm afraid not," Nolan said. "But I'd like to introduce you to my younger brother, Tyler."

"He's here?"

Tyler appeared in the doorway and strode over to join them.

"I wondered why we had a spare seat," Hailee said. "Jennifer has sprung this on me too, folks. So, firstly, Nolan, how long have you known about Tyler and Susan?"

"Not for long. Tyler and I had a conversation a few days ago," Nolan said.

"I would've liked to eavesdrop on that little chat," Hailee said. "Did they tell you what happened, Susan?"

"No," Susan said. "I know nothing."

"Now that's not quite true," Hailee said. "I want to know the truth. Did Nolan and Tyler come to blows over you?"

"No," Susan said. "As you can see, they're both fully intact without bruises."

"You'd have us believe the three of you are friends with no hard feelings?"

Nolan took the floor. "I have no bad feelings toward Tyler or Susan. Hell, I've never seen my brother happier, and I get a great sister-in-law into the bargain. I'm delighted for both of them."

"Susan, what do your friends and family think of the situation?"

Susan forced a smile at the thought of her mother. Given time, her mother would come to love Tyler as much as she did, especially since she'd score a granddaughter. "If I'm happy, then my family and friends are too."

"Have they met Tyler?"

"Yes," said Susan. "They're excited for me."

"When are you going to get married?" Hailee asked.

"Soon," Tyler said before Susan could answer.

"We don't want her to get away," Nolan said.

Hailee blinked, cast a speculative at Susan and the two men. Finally, she said, "Are you saying what I think you're saying?"

"What's that?" Nolan asked.

"That the three of you..."

"No," said Susan.

"Yes," said Tyler and Nolan at the same time.

"Well," Hailee said, apparently at a loss for words. She picked up again after her brief lapse. "Congratulations. Let's go to greet our other farmers and their chosen ladies."

"Did you have to?" Susan demanded the second the camera switched off. "Now people will think...your mother will think...that we're indulging in kinky acts for three!"

"Yes," said Nolan with a feral grin. "And she'll think twice about trying to organize my love life again."

CHAPTER FOURTEEN

SUSAN LAY IN THE hotel bed, wrapped in Tyler's arms as they watched the closing credits of *Farmer Seeks a Wife*.

"Well," she said. "Did you see the color I went when Nolan announced he'd played Peeping Tom down at the dam?" She moaned aloud. "And my mother probably won't speak to me again for dropping an F bomb on public television. I never say that word. I'd hoped they'd bleep it out."

Tyler chucked and pointed the remote at the TV.

"Wait, that's Jennifer," she said when the news commenced. "I'd love to hear her reaction."

"Your reality show has proved very successful," a male interviewer said. "Did you think the public would get behind the show as much as they did?"

"I'd hoped they would. The reality actually surpassed my expectations and the show took on a life of its own."

"Are you disappointed Farmer Nolan didn't end up with Susan?"

"Not at all. Two of our farmers have found women with whom they want to pursue a relationship. It's not my job to force relationships on our farmers. I like to think we give them opportunities to grasp if they seem right for them. Besides, Susan did find a happy ending with Nolan's brother, Tyler. If it weren't for *Farmer Seeks a Wife*, the two wouldn't have met."

"What's next for you?" the interviewer asked.

"*Farmer Seeks a Wife* has proved so successful the network has given the go ahead for me to produce another reality show. We hope to have more seasons of *Farmer Seeks a Wife*, but meantime I'm heading back to the township of Clare. The Shakespeare sextuplets have agreed to a reunion show, and we're going to film them in their hometown."

"Now that is exciting. I thought they refused to film after the age of twelve because they wanted privacy," the interviewer said.

Jennifer beamed with excitement. "I obviously approached them at the right time. We intend to start filming early next month."

The news station cut back to the newsreader who continued to report the day's events, and Tyler switched off the TV.

"That will get the gossip vine buzzing in Clare. As far as

I know, the Shakespeare sextuplets haven't been together as a family since their parents divorced," Tyler said.

"Isn't one a famous model?"

"Yeah. I went to school with them. We were in the same class for a while." He ran his fingers down Susan's cheek. "Since we're finally alone without cameras and friends, I think it's time to have a private celebration."

"We've been making merry since we got to your room," Susan said with a grin.

Tyler nipped the fleshy part where her shoulder and neck met, the sharp bite pushing instant messages of lust through her body.

She tipped her head back and fluttered her lashes at him. "But we can do it again."

"I'll never tire of celebrating with you."

Unable to resist, she ran her fingers along his jaw, his dark stubble abrading her skin. "Are you sure? What will you do for a job?"

"Eric and Josie told me I should finish my graphic design course."

"Would you like that? Can you afford not to work?"

"They offered to pay for my course." He frowned. "They said they owed me for all the time I'd put into the farm. As far as I'm concerned, they don't owe me anything."

He'd put his life on hold to help his in-laws on the farm and raise his daughter, but now wasn't the time to fight the point. "You could get a part time job. Julia is always looking for security men who won't hit on the customers. There's no rush to decide."

"That might work." He flashed a grin. "Only one woman I want."

Their lips touched and immediately the air crackled with sensual tension. She rose over him and his muscles jumped beneath her touch.

His lust-filled gaze settled on her breasts. "I want to make love to my fiancée." He reached up and sucked her distended nipple into his mouth.

"That feels good." Already renewed dampness made her ready for him and arousal coiled low in her belly.

He switched his mouth to her other breast, sucking the nipple strongly into his mouth. Each wet pull yanked a corresponding nerve ending in her pussy. Her hand wriggled between them to curl around his cock, the skin smooth and hot beneath her palm. The musky scent of sex swirled around them as she pumped her hand up and down his shaft.

Tyler released her nipple with a wet pop, licked a path over the curve of her breast. His fingers dipped down her body and delved into her swollen labia. The touch made her catch her breath, and the wet rasp of his tongue, the drag of his stubble spiked heady sensations in her. His thumb skimmed her clit, fire whipping through her with each drag of his digit.

"You're very good at that," she said.

"Practice makes perfect. Let me get a condom." He reached over to grab one from the box, and immediately she missed the weight of his hands on her body.

"Hurry," she said.

He laughed. "We have all night."

"We're making up for lost time."

"Touch yourself. I want to watch while I put on this condom."

His eyes were dark, full of love and the little smile she'd come to cherish hovered around his sensual lips. "I love you so much, Suzy. From the moment I saw you on TV, I wanted you, and the more I came to know you, the harder I fell."

"I love you too, Tyler. So much." When he lay back on the bed and grinned up at her, she straddled him and slowly impaled herself with a hot, wet slide. His cock filled her, pushing the velvet tension inside her to new heights. He met each of her downward strokes with an upward surge of his hips.

Each rise and fall packed her beautifully, gave her exactly what she needed. Her vagina flexed and rippled around his shaft, and she increased her pace, sliding a hand down to rub her clit.

Without warning, she came in long, languorous waves, gasping and throwing her head back to better enjoy the pleasure dragging her under.

"You look pretty when you come."

Her breath went shallow while her heart brimmed over with pure joy.

Tyler moved, taking her by surprise, and seconds later, she stared up at him. He powered into her with rapid strokes and sent renewed pulses through her pussy. He froze fully embedded, his eyes squeezed shut as his climax thundered through him. She held tight to his shoulders, aware of the happiness, the rightness of being with Tyler.

She traced patterns over his chest and waited for his orgasmic buzz to pass.

"Hey." His smile was a sexy twist of lips, tinged with sweetness and satisfaction. "Katey is excited about living in Auckland. Once she heard about the zoo and the museum and making new friends, she wanted to pack straight away."

"Does she know about me? About us?"

"That was the tipping point," Tyler said. "She's fallen in love with dancing and wants to be a ballerina. You're going to show her how."

"A daughter," Susan murmured. "I never dared to dream about a child as well as a husband."

"We could have more, once we're settled."

Susan thought about it for a few seconds and nodded. "I'd like that. Maybe in a year or two."

"Anything you want, Suzy." Tyler kissed her again and they didn't stray from the bed for a long, long time.

So what's up with Nolan?

Please turn the page for a glimpse of *Part-Time Lovers*,
the next book in my *Friendship Chronicles* series.

Excerpt — Part-Time Lovers

Lord, her feet hurt.

Yvonne McDonald thumped the spent coffee grounds into her bin and started making a soy latte and two flat whites. While the coffee dribbled into cups, she filled a teapot with peppermint tea leaves and poured over boiling water while trying not to think about her cozy sheepskin slippers waiting for her at home.

The Clare town festival to celebrate the New Zealand spring was great in theory. Aunt Gina was cackling gleefully about their bumper takings this week, but they needed someone stationed at the door to draft customers into their bookstore café in manageable groups rather than massive herds. A set of the mobile yards the local farmers used for their cattle would do the job.

The bell over the door dinged a cheerful welcome. Yvonne didn't bother to glance up since they'd hired two students to help. The two teenage girls could do the smiling thing. She bashed her bell to signal order up.

"My feet hurt." Kelsey loaded her tray with the coffee, tea and a plate of fresh scones, jam and clotted cream.

"We need to hit Gina up for spa visits," Yvonne said, almost moaning at the decadent thought. What she wouldn't give for a man to greet her at home. Never mind the hot sex. She'd settle for a foot rub.

A flood of whispers stormed the café. Stray words struck Yvonne like bullets. *Farmer. Reality show. Susan. Nolan.*

"Yvonne." The familiar masculine voice hurled her into the past...

A dark bedroom.

Naked bodies sliding together.

Mind-zapping touches.

Pleasure storming her body, culminating in sweet, sweet bliss.

Stellar sex. Superior and awesome and stellar sex.

Another word bullet hit, and her head jerked up at the repeat of her name.

Nolan.

Damn, the man.

Her gaze settled, and irritation punched her in the chest, stealing her ability to breathe for a few seconds. She glared at Nolan Penrith, the bane of her life. Tall and lean from hard physical farm work, he was a male in his prime. His light brown hair—currently full of blond streaks from a fortnight of spring sunshine—needed a cut but he suited the unruly curls. His brown eyes sparkled with open admiration as he stared at her, and his sensual lips curved upward in a smile of greeting.

This acknowledgement with the underpinning of lust was a new development, and the hair lifted at the back of her neck in a silent warning to take care.

She directed her scowl away from his tempting smile and started to build the next order. A skim milk latte and a hot chocolate. Her disobedient mind refused to focus and like a rambunctious child, darted back to thoughts of sexy Nolan.

The man owned a farm on the outskirts of Clare and recently he'd brought fame and notoriety to the country town when he took part in the reality show *Farmer Seeks a Wife*. The minute he'd started dating women from the show, their...fling—the best description for their relationship—ended.

Kaput. A full stop on her sex life.

Yvonne frothed a jug of milk, the hiss and whir of the coffee machine overly loud and rubbing her nerves raw. The café section of the bookshop had become library quiet, but she didn't intend to glance up to see why.

She. Would. Not.

She sucked in a deep breath, tried to ignore the zing of sensual awareness tugging her breasts, the tremor of her hand guiding the coffee machine, the clamp of invisible hands constricting her ribs. She brushed off her hormones' celebratory rumba.

"Yvonne."

Cursing under her breath, she gave up the fight. She tore her gaze from the steaming milk and glowered at the man. "Nolan, what can I get you today?"

"I'm here to ask you to dinner," he said in a husky, jump-in-bed-with-me-now voice. "Tonight."

Yvonne's mouth dropped open. Shock kicked her square in the solar plexus while irritation charged like a mad bull seconds later. "You have *got* to be kidding me."

Her voice emerged in a high-pitch shriek, the register of her tone reminding of her of a squeaky cartoon character. The customers in the café were pin-drop quiet now, entertained by the impromptu *Nolan and The Dumped Girlfriend* show.

Nolan straightened, his good humor visibly cooling. He shot a glance to his left, one to his right. "No. I'm asking you on a date. If tonight doesn't work, we can try another night."

"You've treated me like a dirty secret," she snapped. "And I don't need your mother's shrewish attention focused on me again."

The man had rocks in his head if he thought she'd come running after his behavior. And the way his witch mother had flown around town on her broomstick to spread rumors about Yvonne's morals. *Bah*. Elizabeth Penrith might consider herself Clare royalty, but that didn't give her the right to treat people like crap for not measuring up to her lofty standards.

"Our dating has nothing to do with my mother. Look, we can't discuss this here. The café is too busy. I'll see you later at your place."

The bell tinkled as someone left the café.

Yvonne didn't blink. "I'm not a disposable commodity for you to discard then pick up when you have no better offers. I'm tired, my feet hurt and all I want to do is go to bed." Her good-for-nothing husband had left her and walked away with another man. Nolan had searched for a wife elsewhere. The third time was *not* a charm.

"You tell him, love," an elderly woman called from her table over by the magazine stand.

"Make him grovel," another woman shouted out her advice.

"Don't throw him away," a teenage girl called. "Give him a chance, or better yet, toss him my way."

"Make him work for you. He should apologize." Elderly Mrs. Wright added her two cents in a deep voice.

Yvonne felt heat rise up her neck to take residence in her cheeks and gave silent thanks to her Māori grandmother. Not many people would notice her discomfort.

"Tonight," Nolan repeated in a firm voice. He turned to face the café patrons and bowed from the waist, straightened and strode from the café. The doorbell tinkled for long moments then silence fell—a long one in which everyone studied Yvonne.

Does Yvonne make Nolan grovel?

Purchase Part-Time Lovers to find out!
(www.shelleymunro.com/books/part-time-lovers)

ABOUT AUTHOR

USA Today bestselling author Shelley Munro lives in Auckland, the City of Sails, with her husband and a cheeky Jack Russell/mystery breed dog.

Typical New Zealanders, Shelley and her husband left home for their big OE soon after they married (translation of New Zealand speak - big overseas experience). A twelve-month-long adventure lengthened to six years of roaming the world. Enduring memories include being almost sat on by a mountain gorilla in Rwanda, lazing on white sandy beaches in India, whale watching in Alaska, searching for leprechauns in Ireland, and dealing with ghosts in an English pub.

While travel is still a big attraction, these days Shelley

is most likely found in front of her computer following another love - that of writing stories of contemporary and paranormal romance and adventure. Other interests include watching rugby (strictly for research purposes), cycling, playing croquet and the ukelele, and curling up with an enjoyable book.

Visit Shelley at her Website
www.shelleymunro.com

Join Shelley's Newsletter
www.shelleymunro.com/newsletter

OTHER BOOKS BY SHELLEY

Fancy Free

Protection

Romp

Buzz

Festive

Friendship Chronicles

Secret Lovers

Reunited Lovers

Clandestine Lovers

Part-Time Lovers

Enemy Lovers

Maverick Lovers

Sports Lovers

Military Men

Innocent Next Door

Soldiers with Benefits

Safeguarding Sorrel

Stranded with Ella

Josh's Fake Fiancée

Operation Flower Petal

Protecting the Bride